6/19

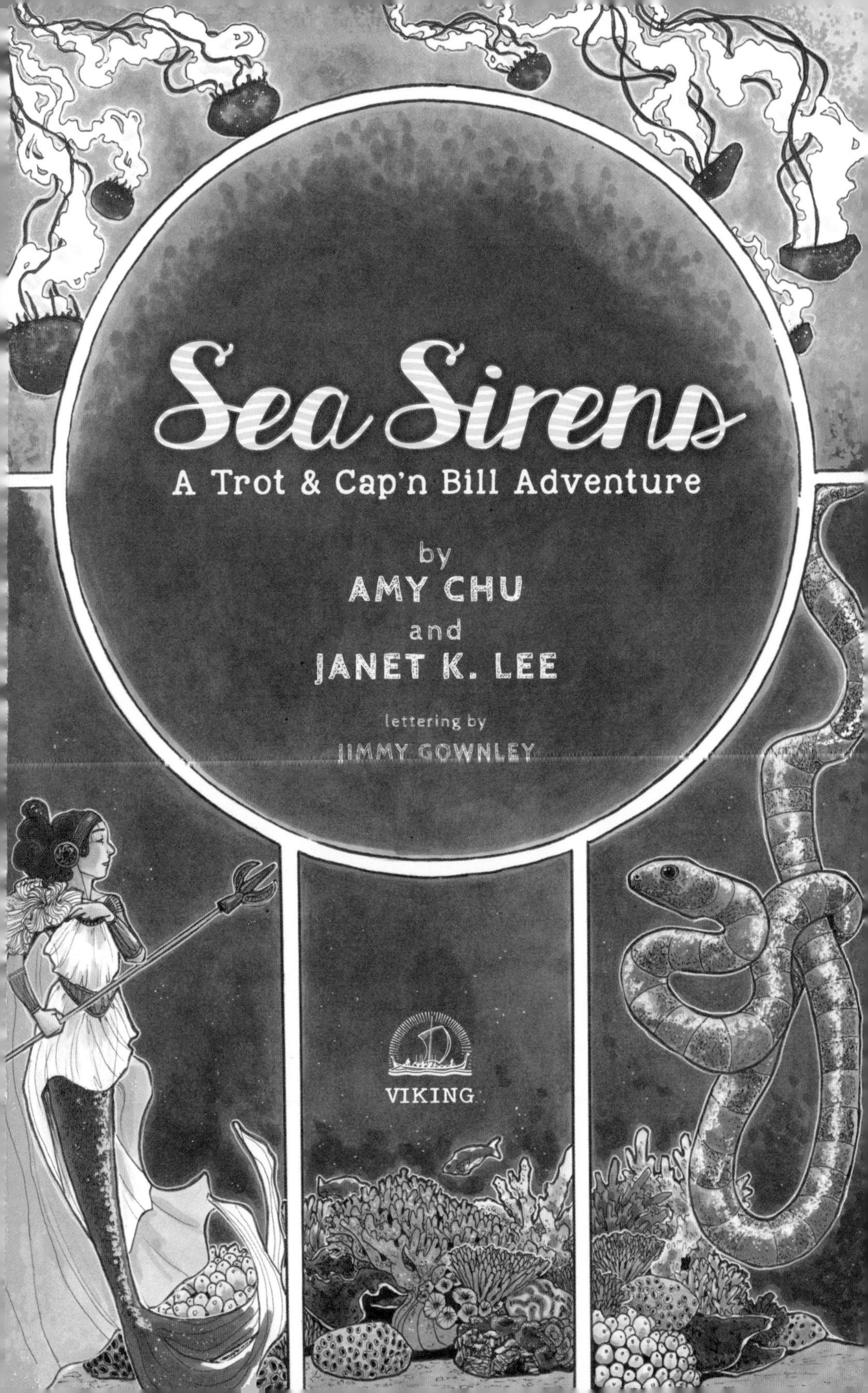

Sea Sirens

A Trot & Cap'n Bill Adventure

by

AMY CHU

and

JANET K. LEE

lettering by

JIMMY GOWNLEY

VIKING

VIKING

An imprint of Penguin Random House LLC, New York

First published in the United States of America by Viking,
an imprint of Penguin Random House LLC, 2019

Copyright © 2019 by Amy Chu and Janet K. Lee

Visit us online at penguinrandomhouse.com

LIBRARY OF CONGRESS CATALOGING-IN-PUBLICATION DATA IS AVAILABLE.
ISBN 9780451480163 (hardcover)
ISBN 9780451480170 {paperback}

Manufactured in China   Book design by Nancy Brennan
1 3 5 7 9 10 8 6 4 2

Contents

To my friend and collaborator Janet Lee who had the initial vision for the book, and L. Frank Baum for the inspiration. Immense gratitude to the incredible force of nature Judy Hansen and the ever patient Sheila Keenan. And much love to my boys Alexander and Adrian for their support, honest feedback and proofreading eyes. —A.C.

For my sister who believed my stories no matter what, for my dad who taught me how to draw, and for my husband who loves me. —J.K.L

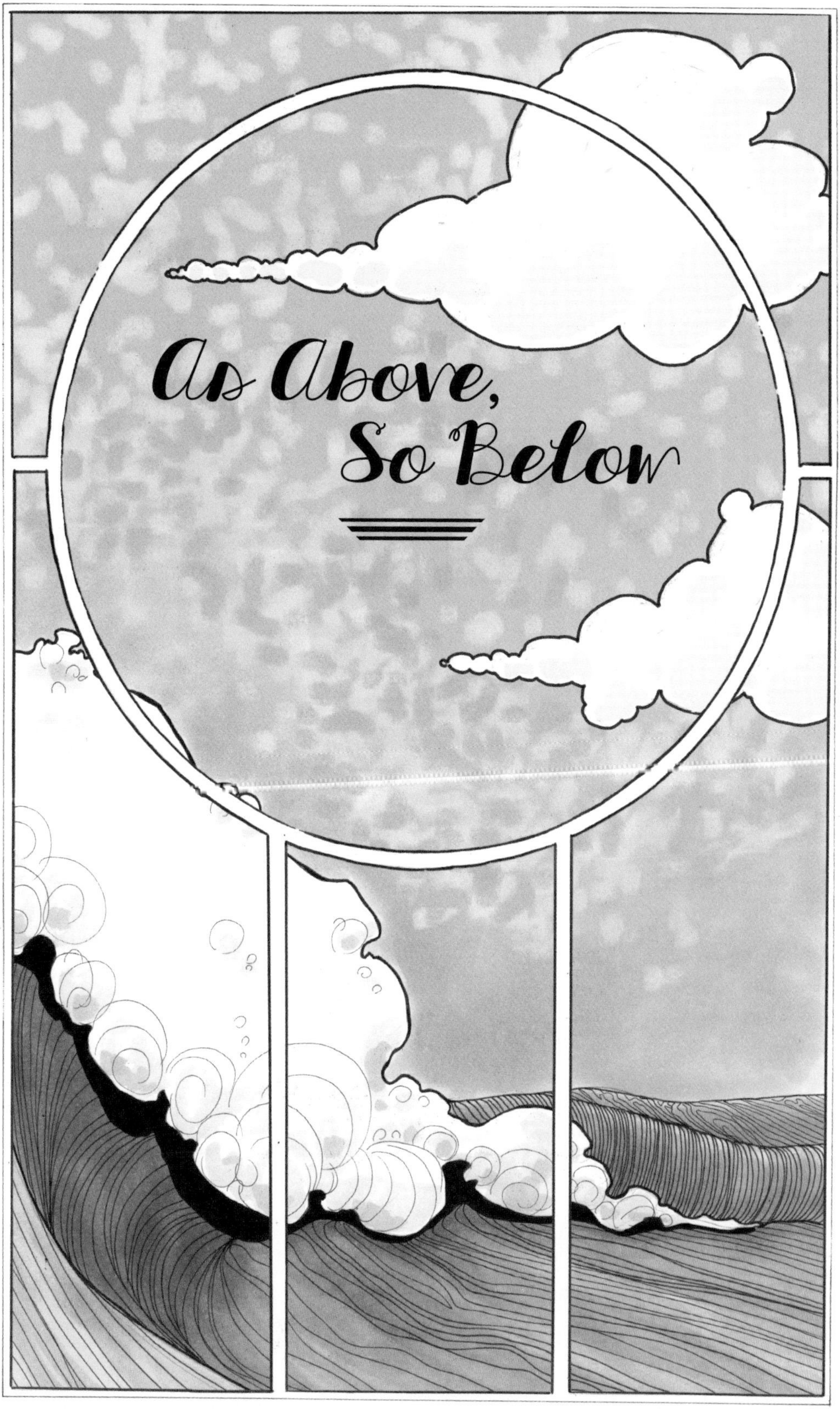
As Above,
So Below

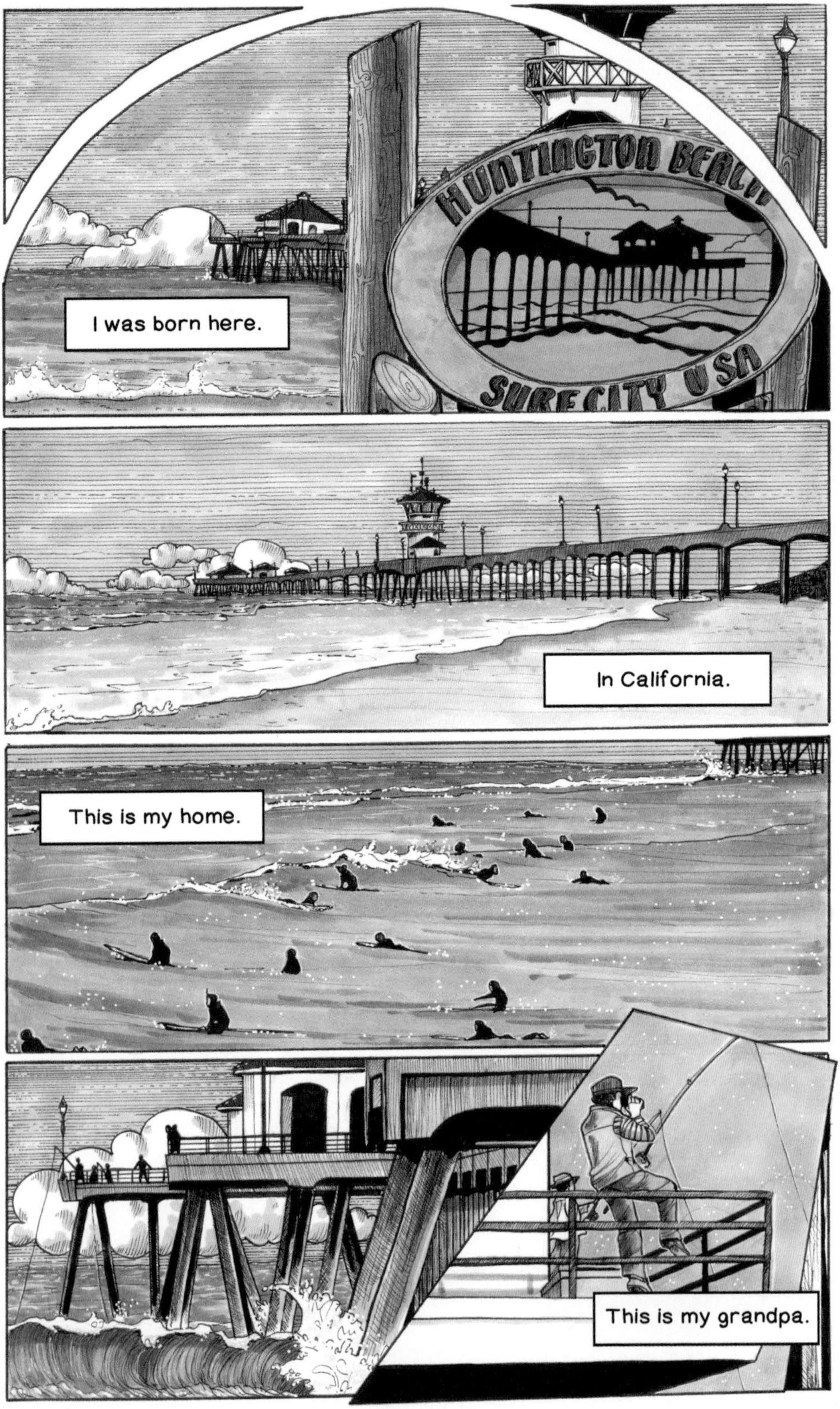
HUNTINGTON BEACH
SURF CITY USA
I was born here.
In California.
This is my home.
This is my grandpa.

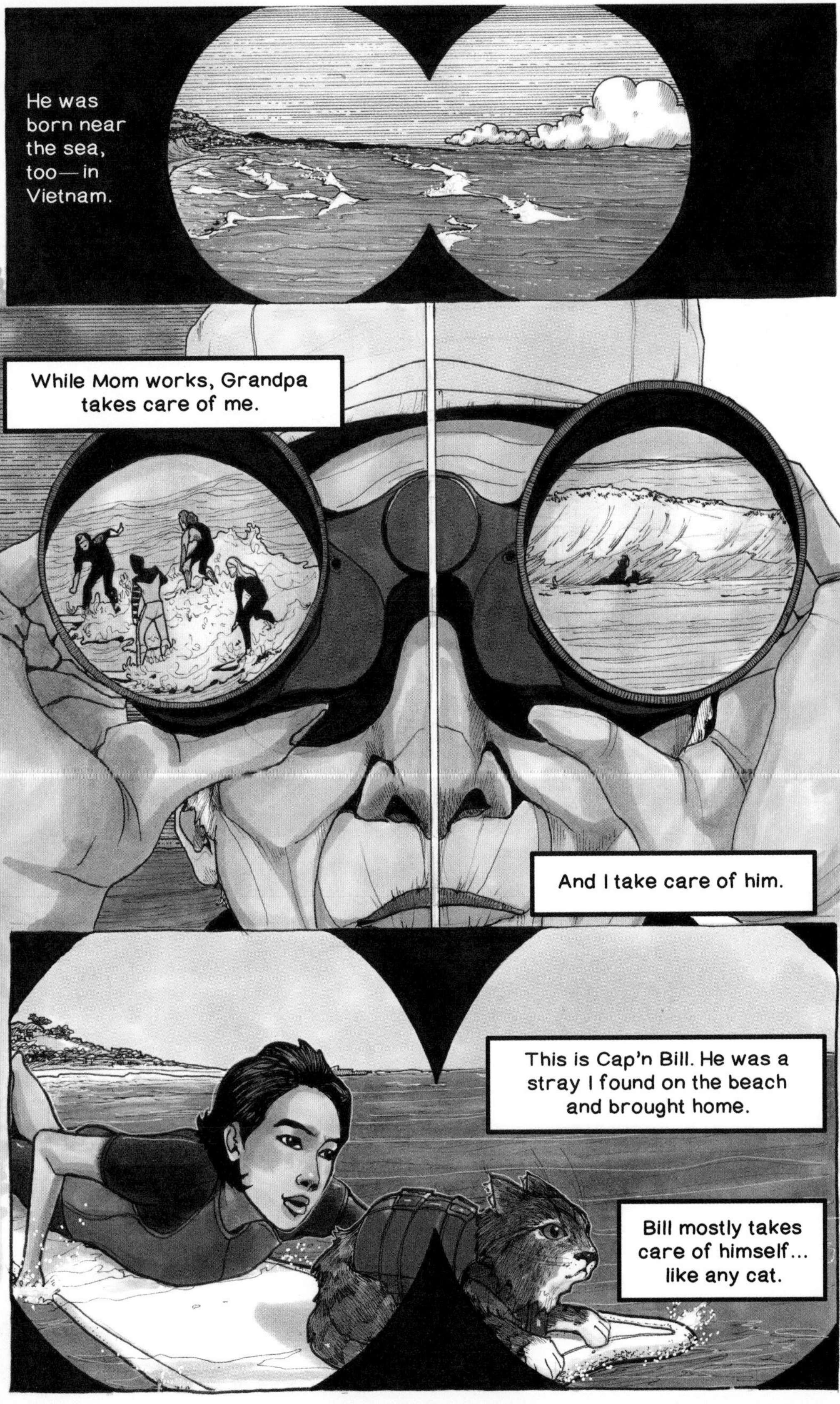
He was born near the sea, too— in Vietnam.
While Mom works, Grandpa takes care of me.
And I take care of him.
This is Cap'n Bill. He was a stray I found on the beach and brought home.
Bill mostly takes care of himself... like any cat.

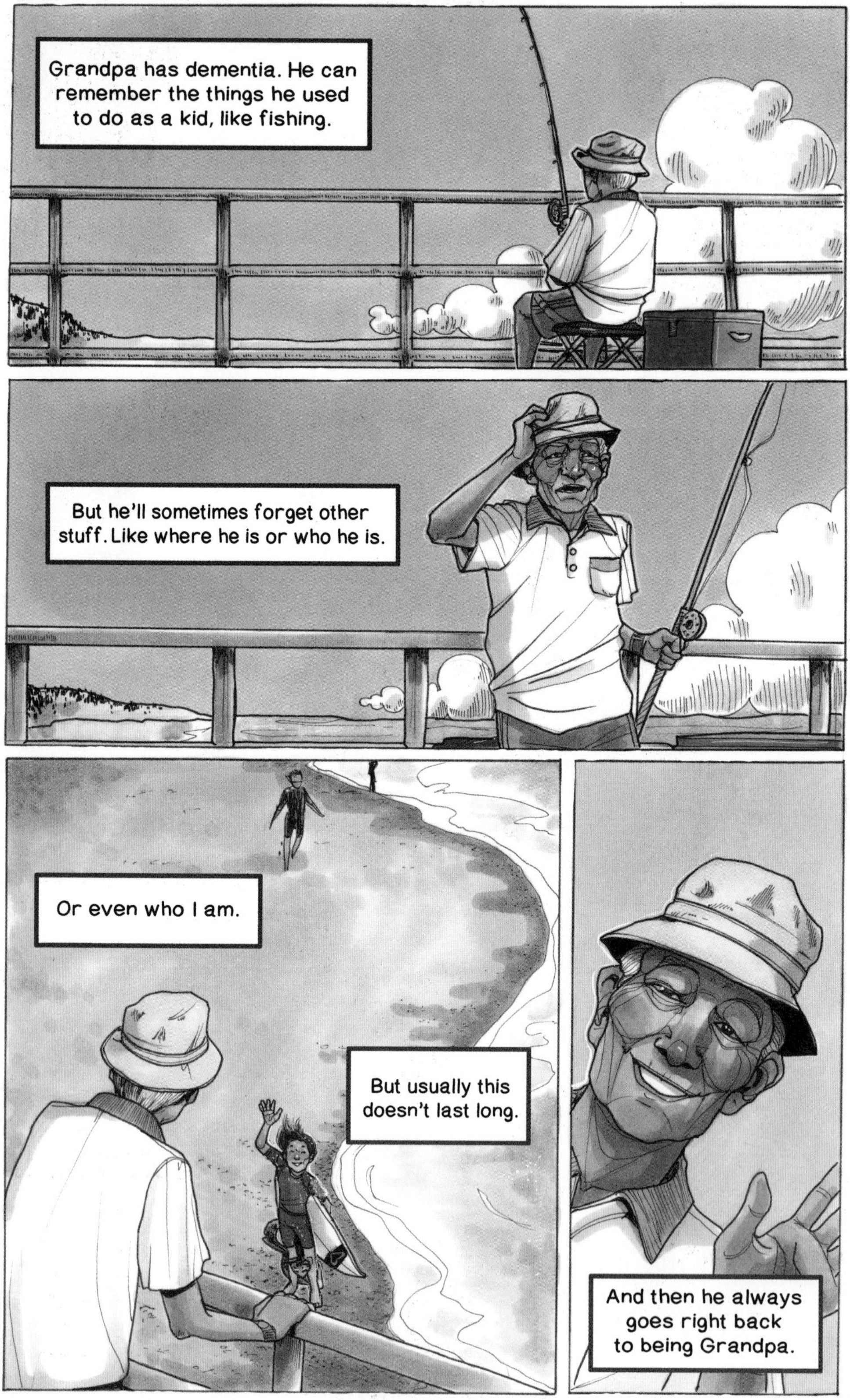
Grandpa has dementia. He can remember the things he used to do as a kid, like fishing.
But he'll sometimes forget other stuff. Like where he is or who he is.
Or even who I am.
But usually this doesn't last long.
And then he always goes right back to being Grandpa.

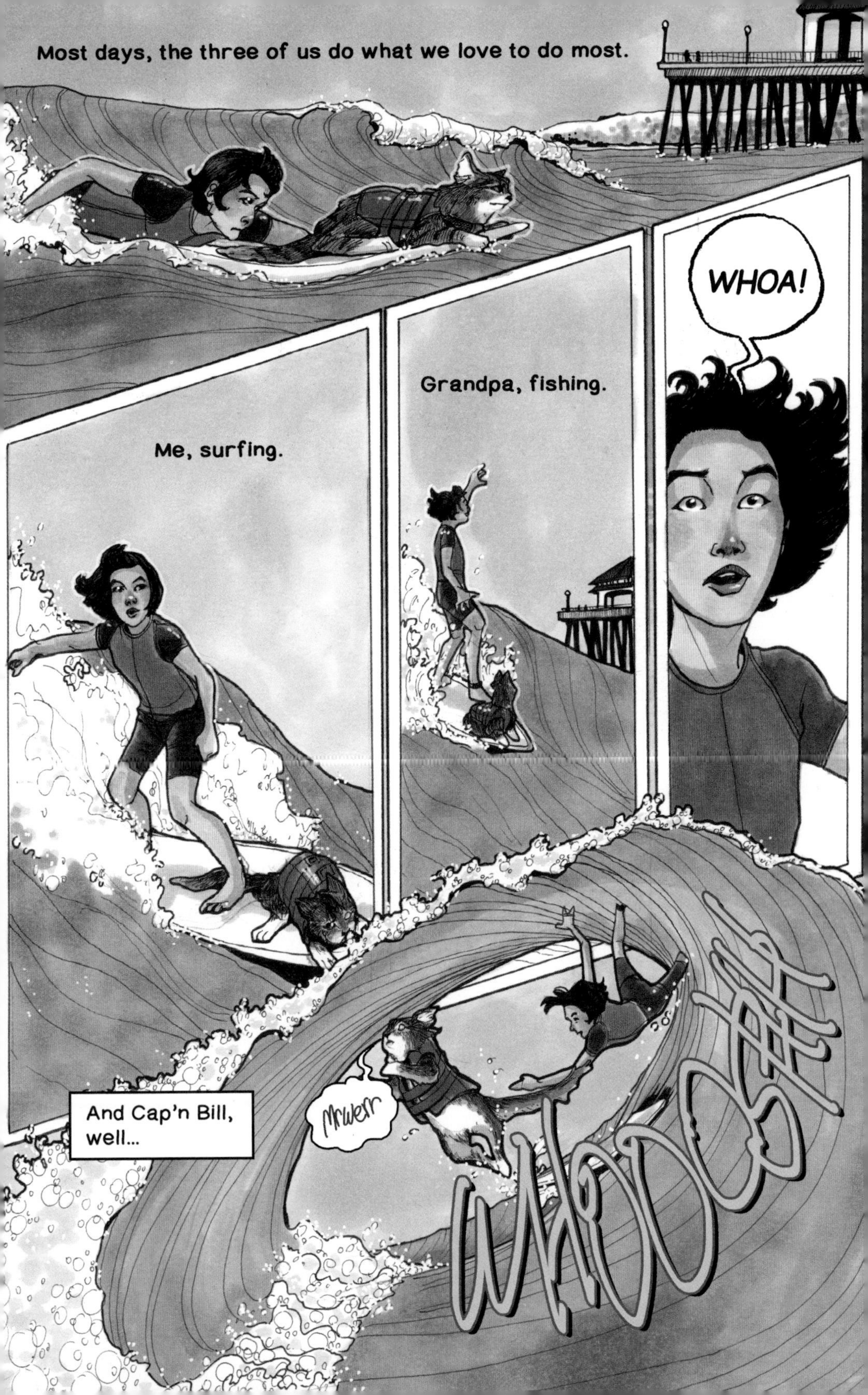
Most days, the three of us do what we love to do most.
Me, surfing.
Grandpa, fishing.
WHOA!
And Cap'n Bill, well...
Mrwerr
WHOOSH

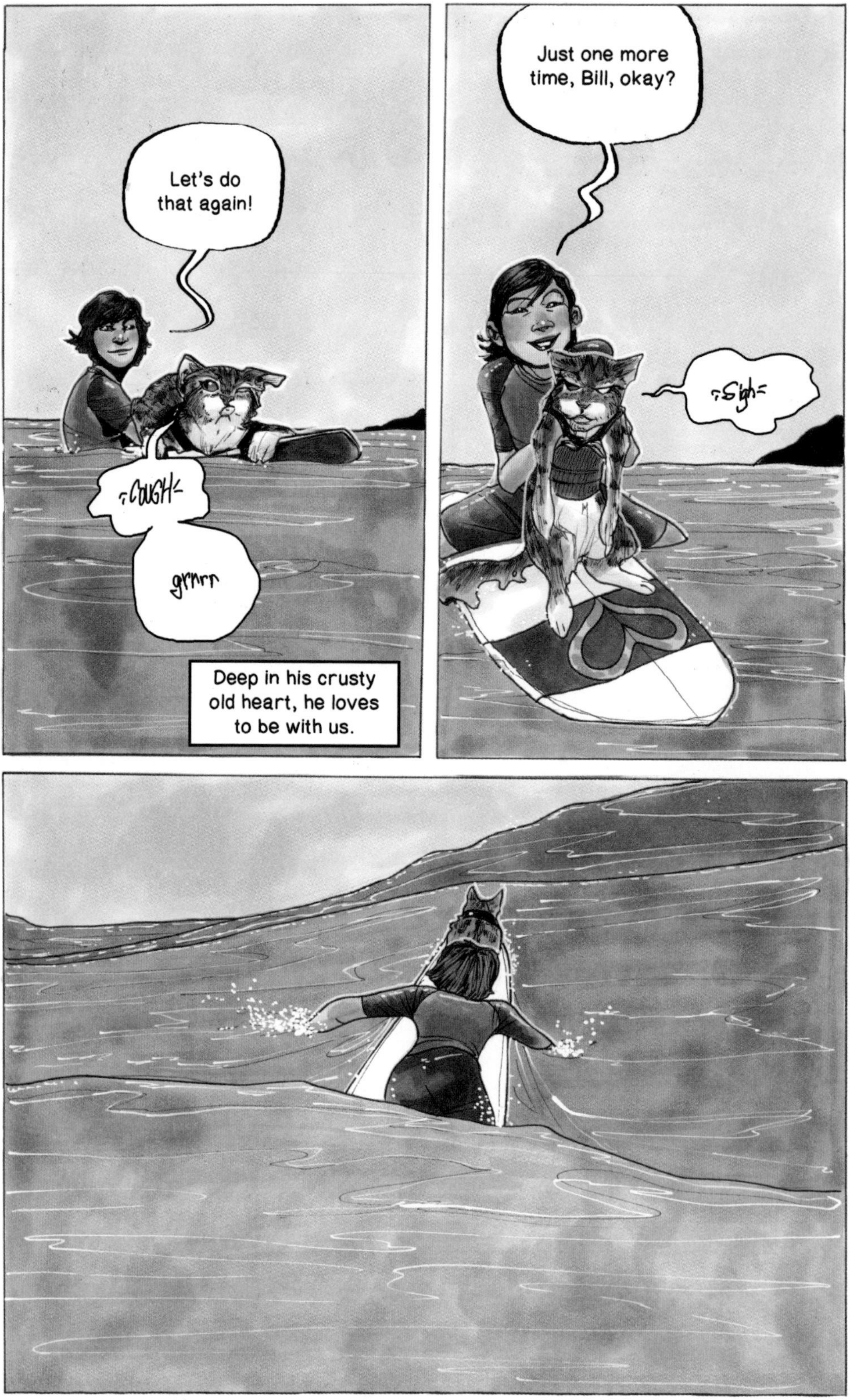
Let's do that again!
COUGH
grrrr
Deep in his crusty old heart, he loves to be with us.
Just one more time, Bill, okay?
Sigh

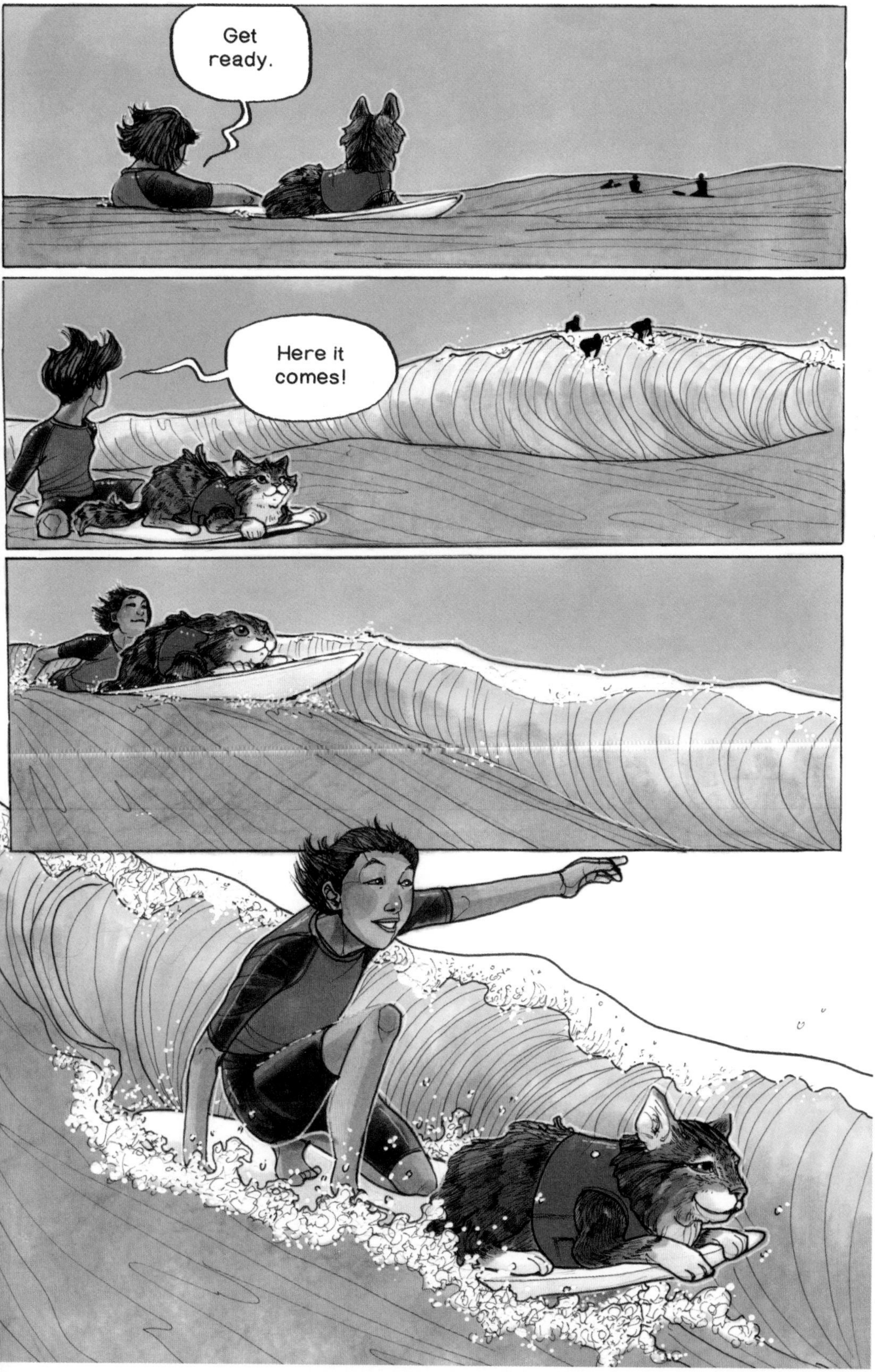
Get ready.
Here it comes!

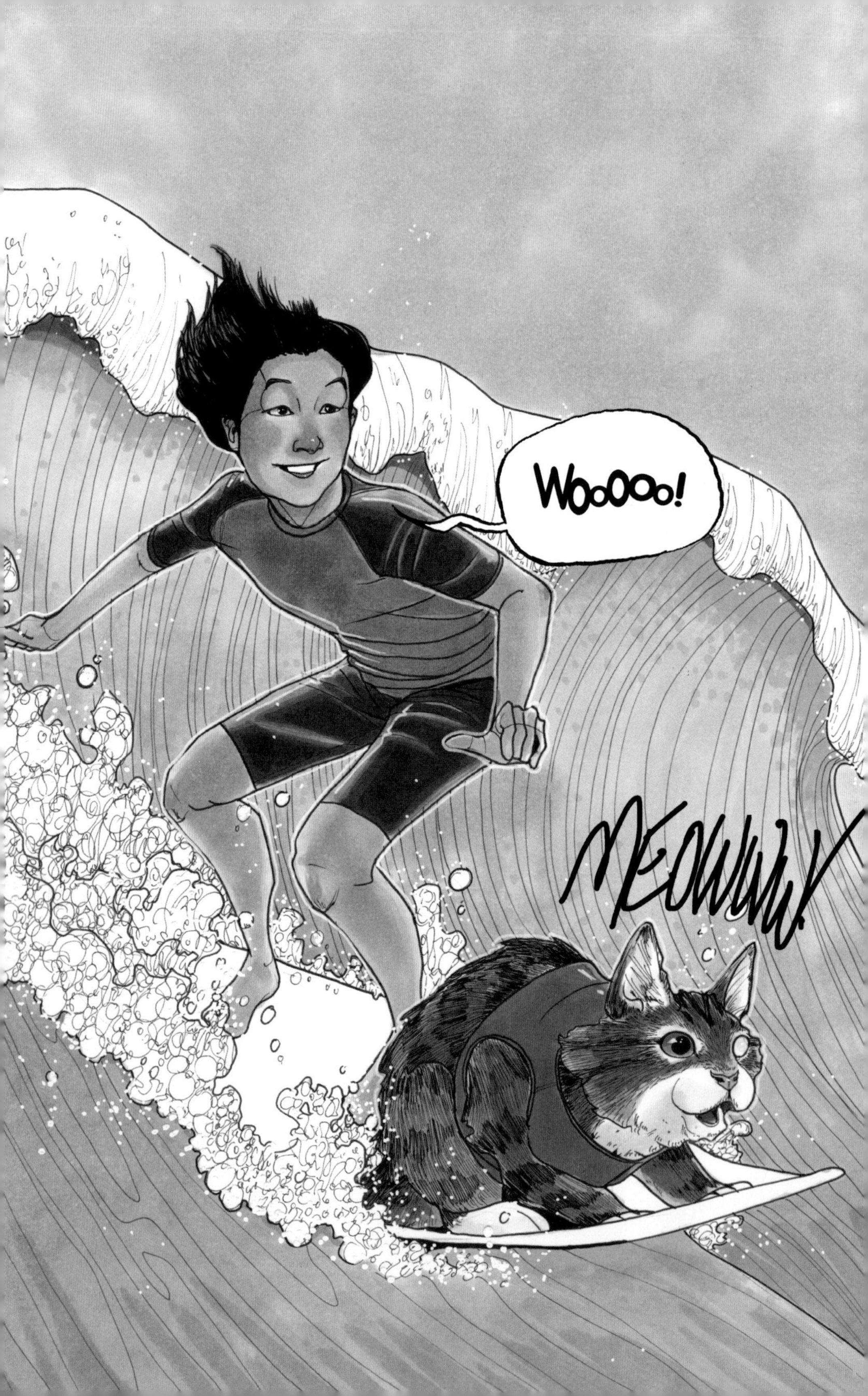
WOoOOo!
MEOWWW!

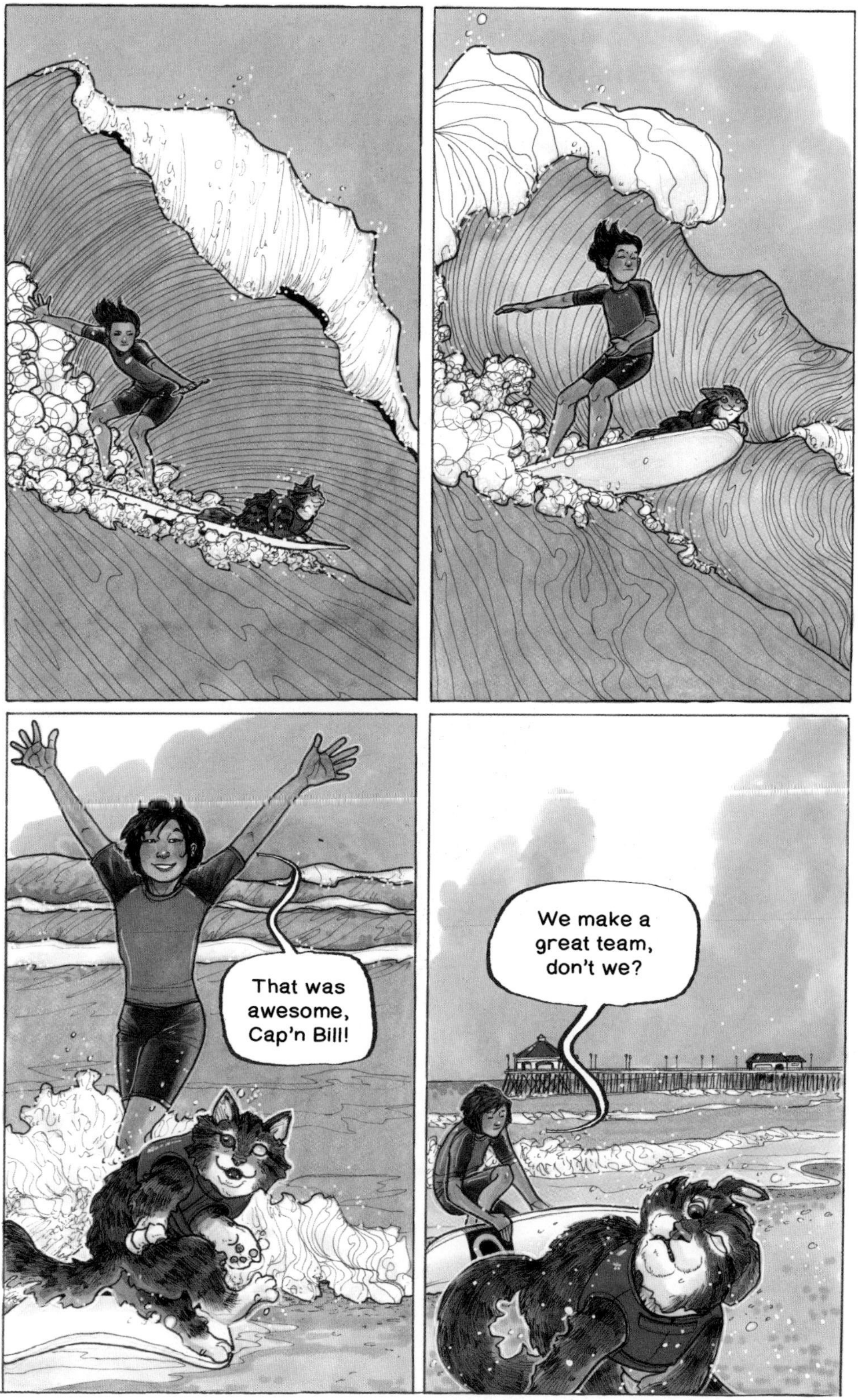
That was awesome, Cap'n Bill!
We make a great team, don't we?

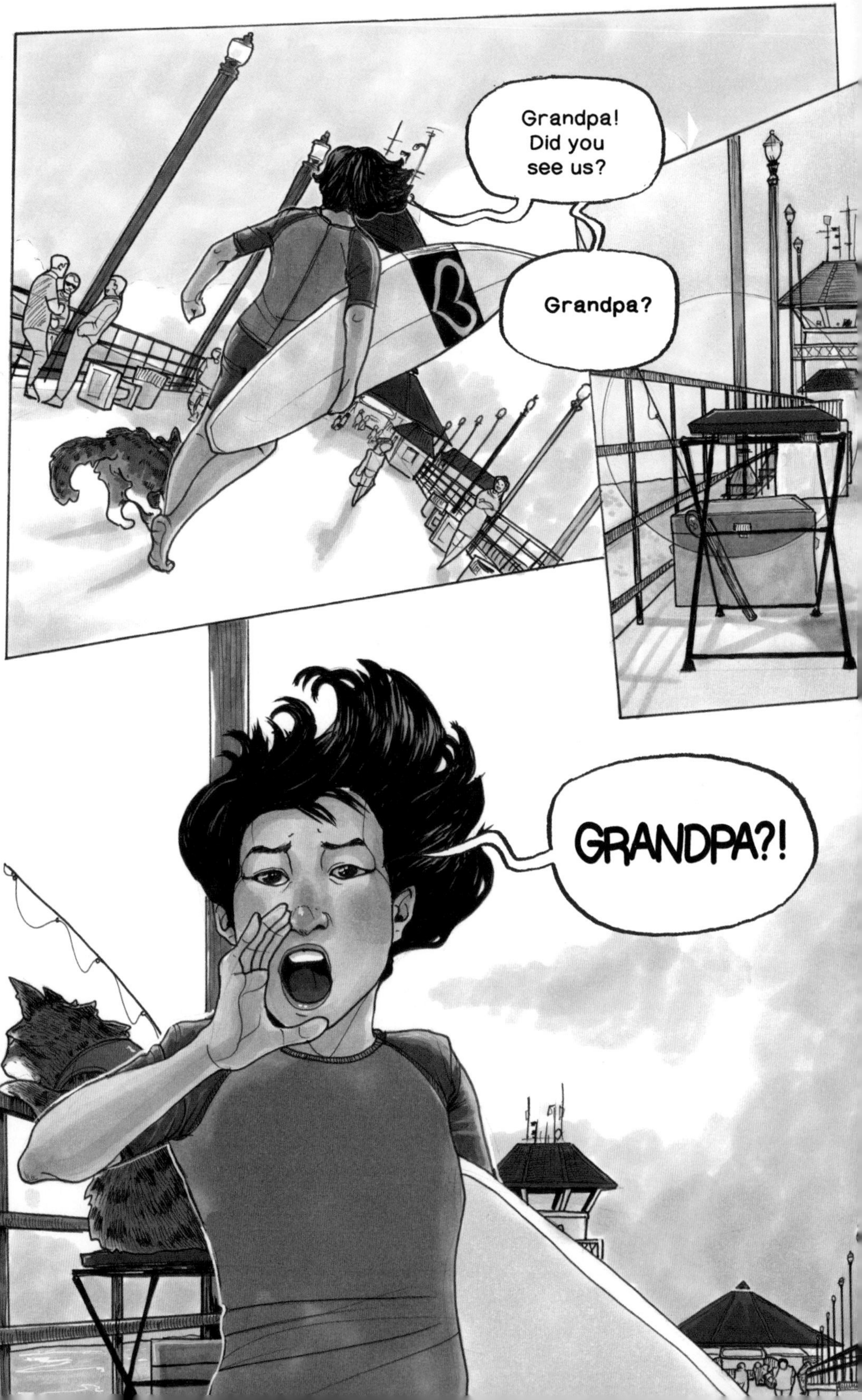
Grandpa! Did you see us?
Grandpa?
GRANDPA?!

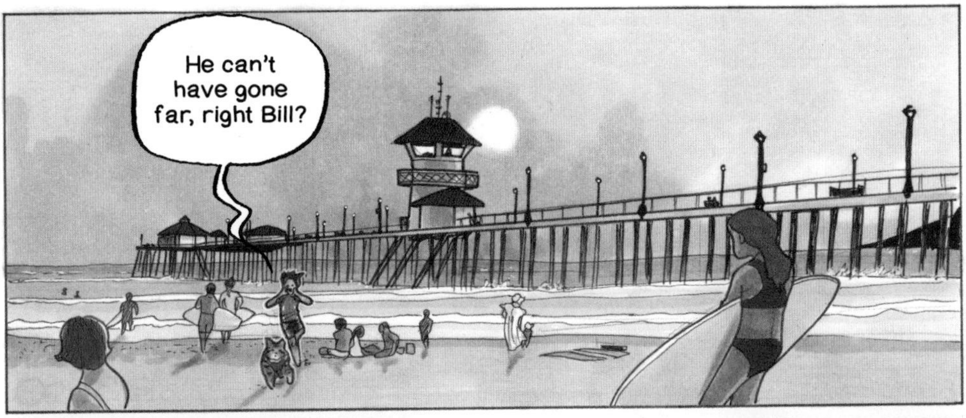
He can't have gone far, right Bill?

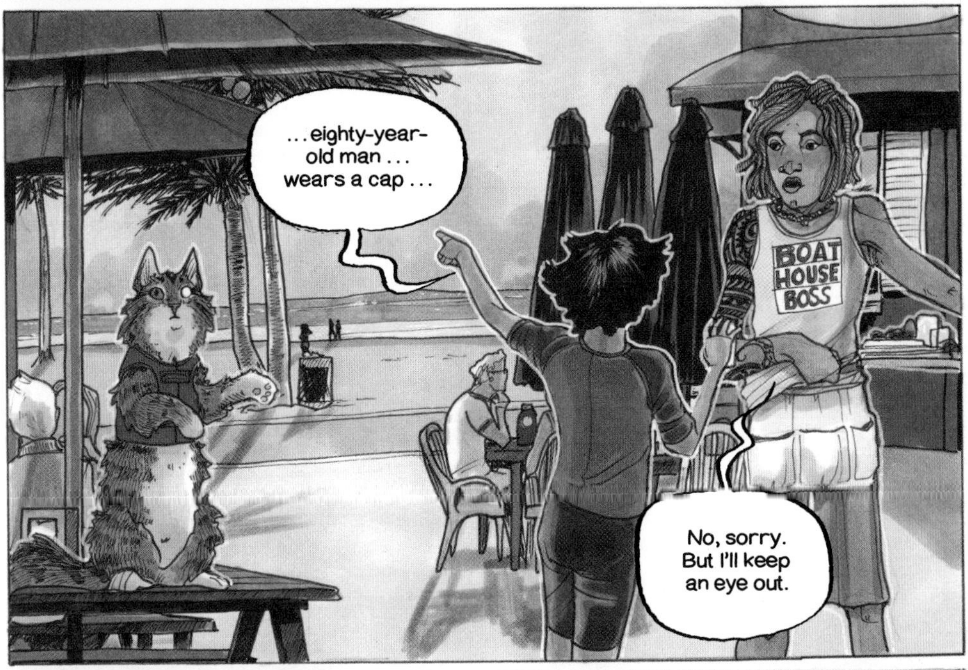
...eighty-year-old man ... wears a cap ...
BOAT HOUSE BOSS
No, sorry. But I'll keep an eye out.

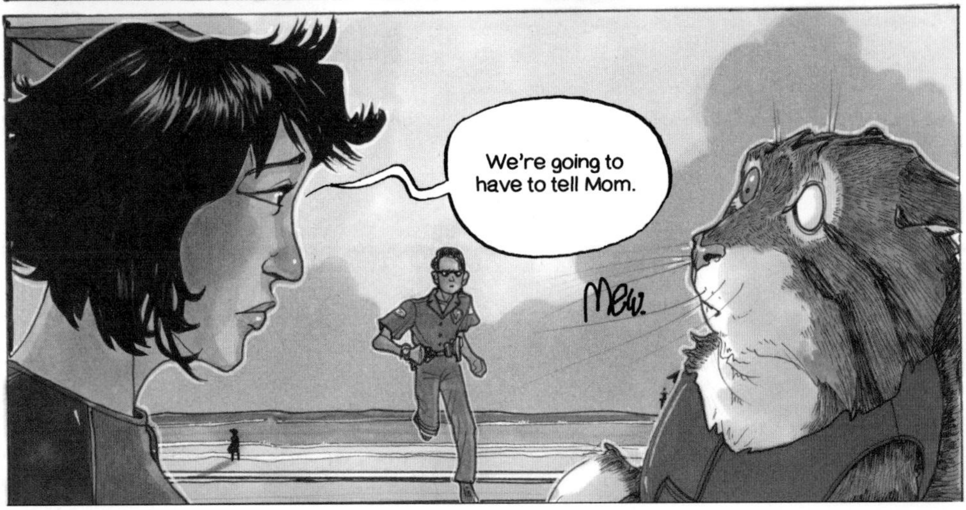
We're going to have to tell Mom.
mew.

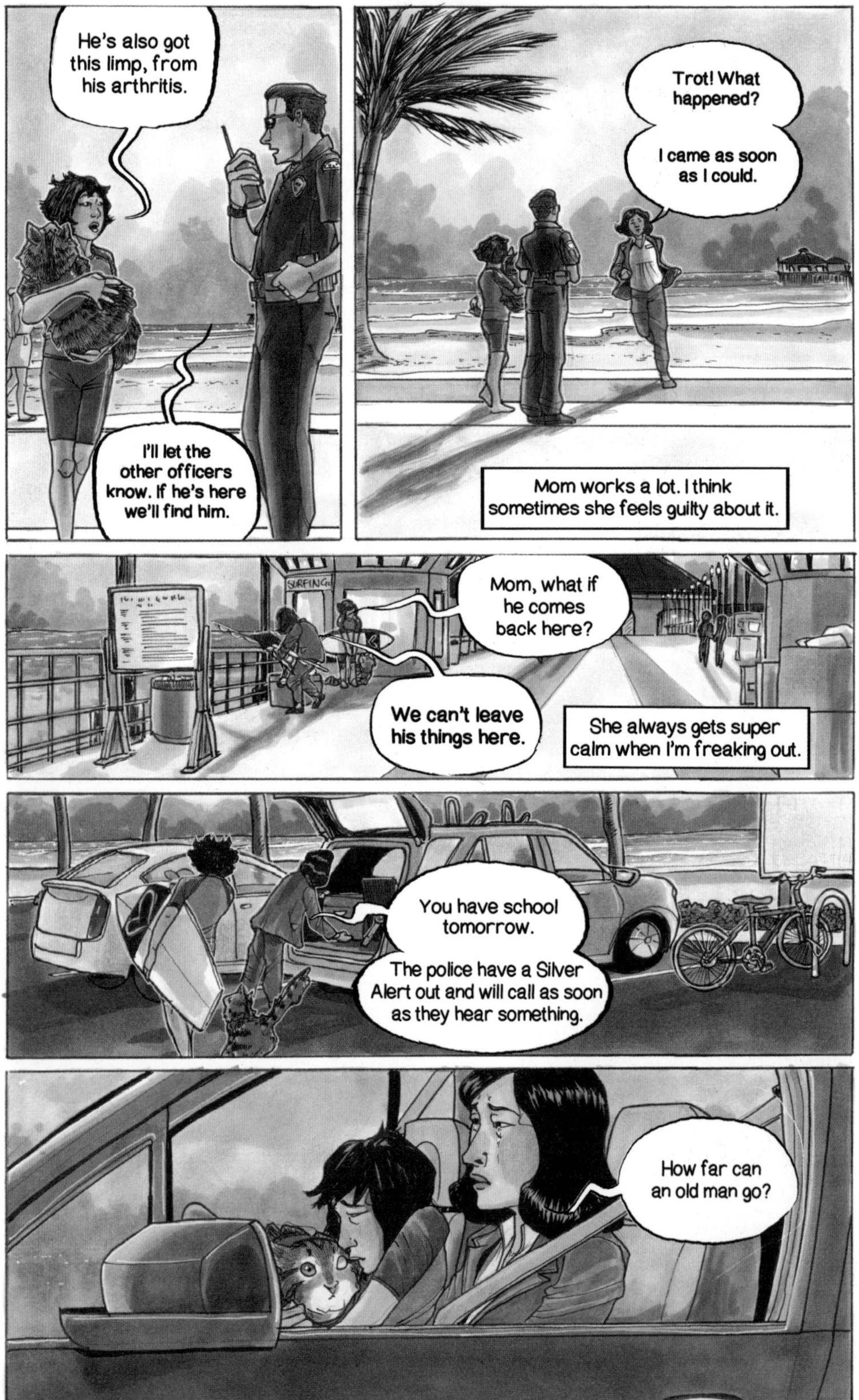
He's also got this limp, from his arthritis.
I'll let the other officers know. If he's here we'll find him.
Trot! What happened?
I came as soon as I could.
Mom works a lot. I think sometimes she feels guilty about it.
SURFING
Mom, what if he comes back here?
We can't leave his things here.
She always gets super calm when I'm freaking out.
You have school tomorrow.
The police have a Silver Alert out and will call as soon as they hear something.
How far can an old man go?

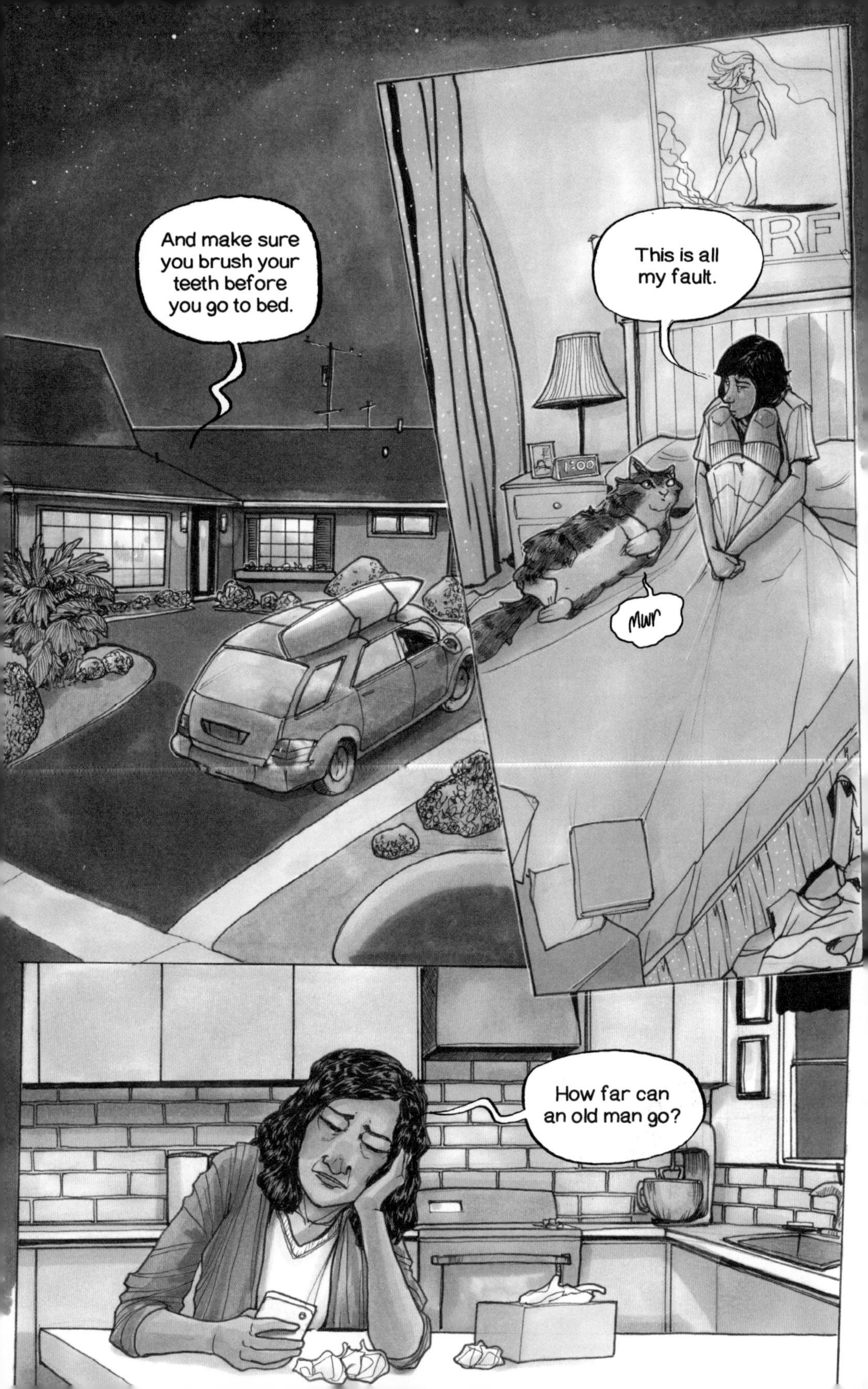
And make sure you brush your teeth before you go to bed.
This is all my fault.
Mwr
How far can an old man go?

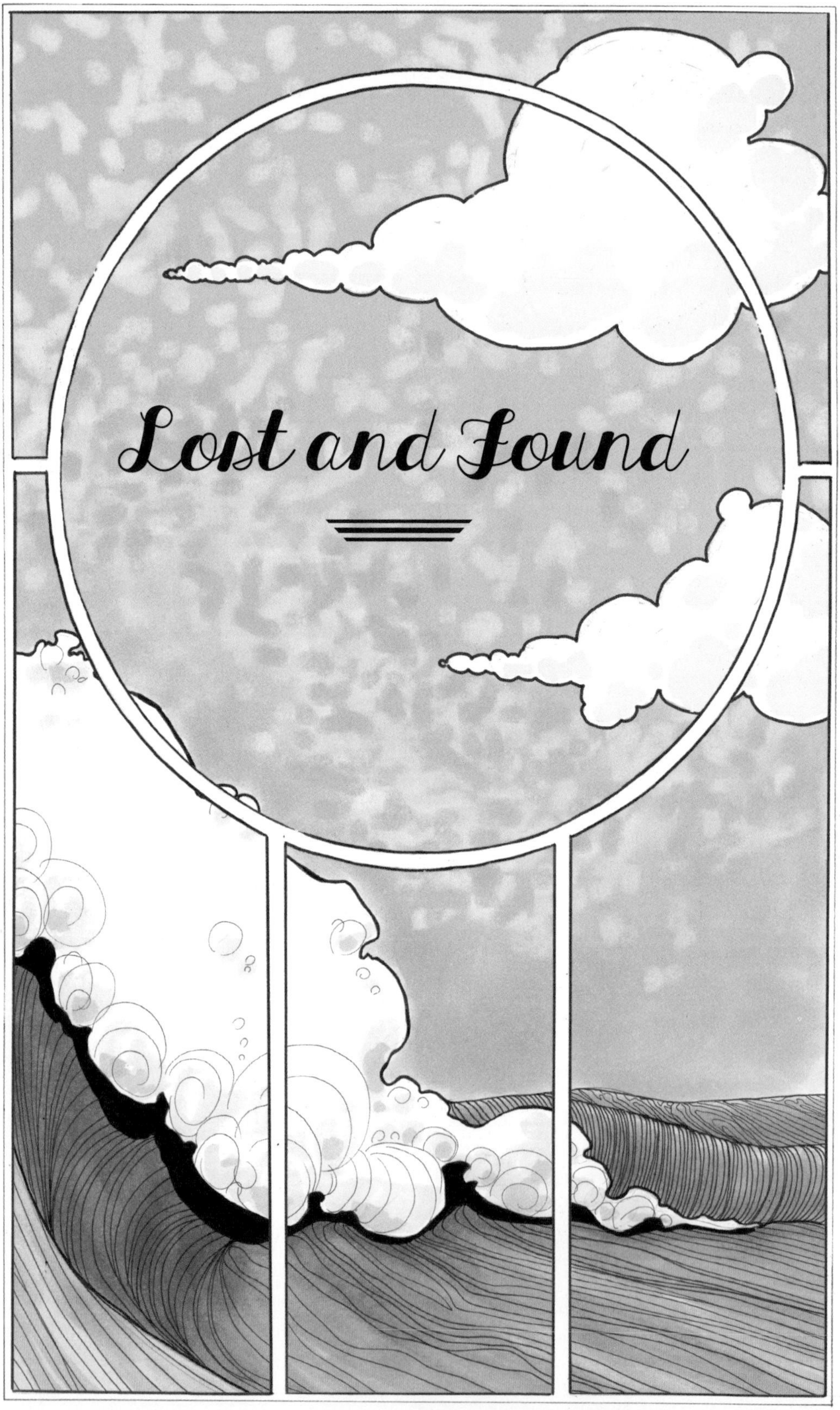
Lost and Found

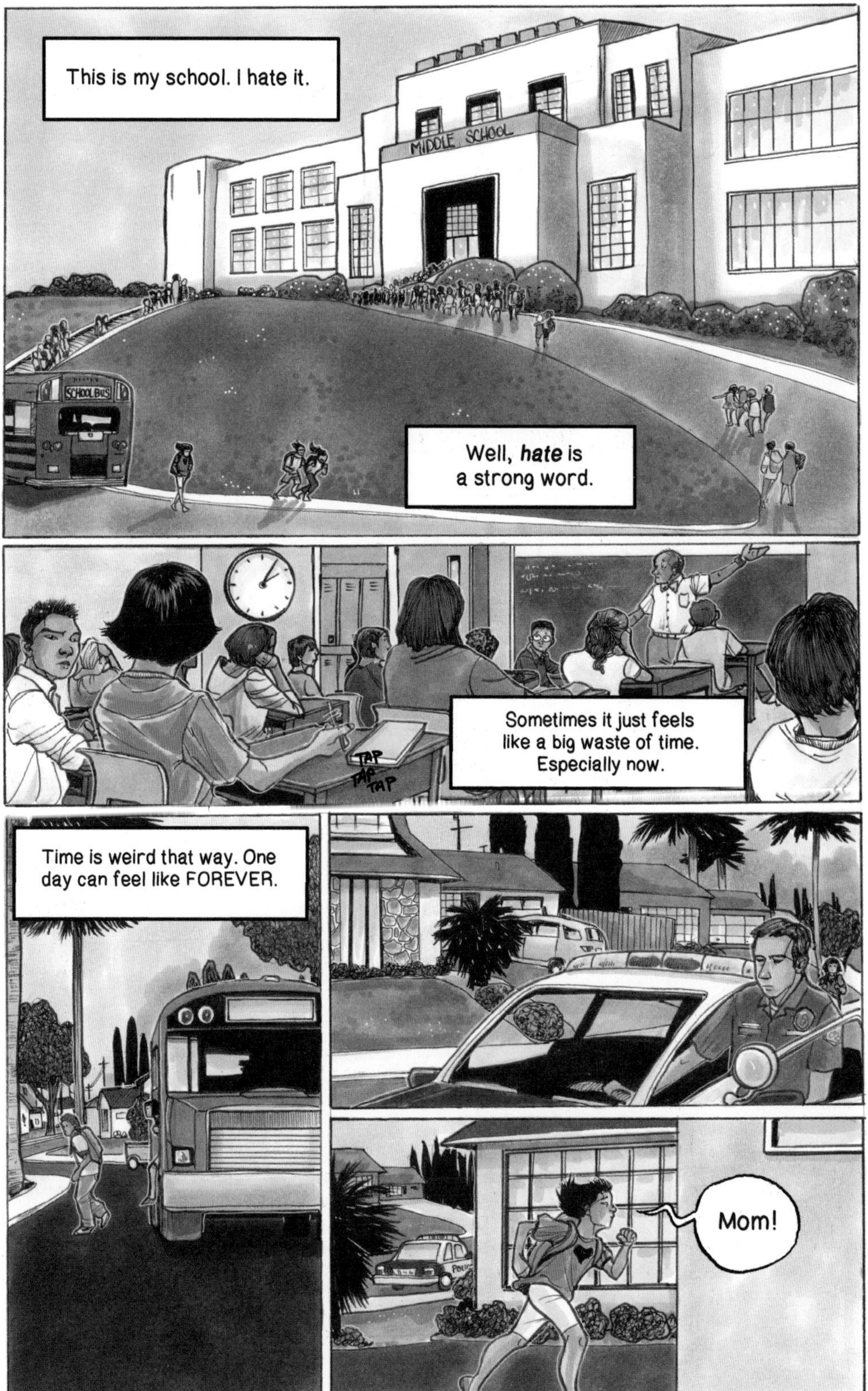
This is my school. I hate it.
MIDDLE SCHOOL
SCHOOL BUS
Well, *hate* is a strong word.
Sometimes it just feels like a big waste of time. Especially now.
TAP TAP TAP
Time is weird that way. One day can feel like FOREVER.
Mom!

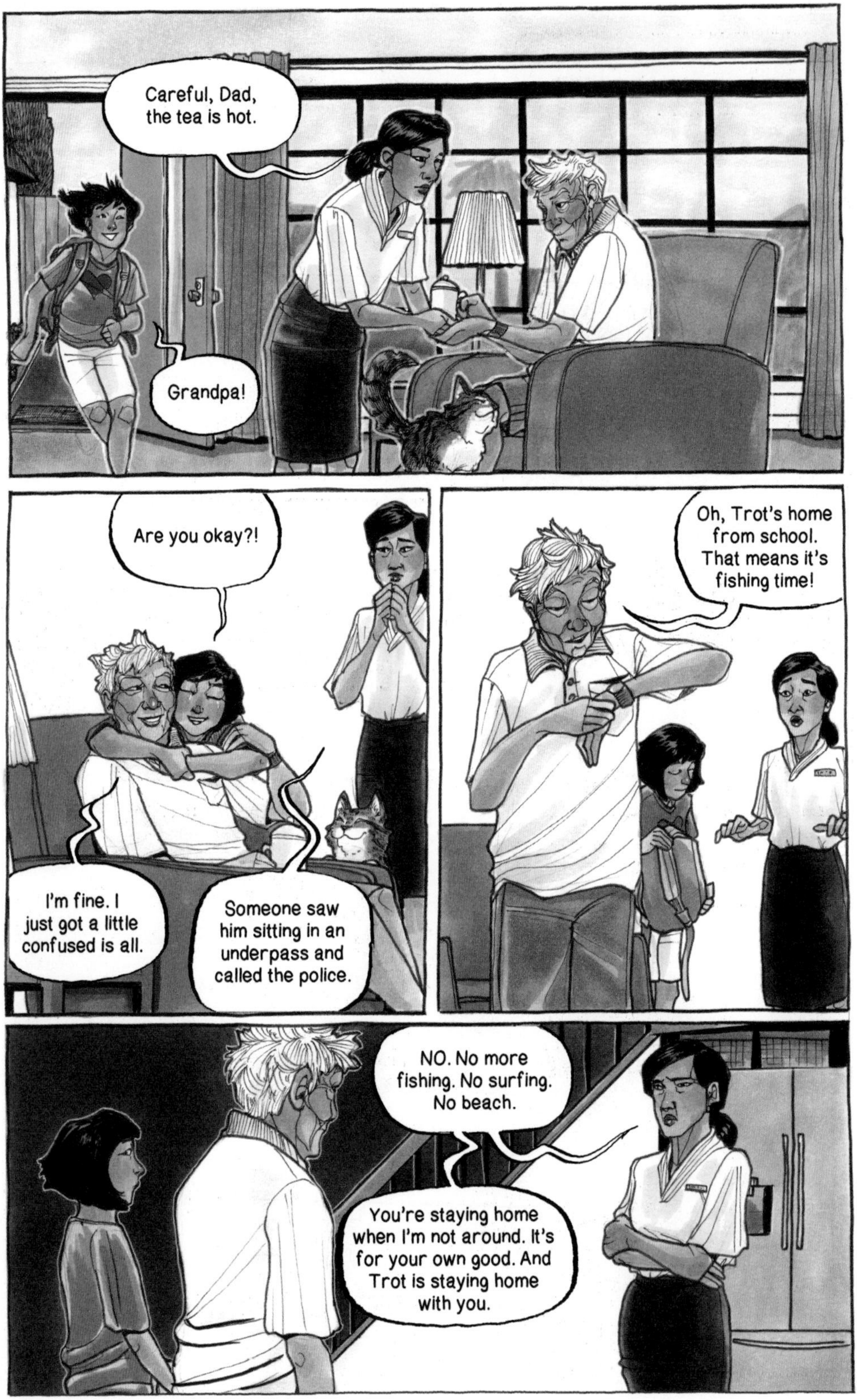
Careful, Dad, the tea is hot.
Grandpa!
Are you okay?!
I'm fine. I just got a little confused is all.
Someone saw him sitting in an underpass and called the police.
Oh, Trot's home from school. That means it's fishing time!
NO. No more fishing. No surfing. No beach.
You're staying home when I'm not around. It's for your own good. And Trot is staying home with you.

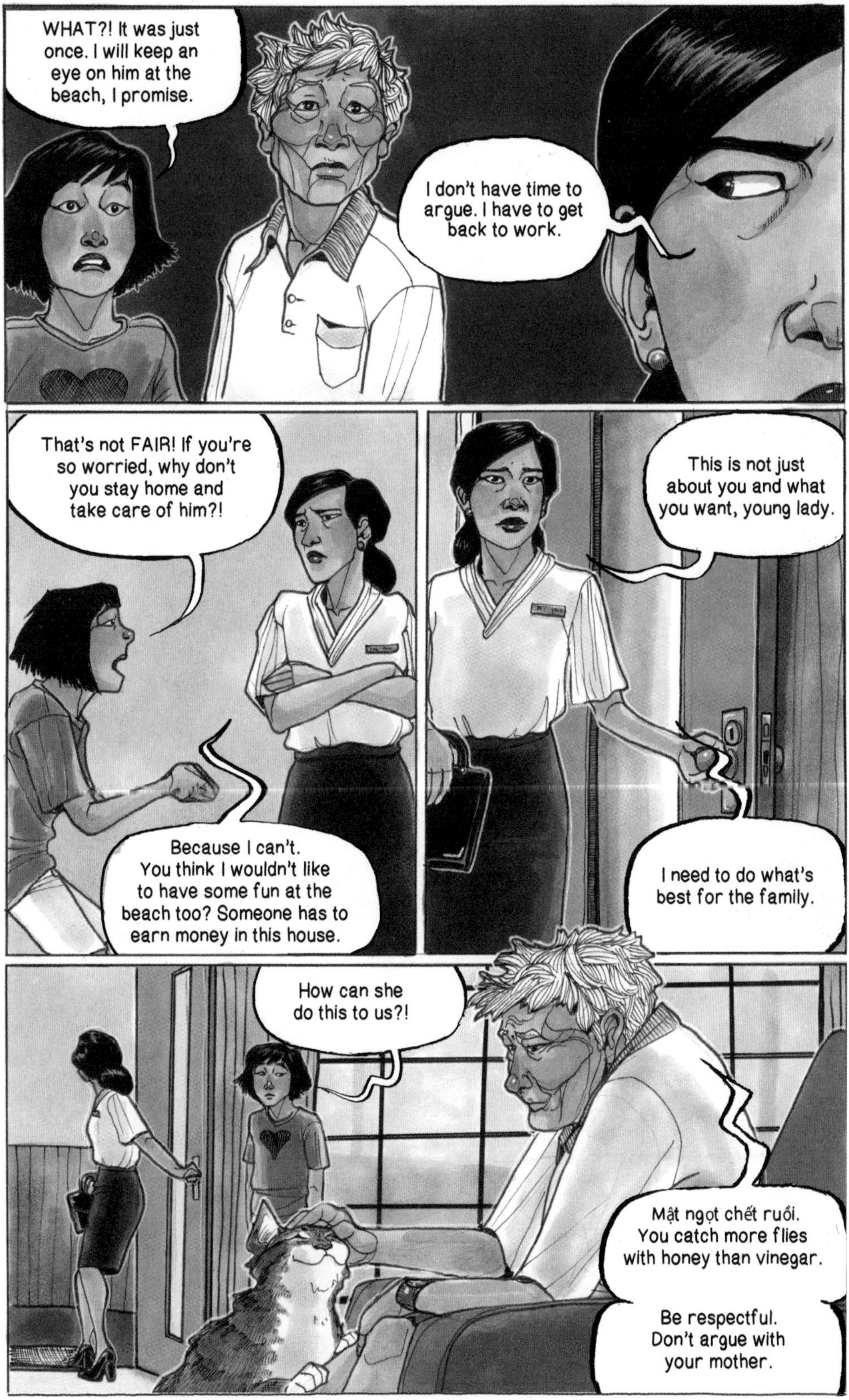
WHAT?! It was just once. I will keep an eye on him at the beach, I promise.
I don't have time to argue. I have to get back to work.
That's not FAIR! If you're so worried, why don't you stay home and take care of him?!
Because I can't. You think I wouldn't like to have some fun at the beach too? Someone has to earn money in this house.
This is not just about you and what you want, young lady.
I need to do what's best for the family.
How can she do this to us?!
Mật ngọt chết ruồi. You catch more flies with honey than vinegar.
Be respectful. Don't argue with your mother.

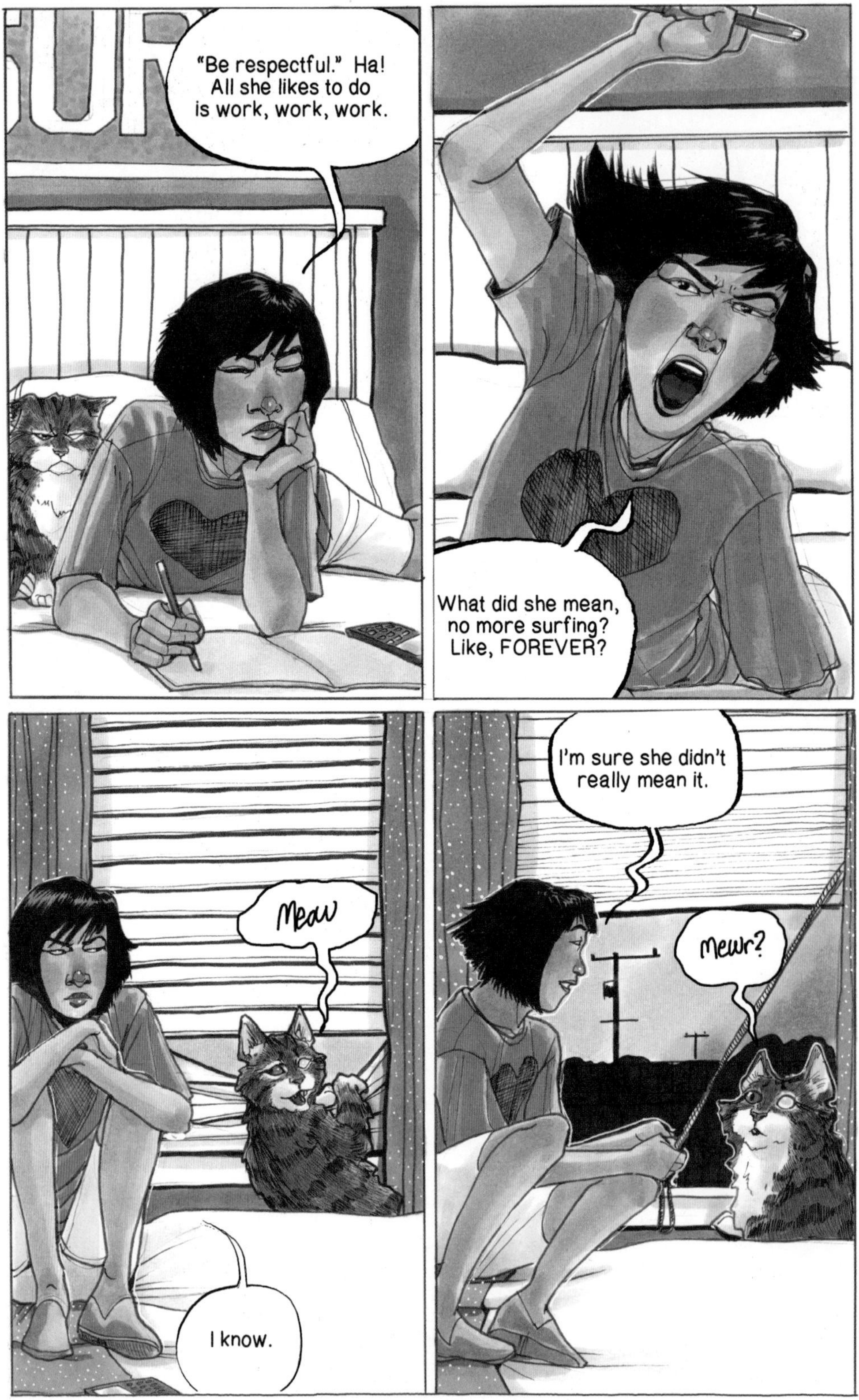
"Be respectful." Ha! All she likes to do is work, work, work.
What did she mean, no more surfing? Like, FOREVER?
Meaw
I know.
I'm sure she didn't really mean it.
Mewr?

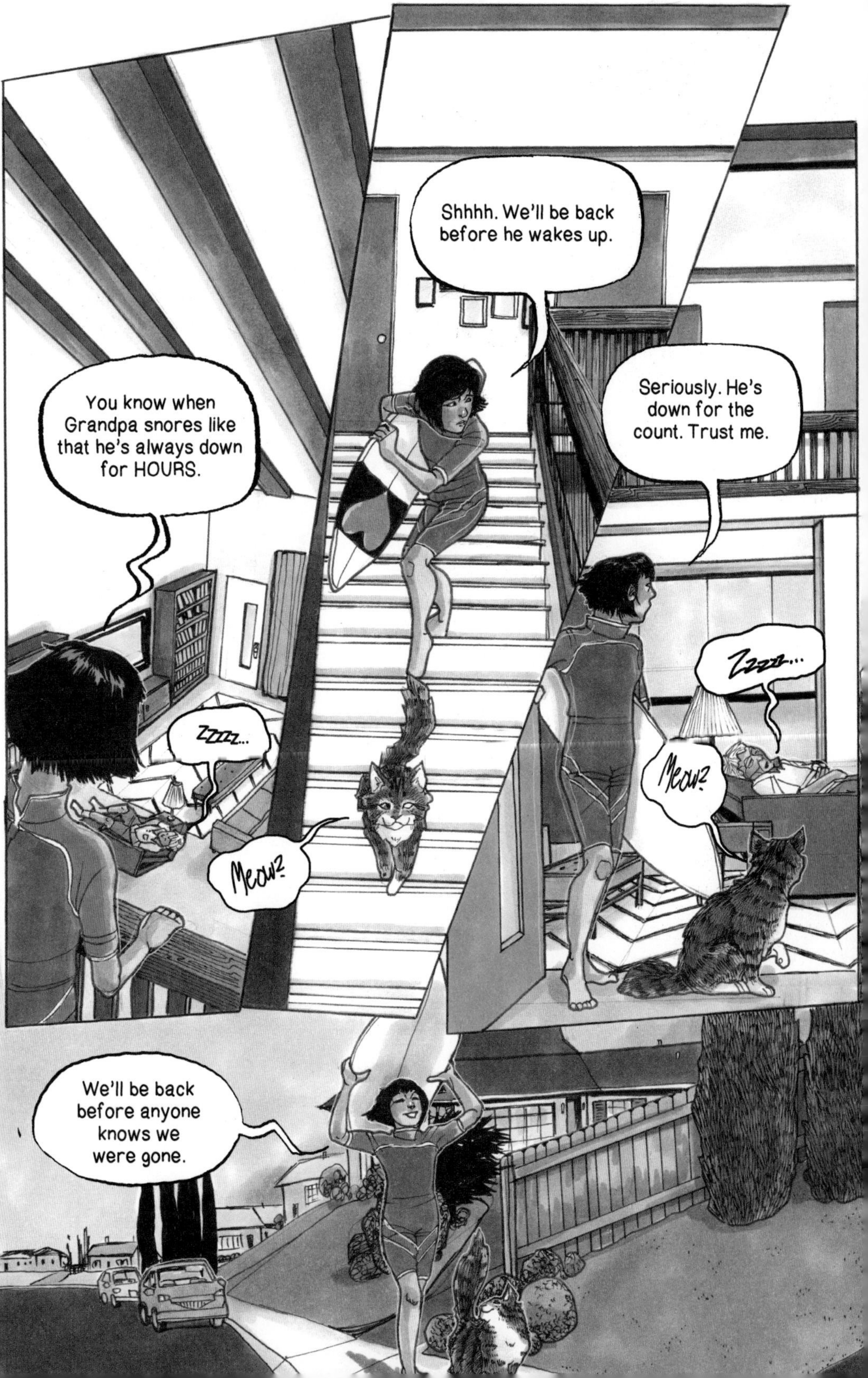
You know when Grandpa snores like that he's always down for HOURS.
Zzzzz...
Meow?
Shhhh. We'll be back before he wakes up.
Seriously. He's down for the count. Trust me.
Zzzzz...
Meow?
We'll be back before anyone knows we were gone.

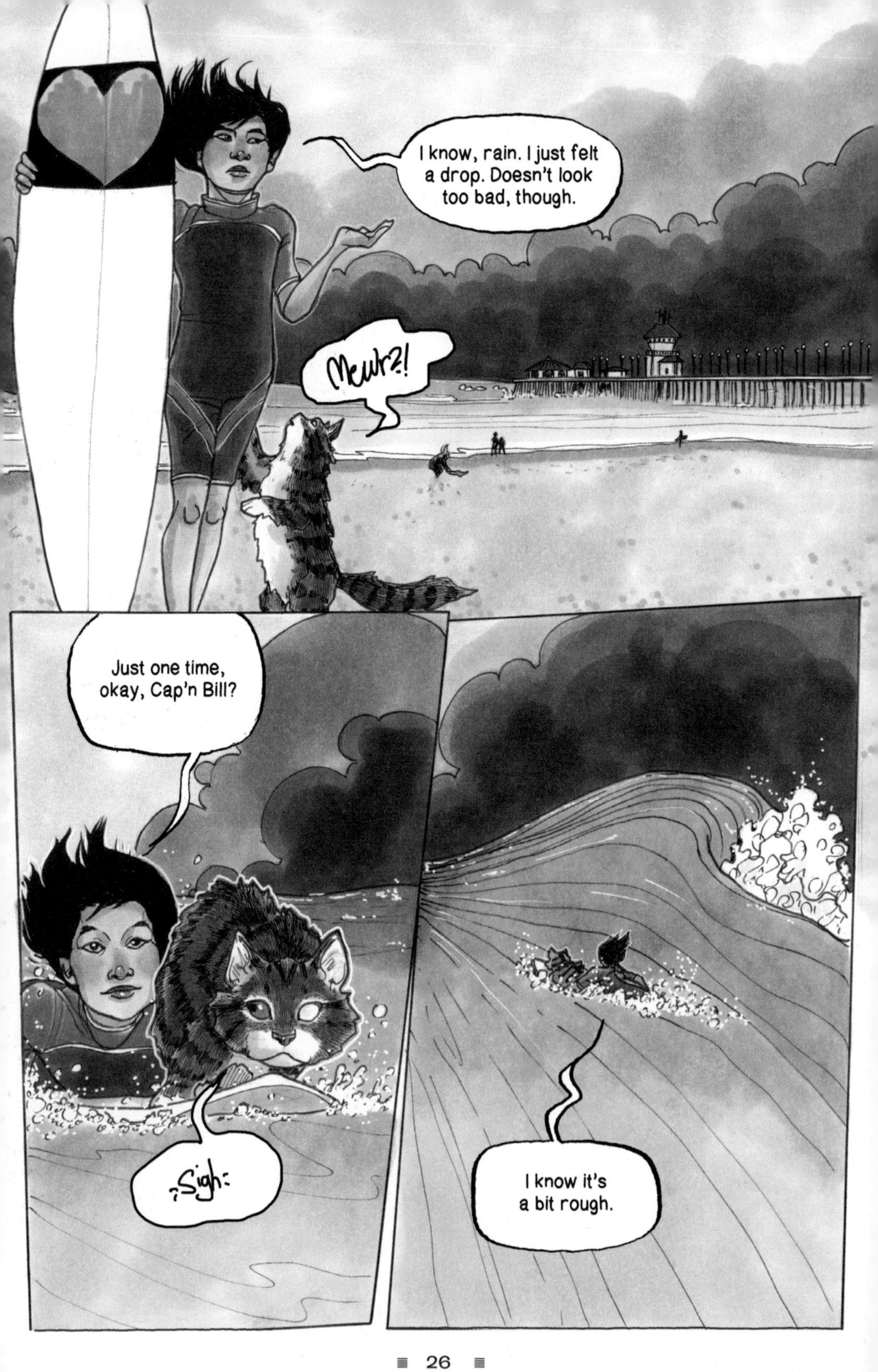
I know, rain. I just felt a drop. Doesn't look too bad, though.
Mewr?!
Just one time, okay, Cap'n Bill?
¿Sigh:
I know it's a bit rough.

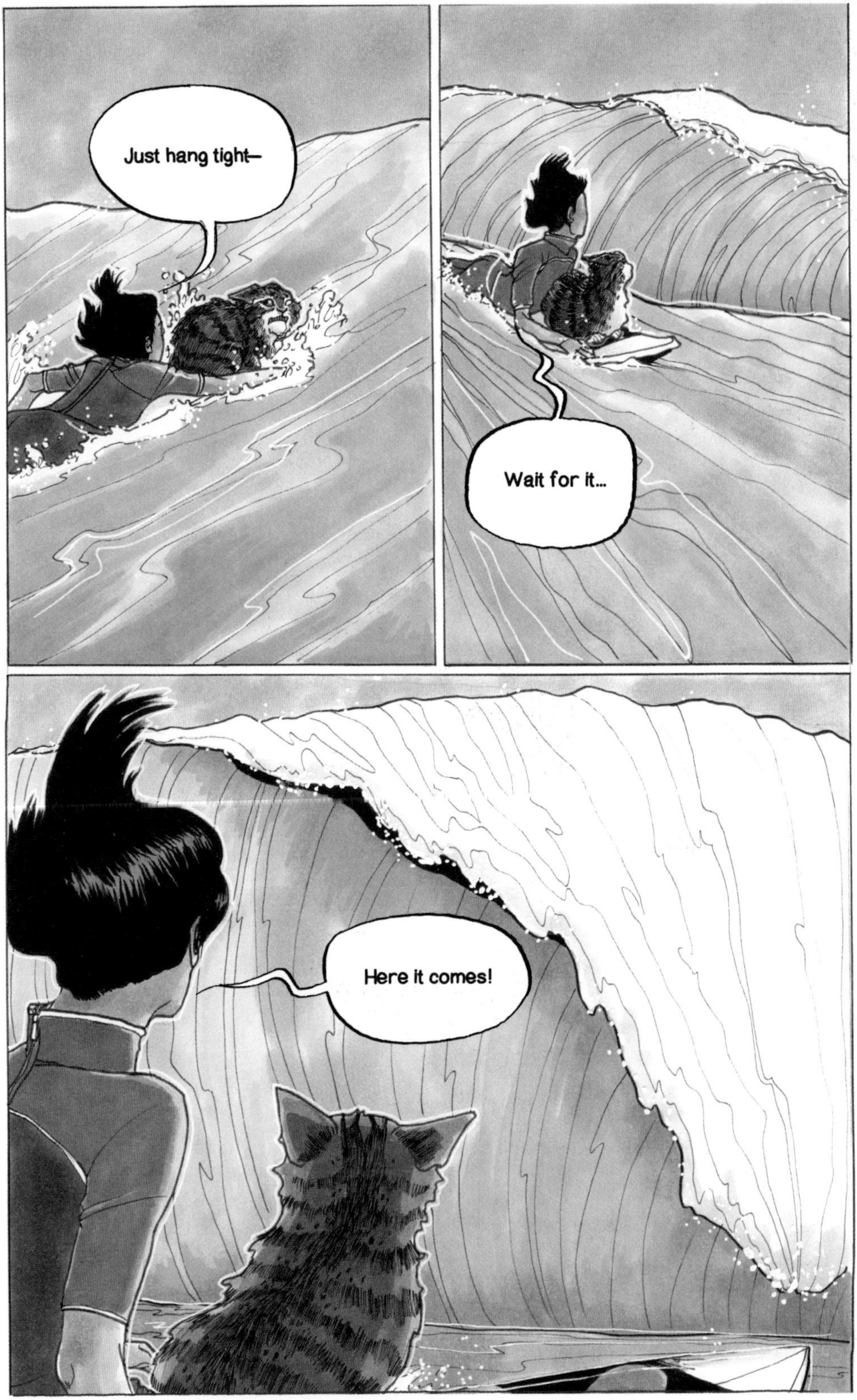
Just hang tight—
Wait for it...
Here it comes!

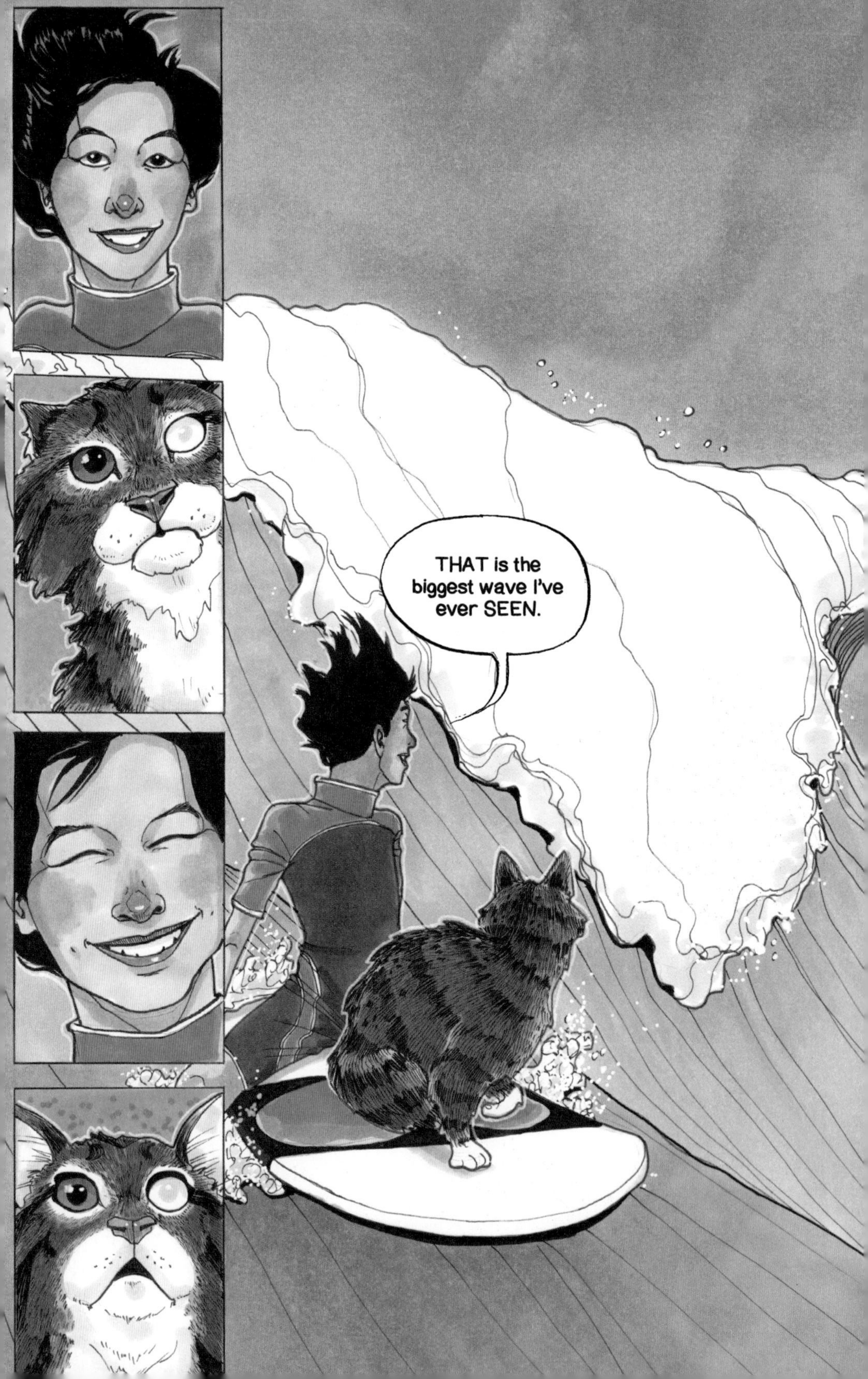
THAT is the biggest wave I've ever SEEN.

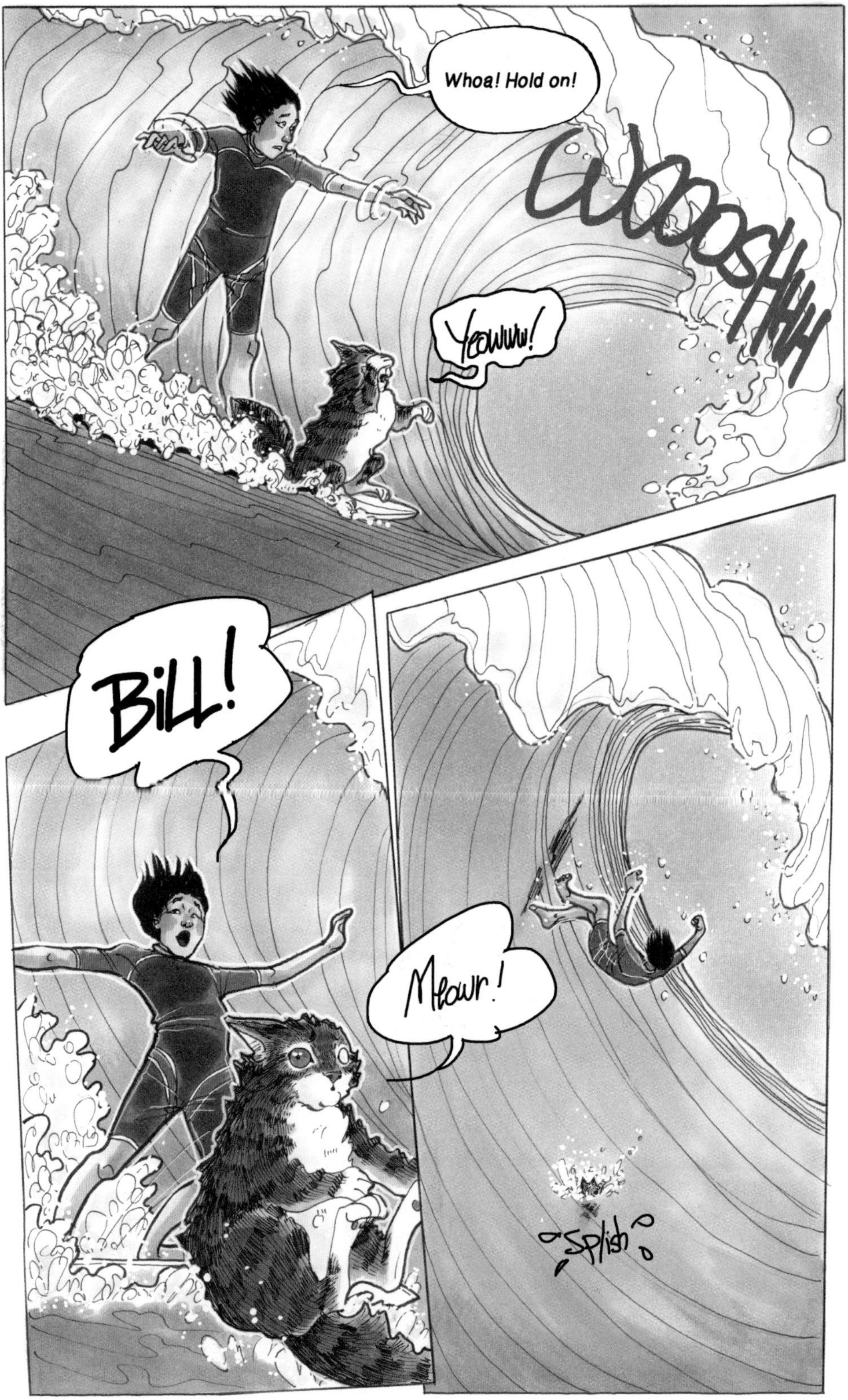
Whoa! Hold on!
WHOOOSHHH
Yeowww!
Bill!
Meowr!
Splish

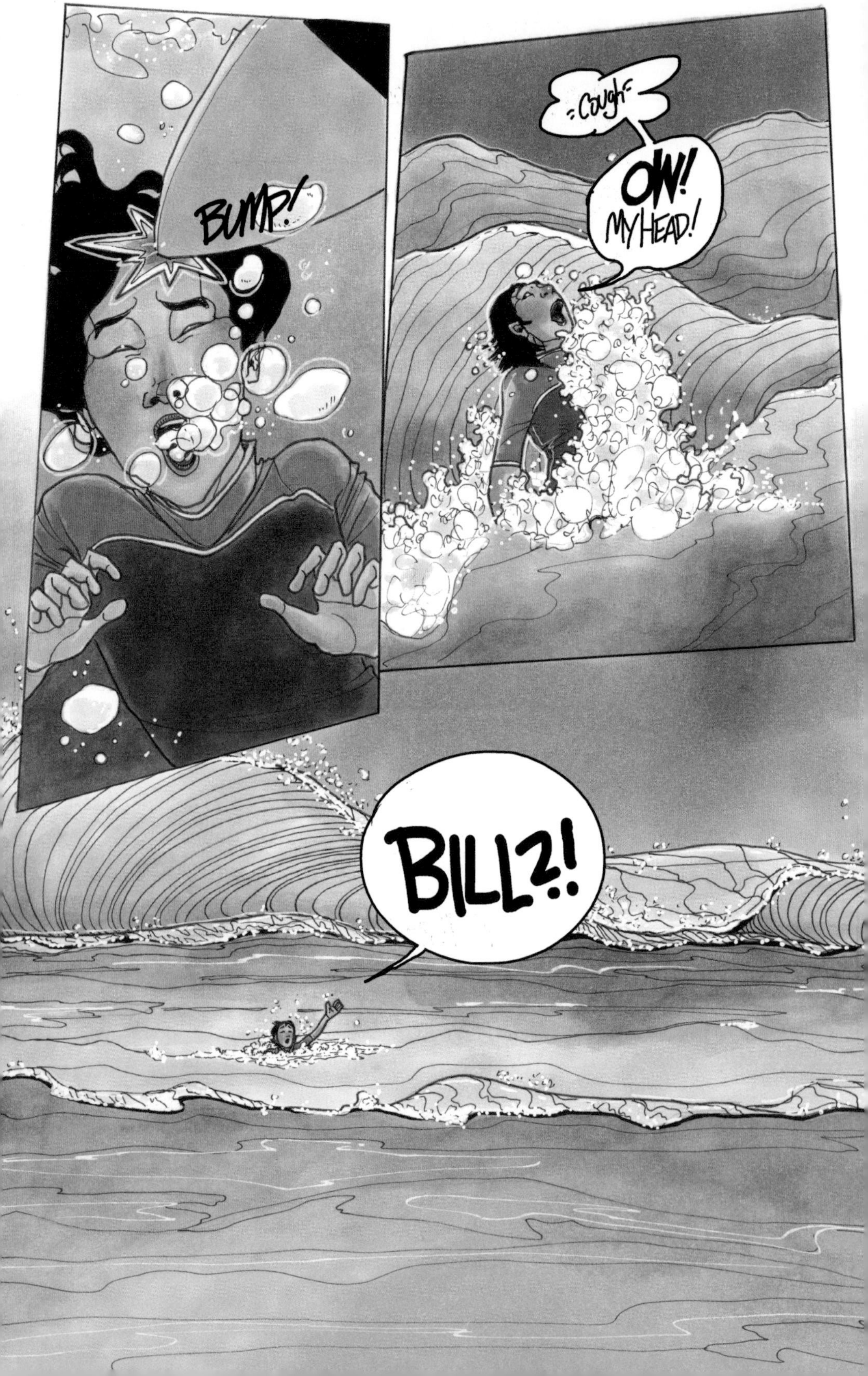
BUMP!
COUGH
OW! MY HEAD!
BILL?!

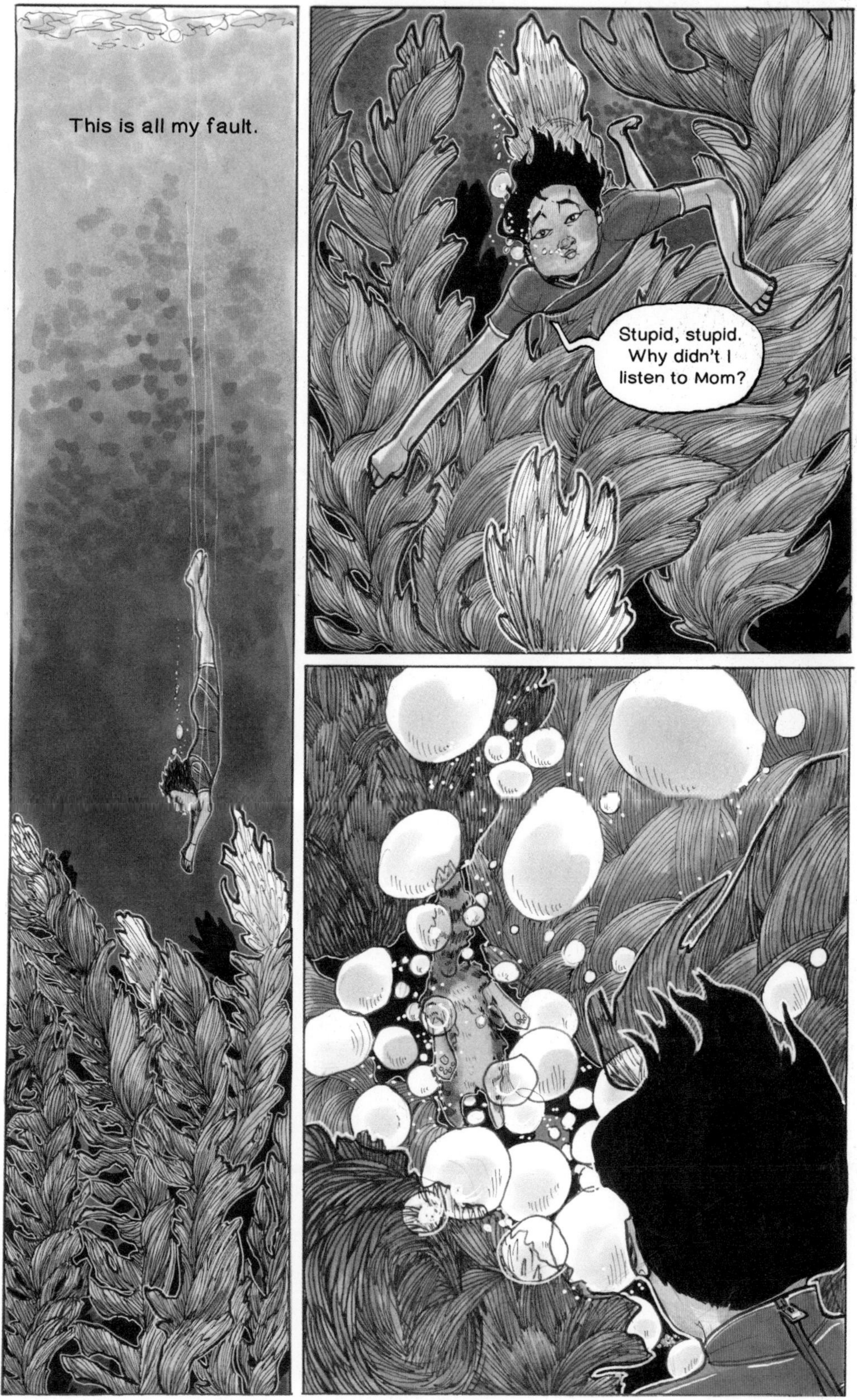
This is all my fault.
Stupid, stupid. Why didn't I listen to Mom?

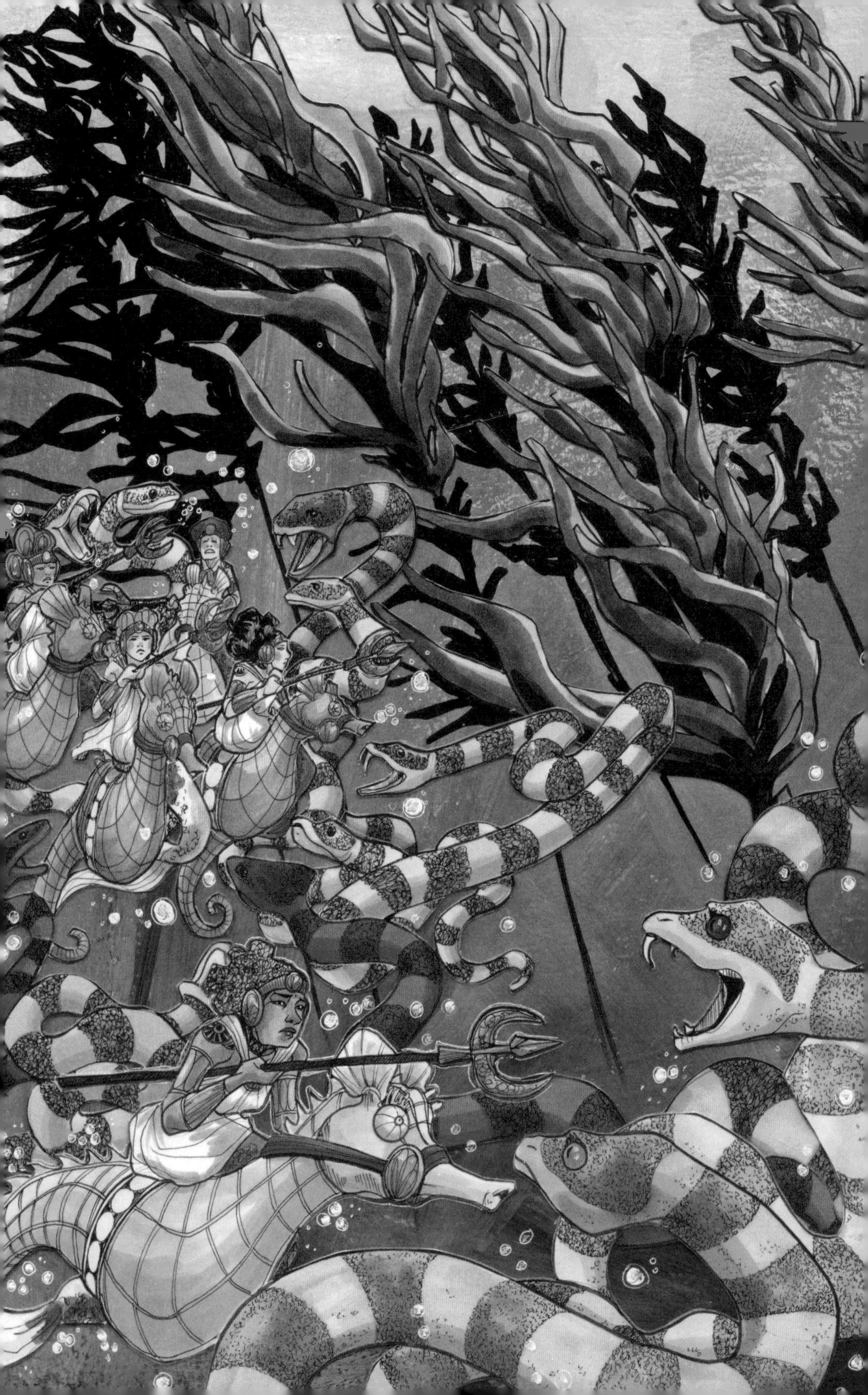

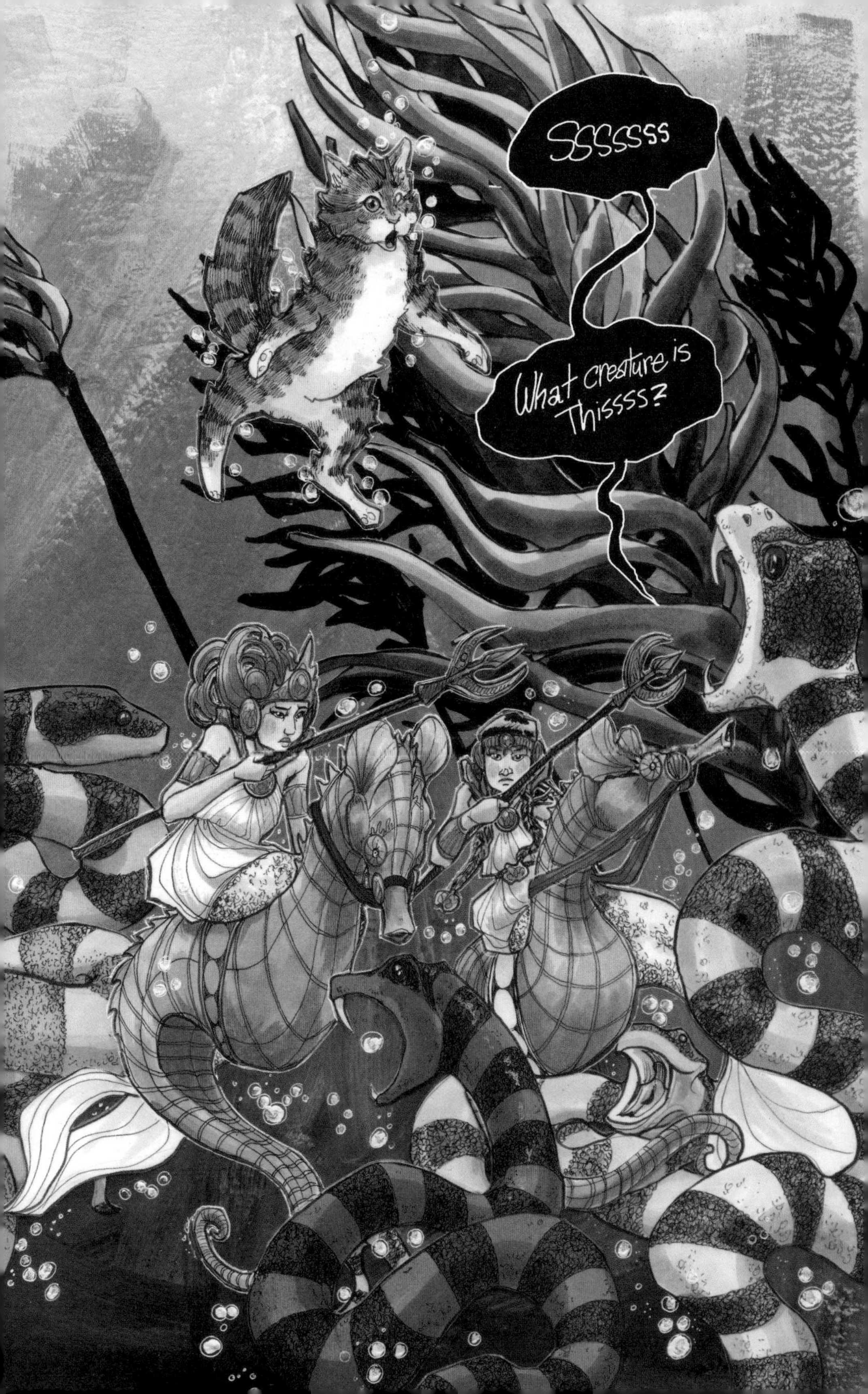
Sssssss
What creature is Thissss?

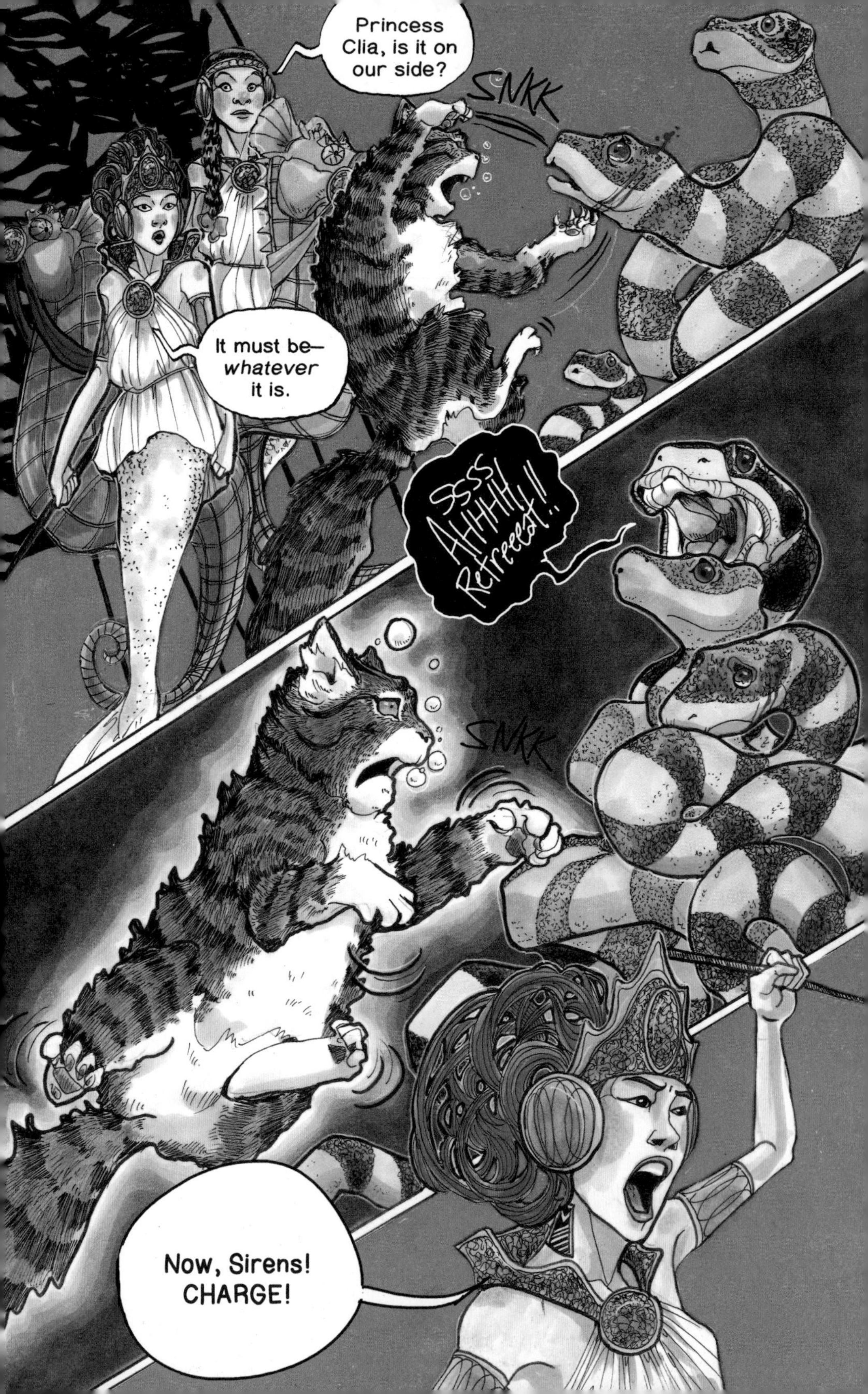
Princess Clia, is it on our side?
SNKK
It must be—*whatever* it is.
SSSS! AHHHH! Retreeeat!!
SNKK
Now, Sirens! CHARGE!

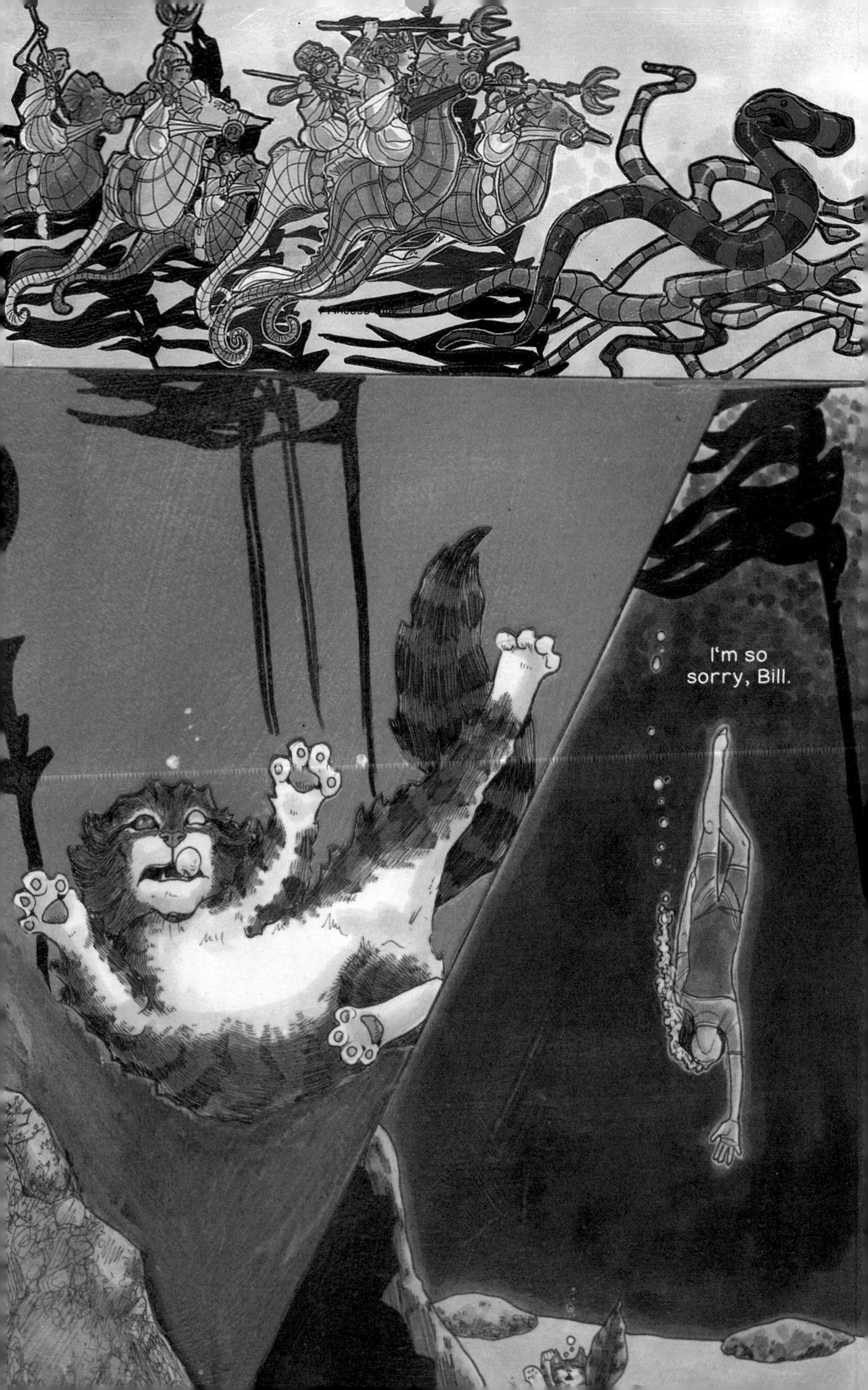
I'm so sorry, Bill.

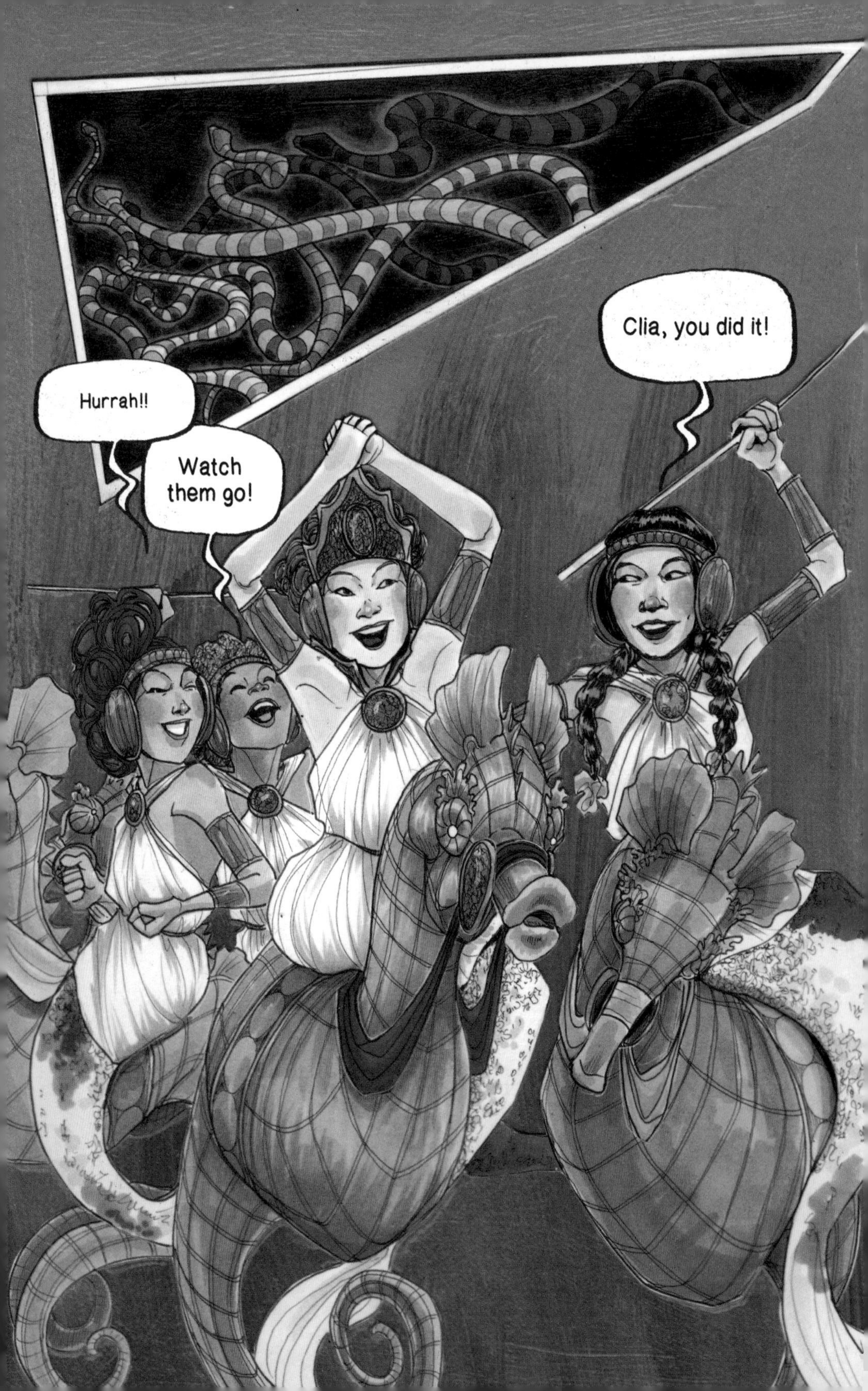
Hurrah!!
Watch them go!
Clia, you did it!

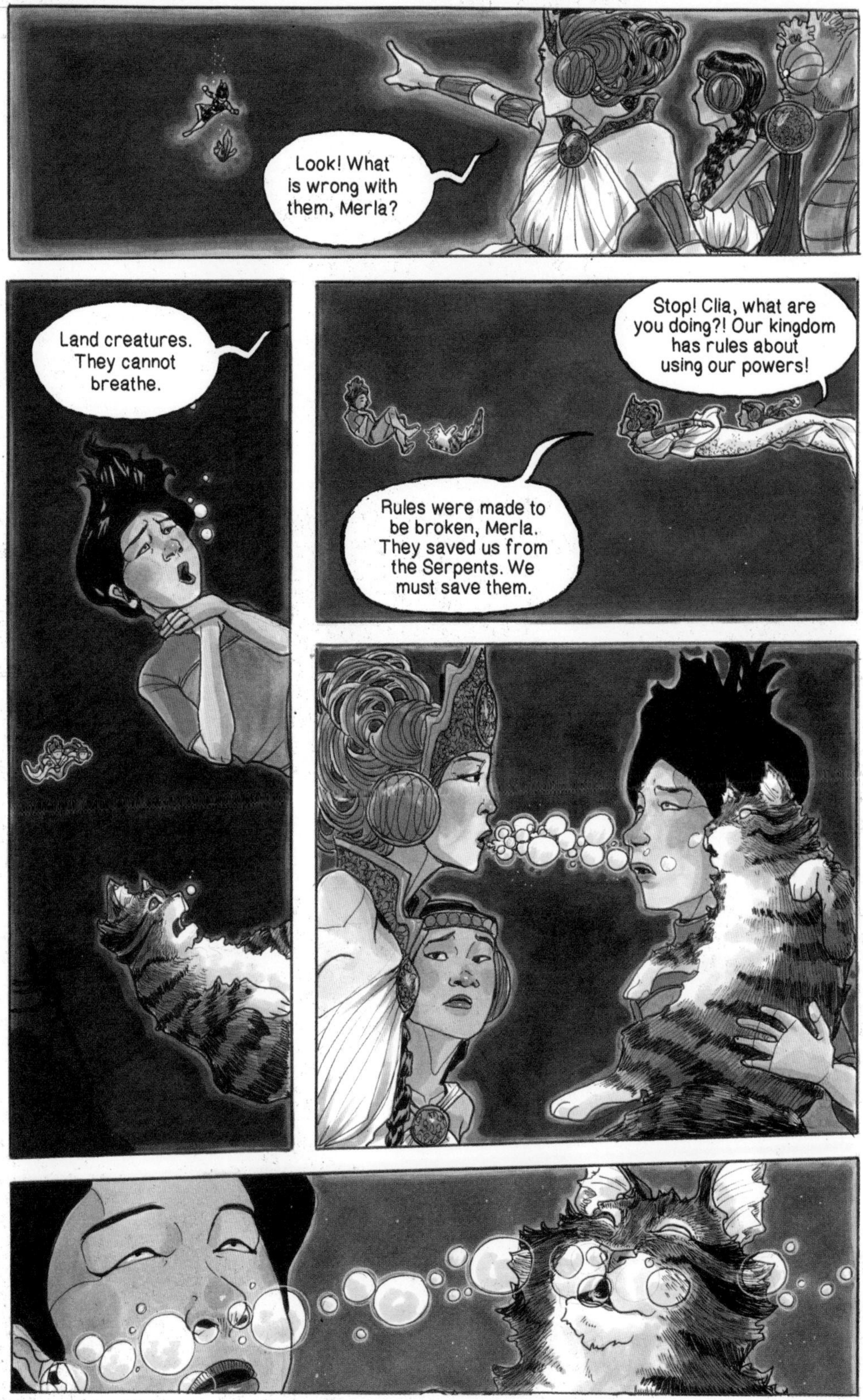
Look! What is wrong with them, Merla?
Land creatures. They cannot breathe.
Stop! Clia, what are you doing?! Our kingdom has rules about using our powers!
Rules were made to be broken, Merla. They saved us from the Serpents. We must save them.

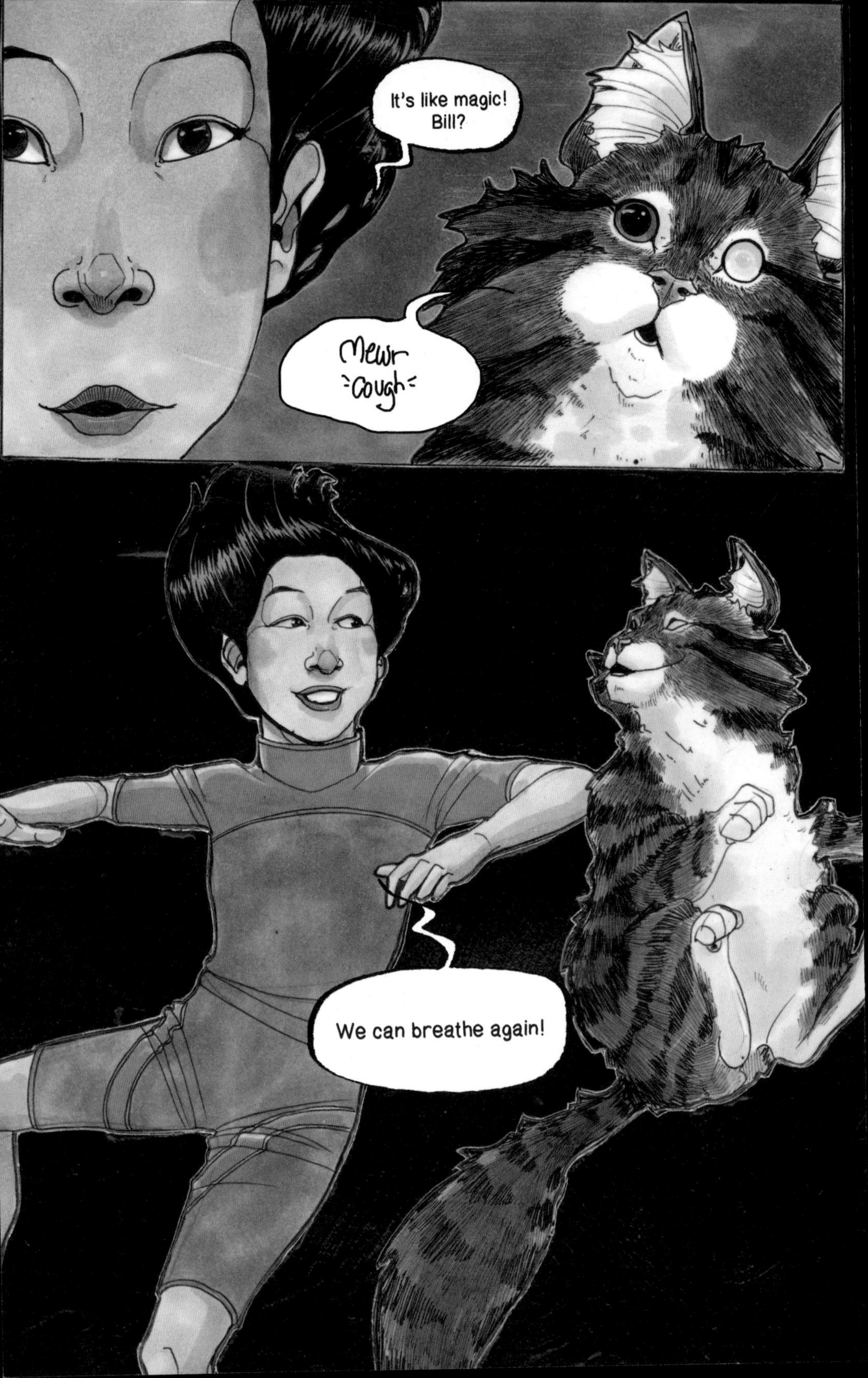
It's like magic!
Bill?
Mewr
=cough=
We can breathe again!

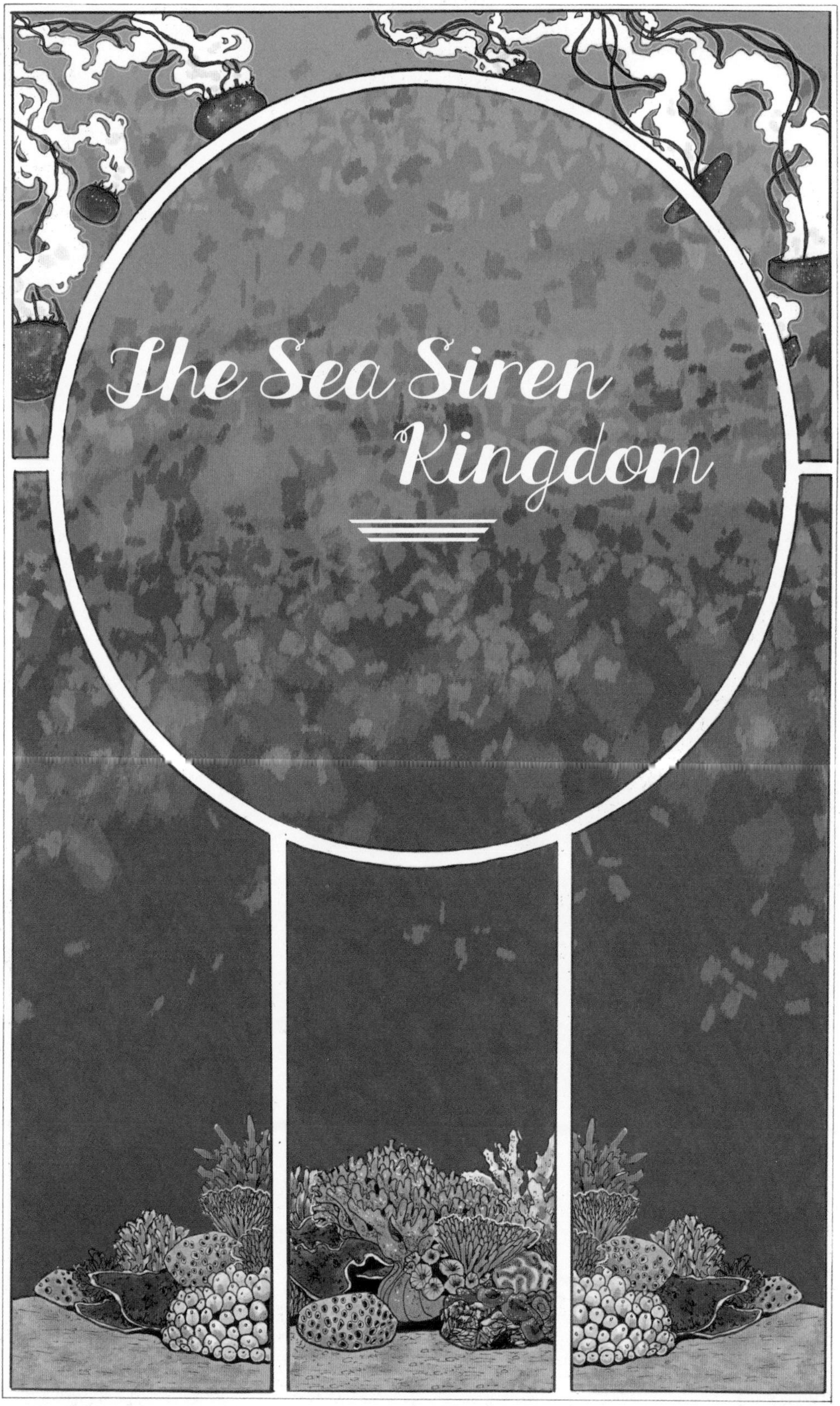
The Sea Siren
Kingdom

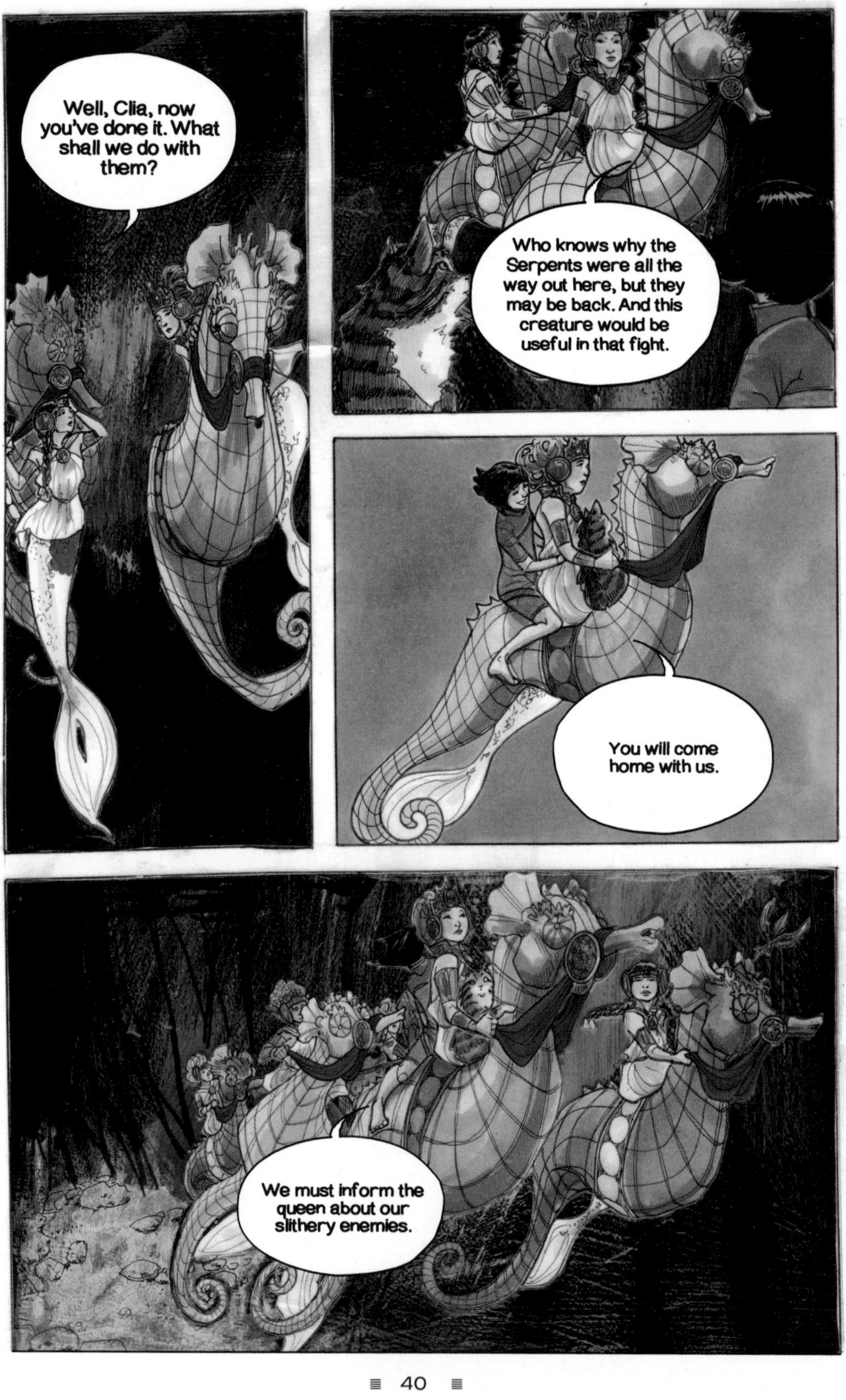
Well, Clia, now you've done it. What shall we do with them?
Who knows why the Serpents were all the way out here, but they may be back. And this creature would be useful in that fight.
You will come home with us.
We must inform the queen about our slithery enemies.

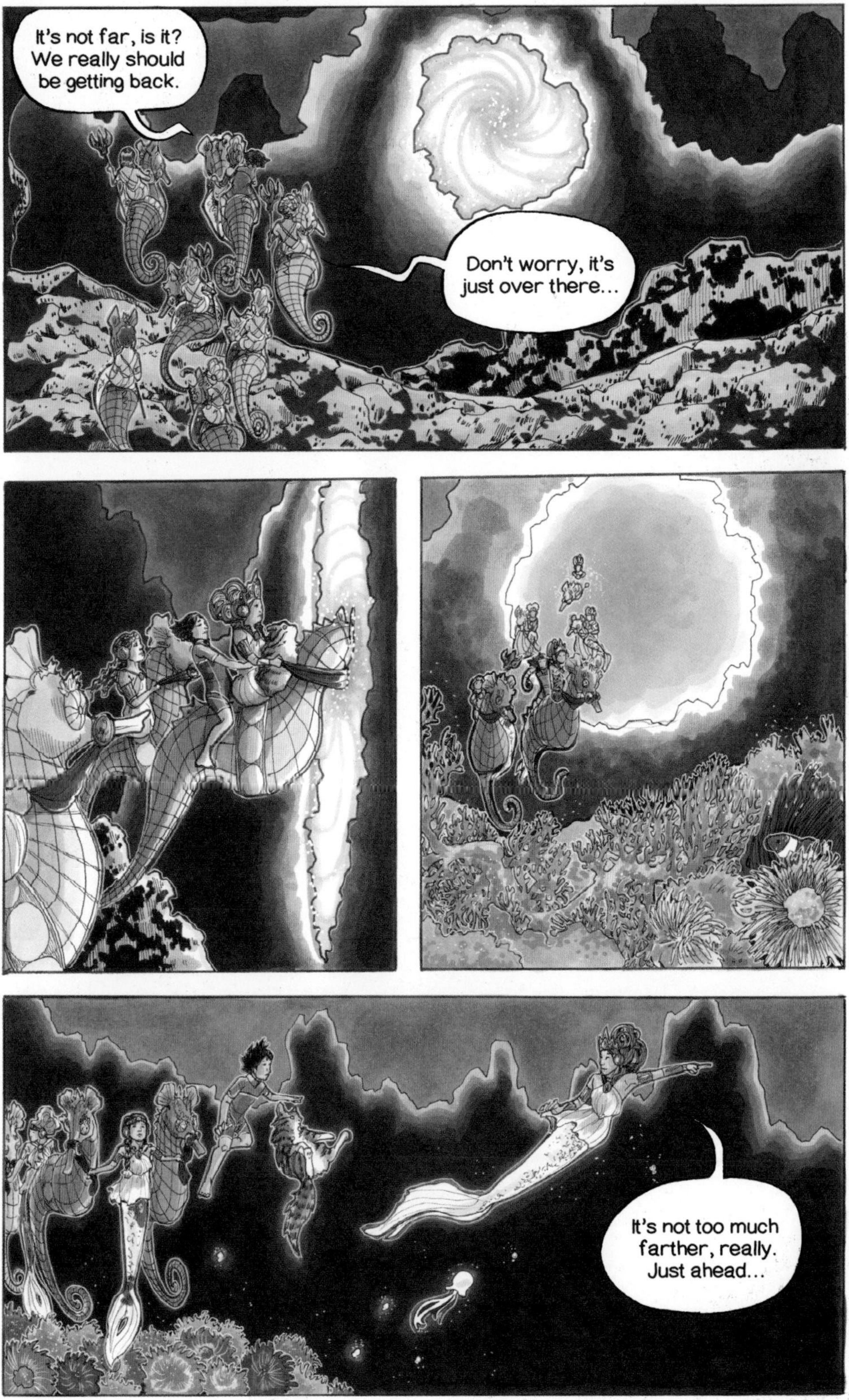
It's not far, is it? We really should be getting back.
Don't worry, it's just over there...
It's not too much farther, really. Just ahead...

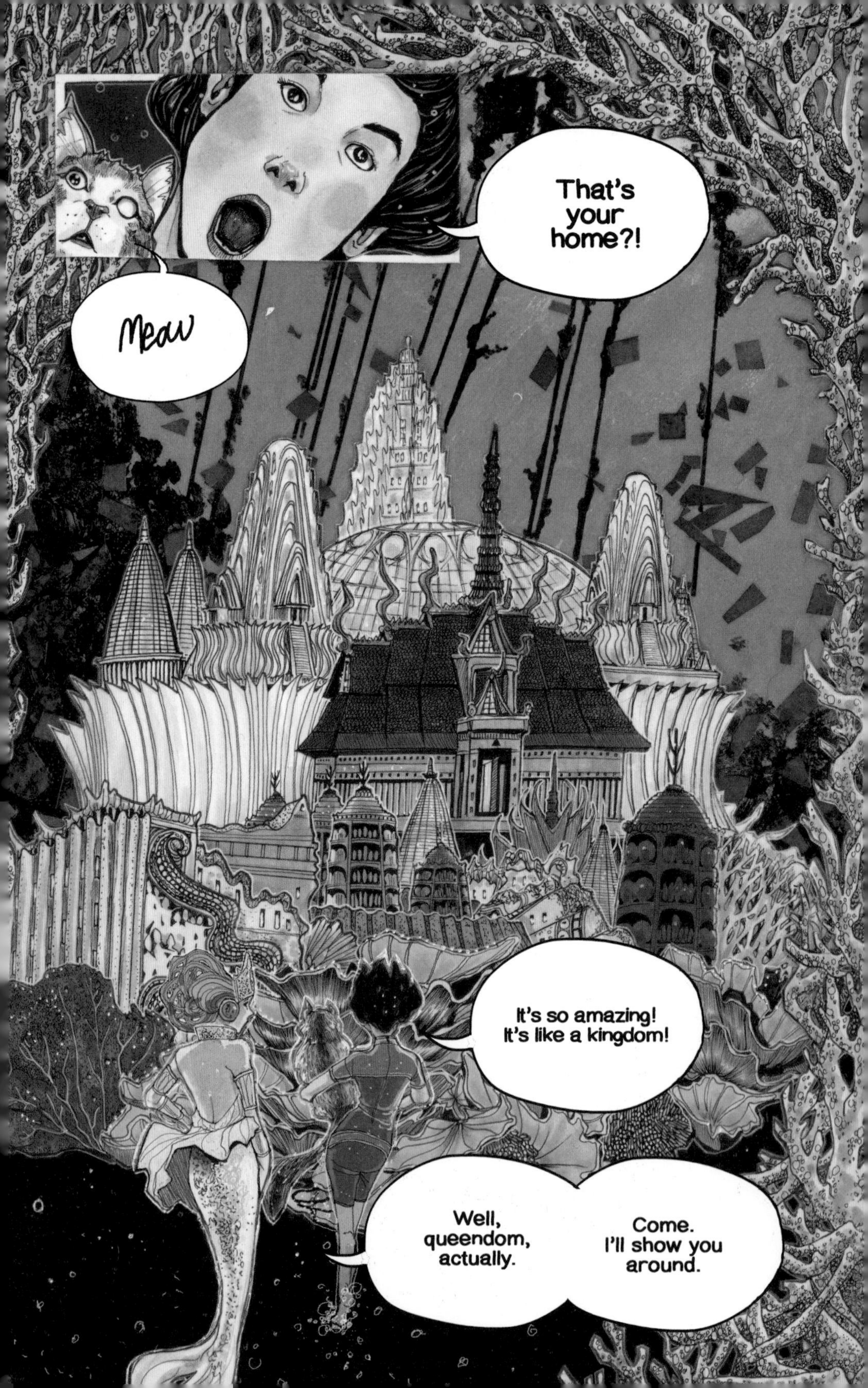
That's your home?!
Meow
It's so amazing! It's like a kingdom!
Well, queendom, actually.
Come. I'll show you around.

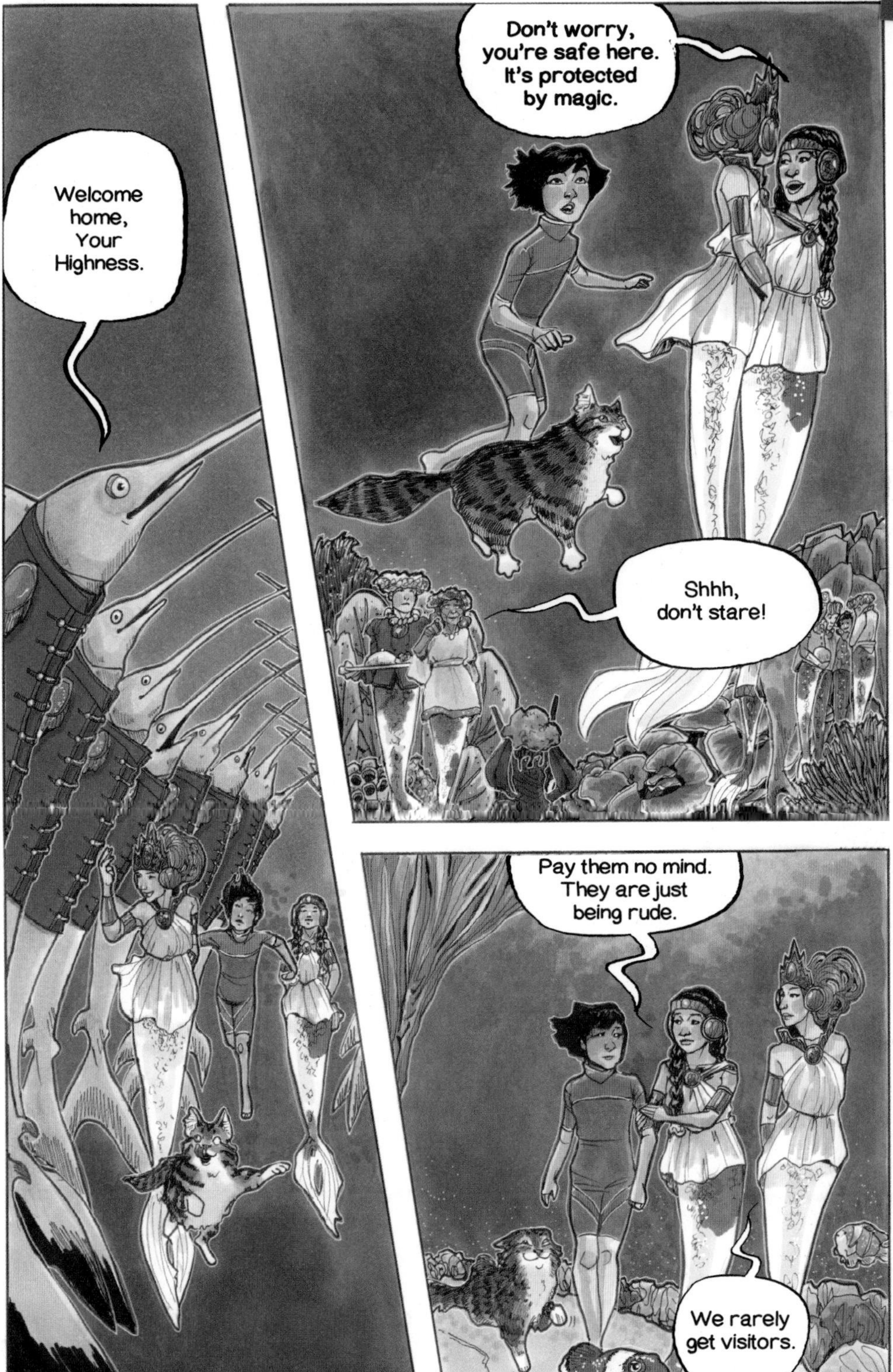
Welcome home, Your Highness.
Don't worry, you're safe here. It's protected by magic.
Shhh, don't stare!
Pay them no mind. They are just being rude.
We rarely get visitors.

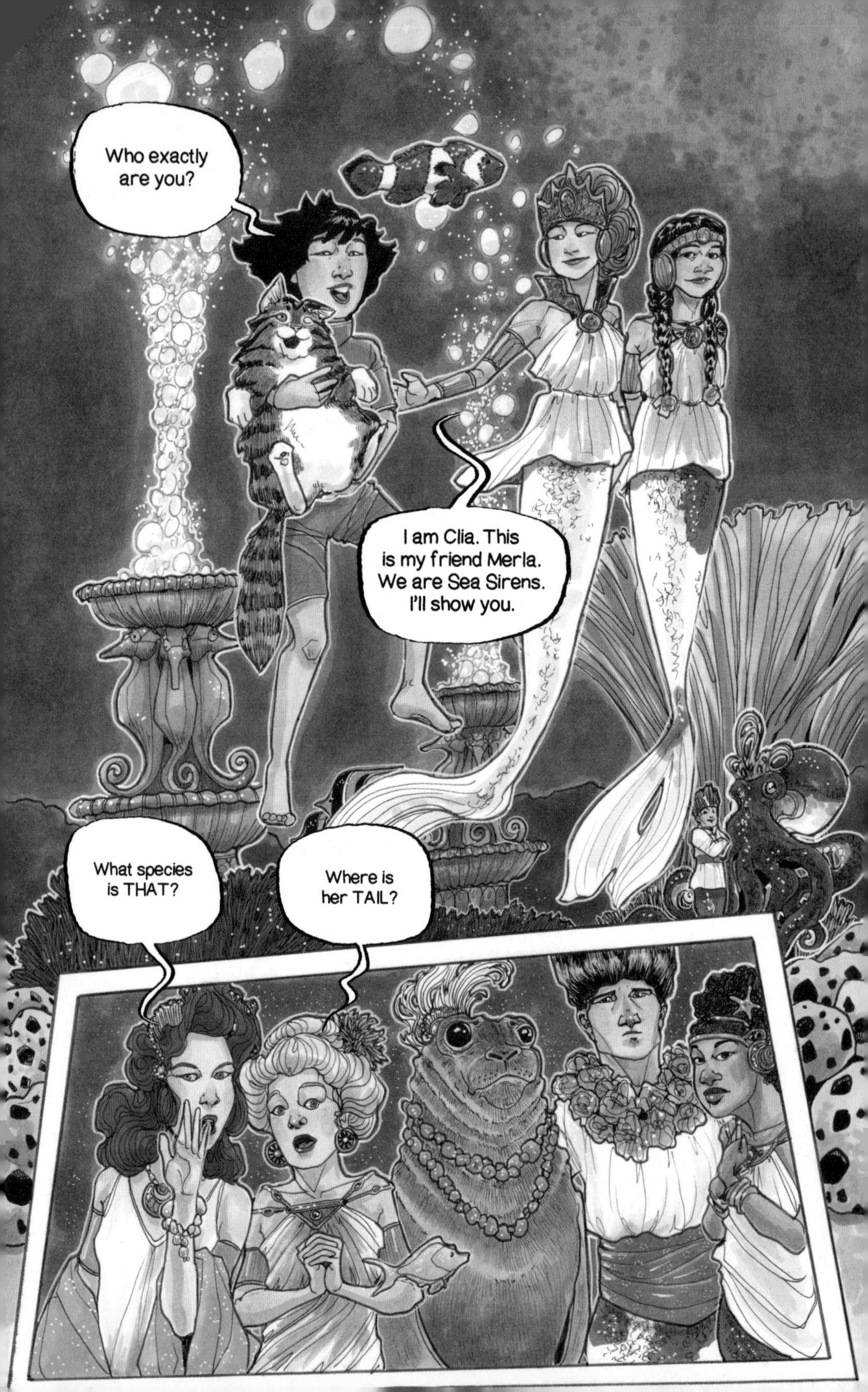
Who exactly are you?
I am Clia. This is my friend Merla. We are Sea Sirens. I'll show you.
What species is THAT?
Where is her TAIL?

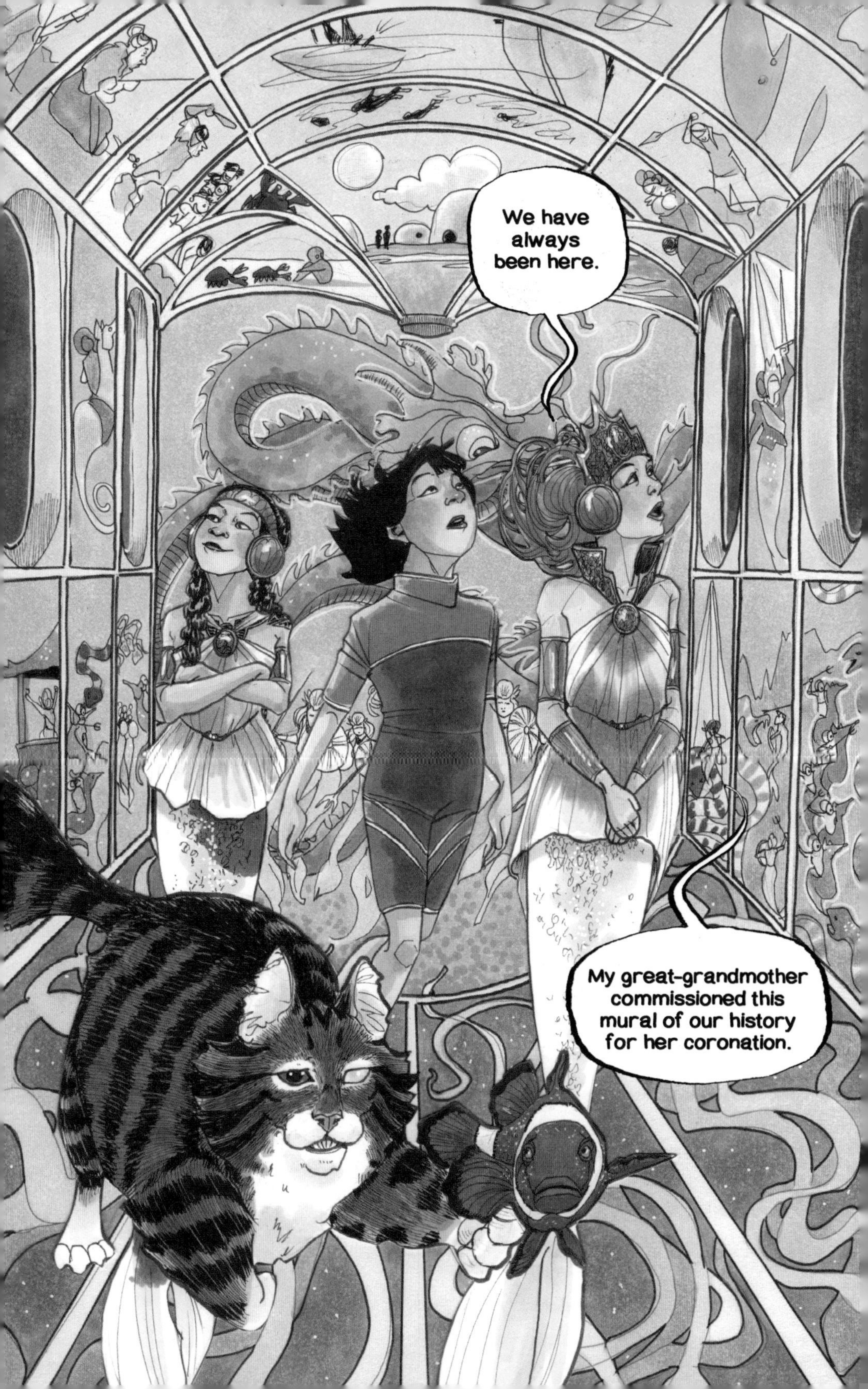
We have always been here.
My great-grandmother commissioned this mural of our history for her coronation.

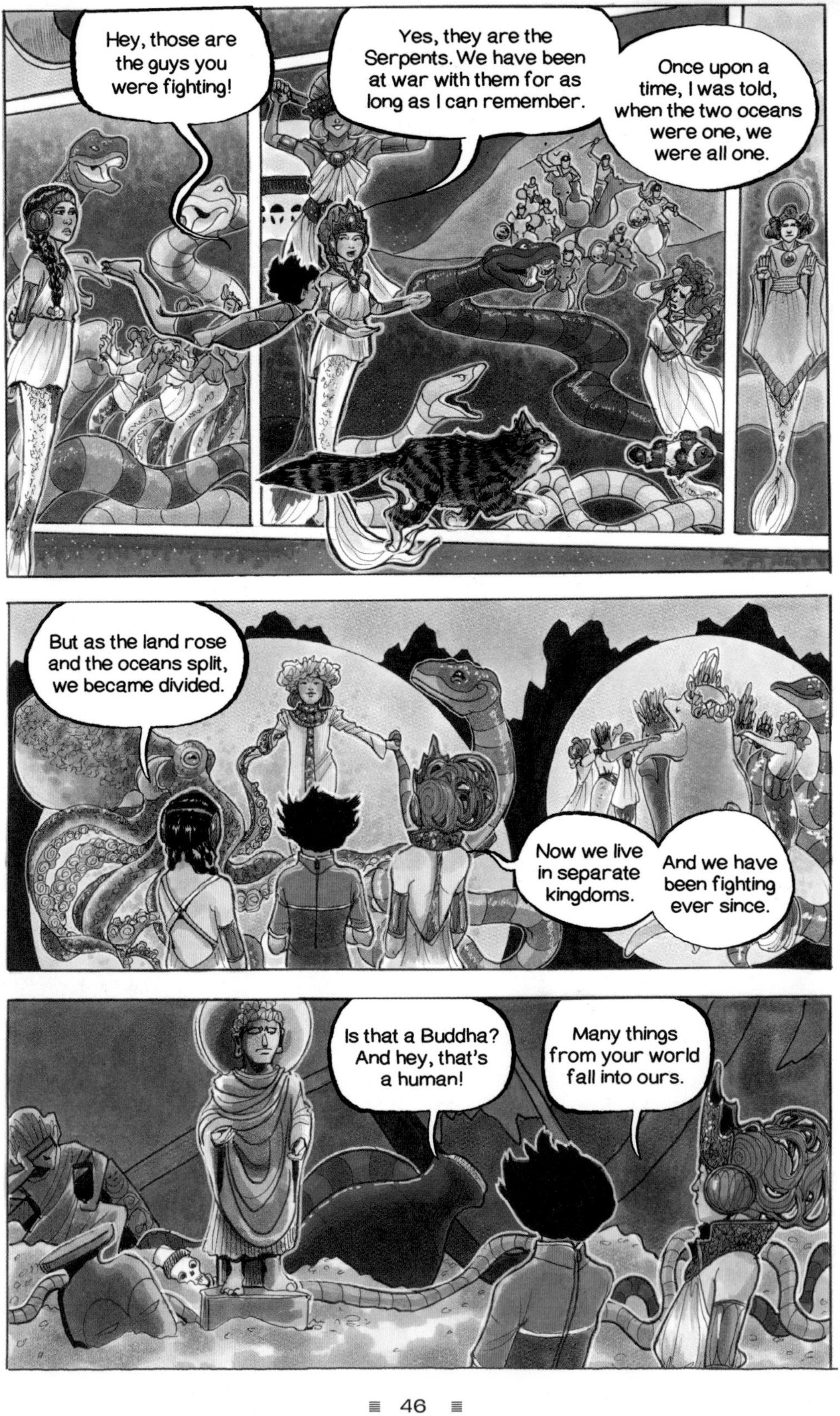
Hey, those are the guys you were fighting!
Yes, they are the Serpents. We have been at war with them for as long as I can remember.
Once upon a time, I was told, when the two oceans were one, we were all one.
But as the land rose and the oceans split, we became divided.
Now we live in separate kingdoms.
And we have been fighting ever since.
Is that a Buddha? And hey, that's a human!
Many things from your world fall into ours.

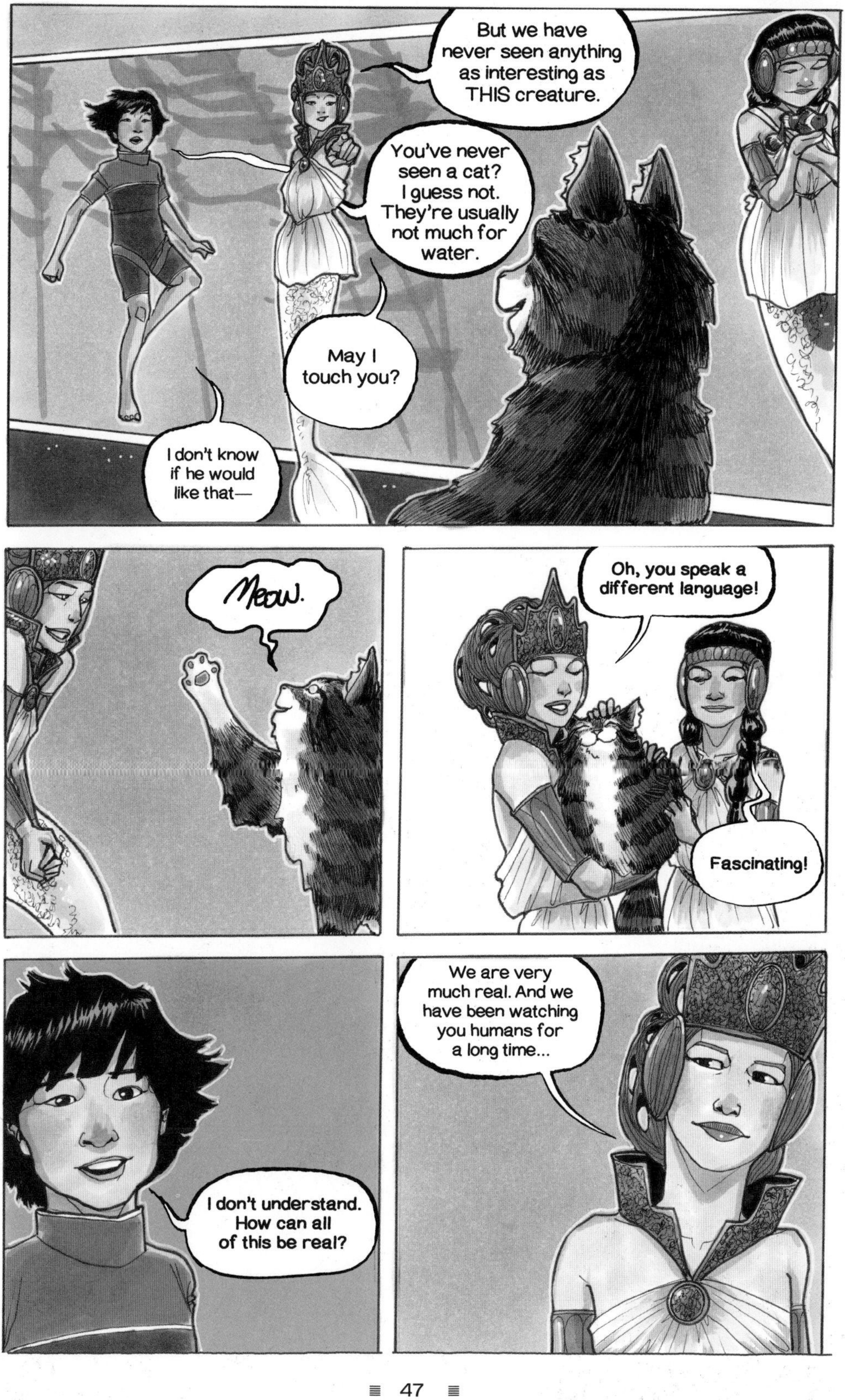
But we have never seen anything as interesting as THIS creature.
You've never seen a cat? I guess not. They're usually not much for water.
May I touch you?
I don't know if he would like that—
Meow.
Oh, you speak a different language!
Fascinating!
I don't understand. How can all of this be real?
We are very much real. And we have been watching you humans for a long time...

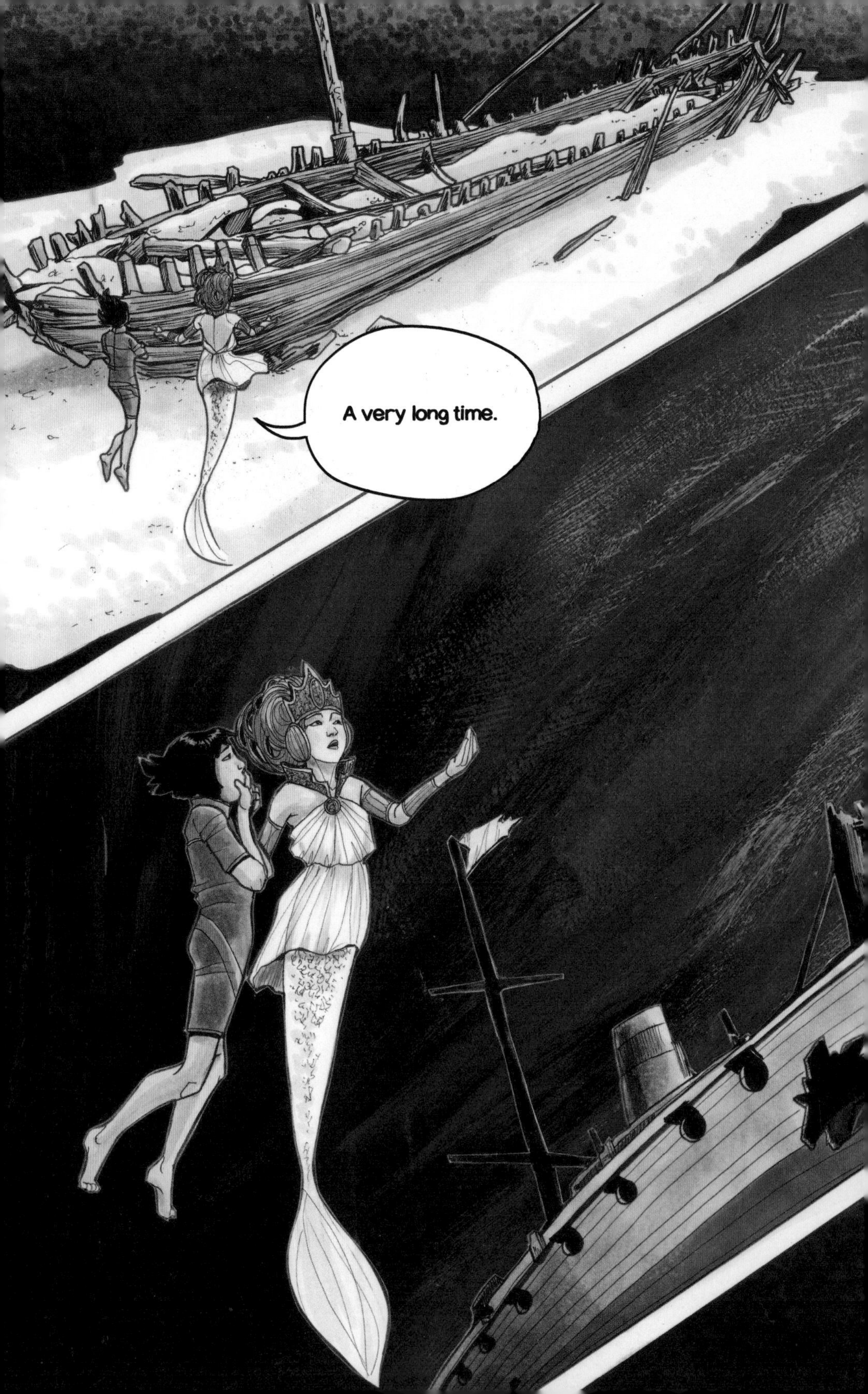
A very long time.

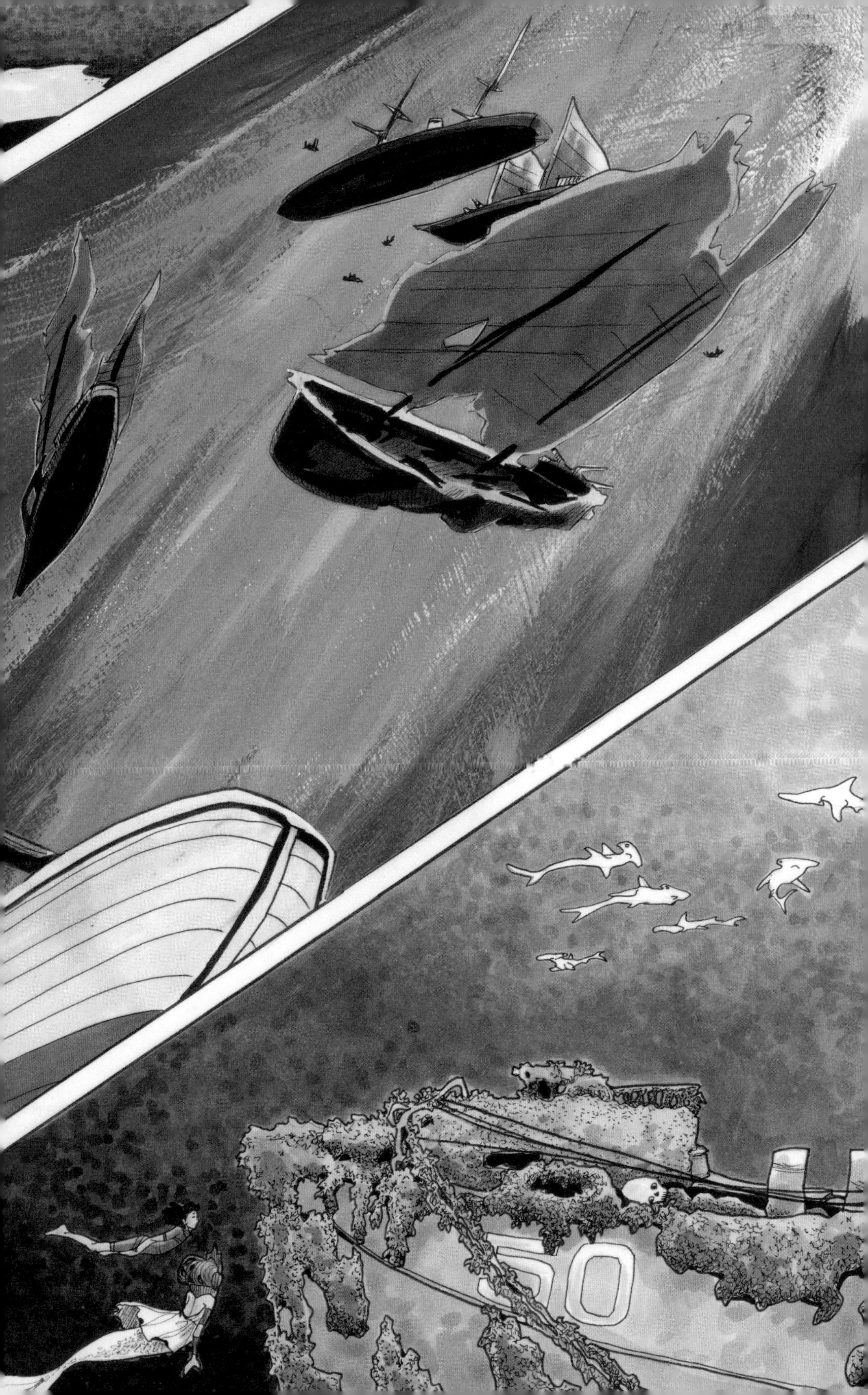
50

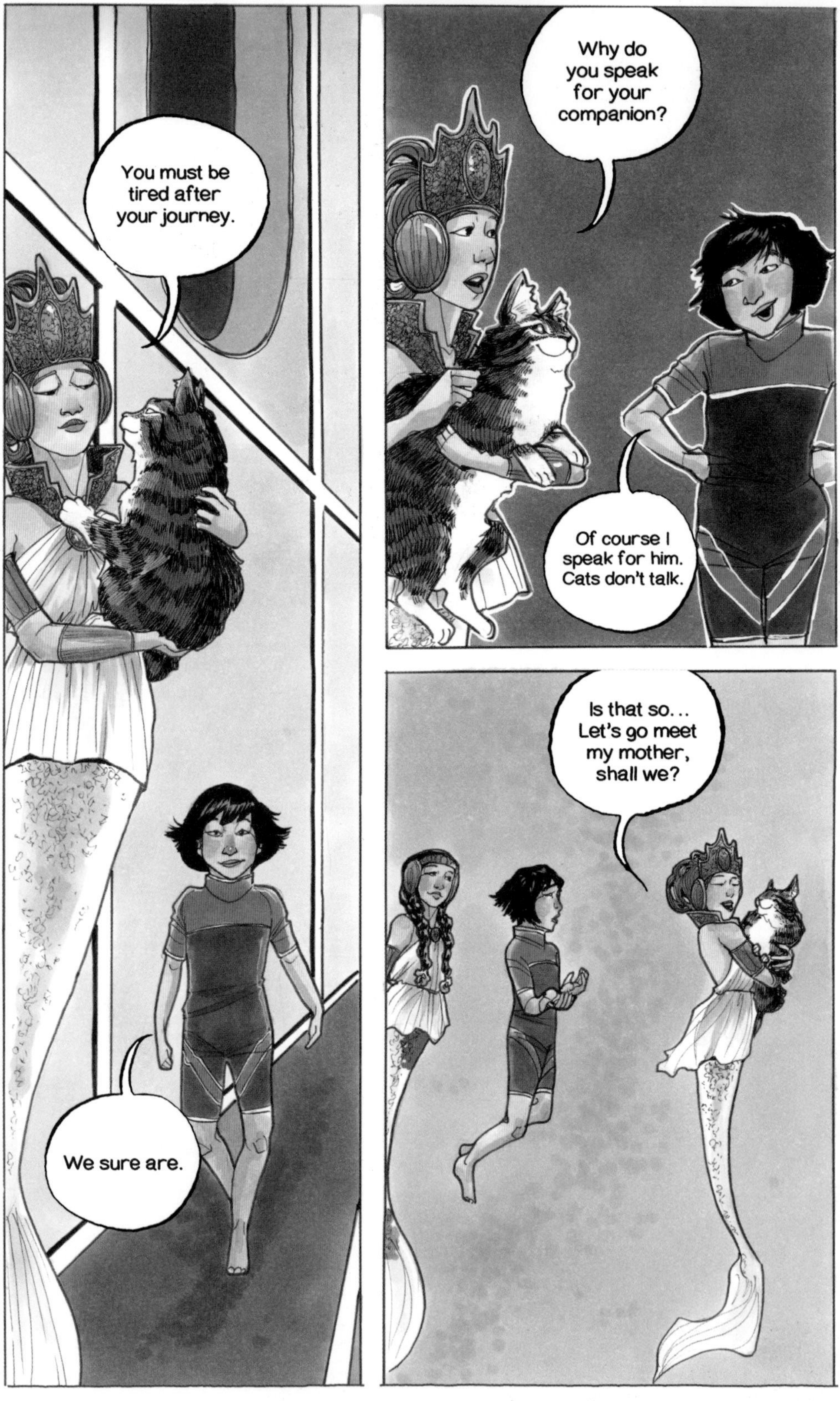
You must be tired after your journey.
We sure are.
Why do you speak for your companion?
Of course I speak for him. Cats don't talk.
Is that so... Let's go meet my mother, shall we?

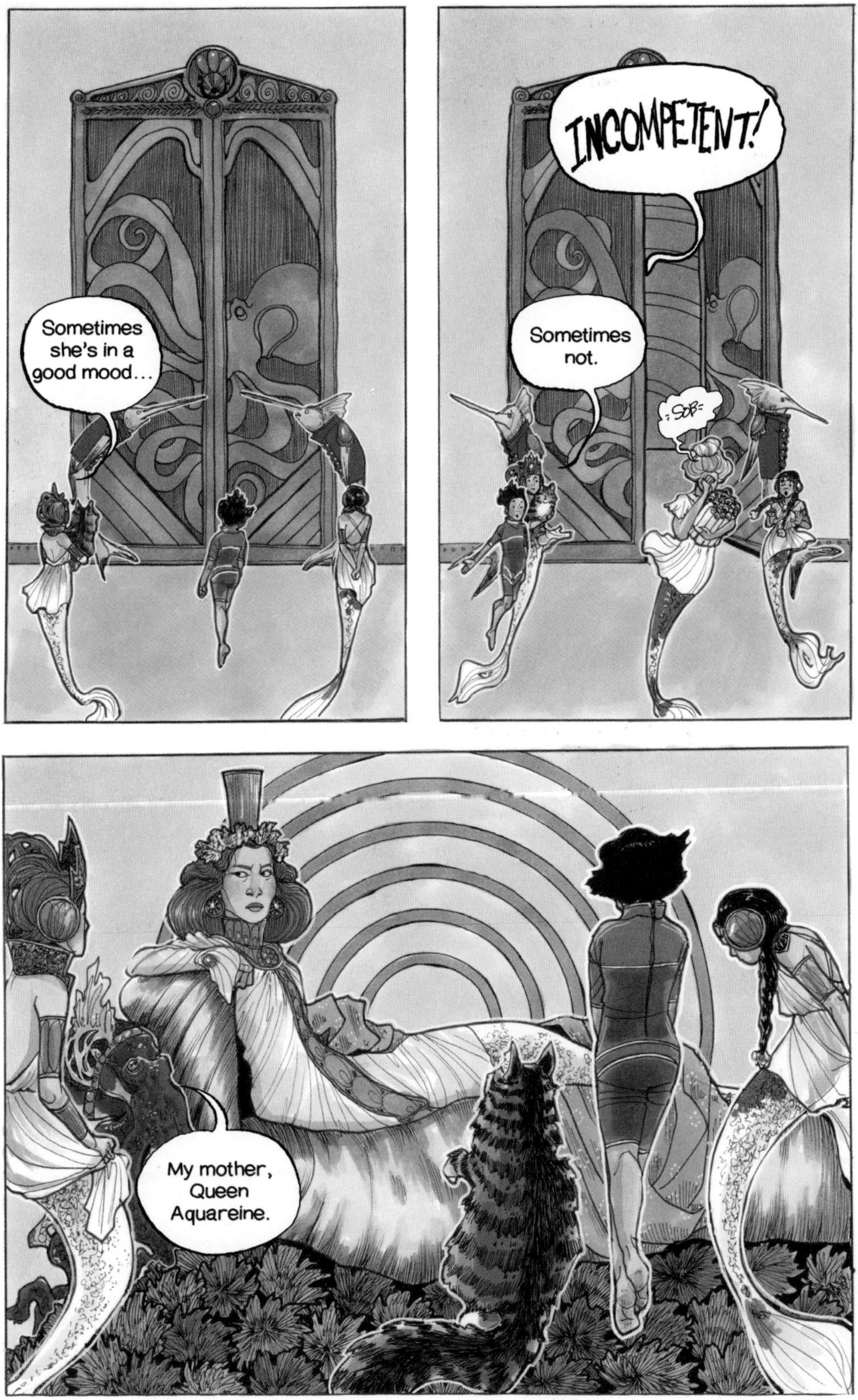
Sometimes she's in a good mood...
INCOMPETENT!
Sometimes not.
=SOB=
My mother, Queen Aquareine.

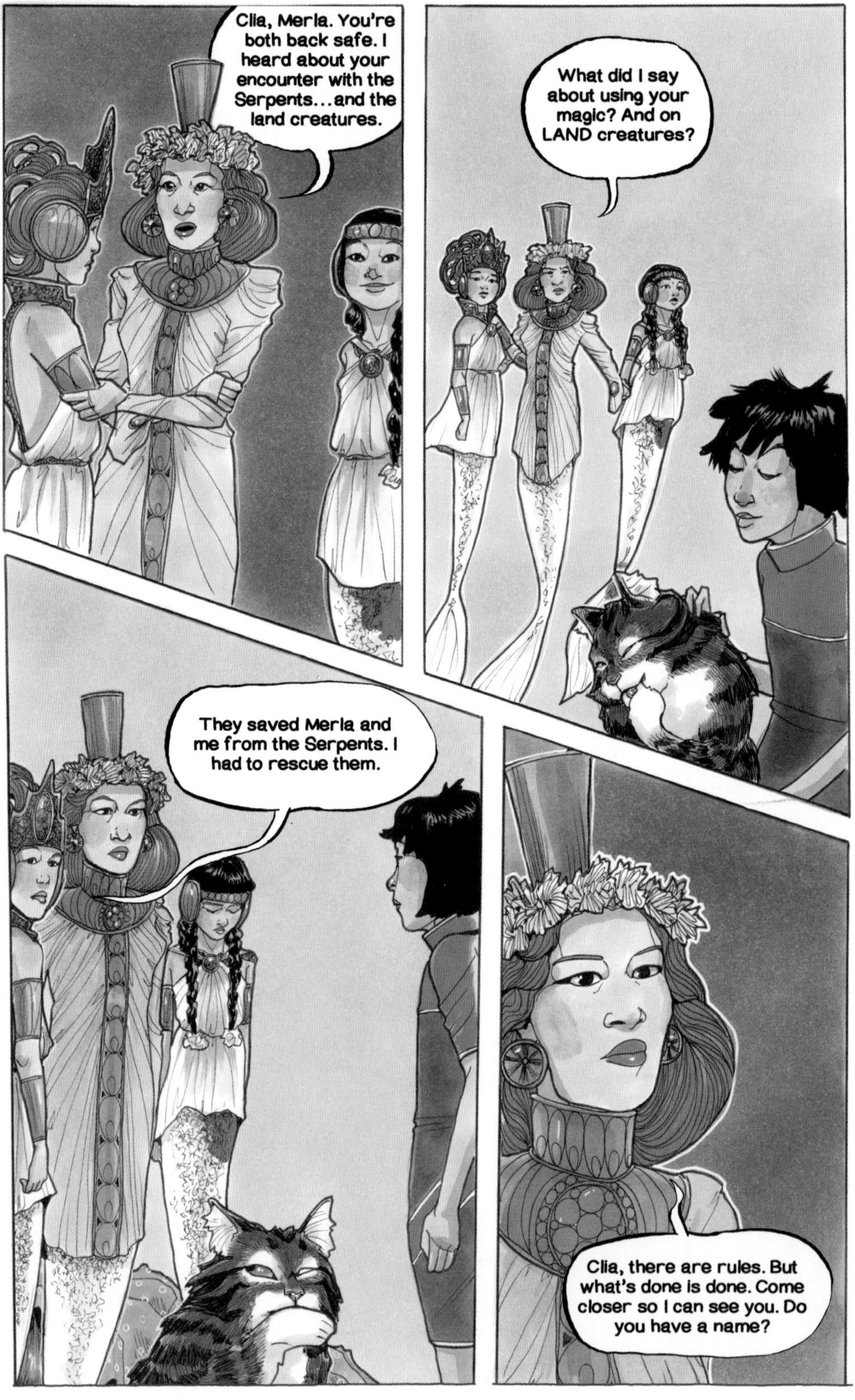
Clia, Merla. You're both back safe. I heard about your encounter with the Serpents...and the land creatures.
What did I say about using your magic? And on LAND creatures?
They saved Merla and me from the Serpents. I had to rescue them.
Clia, there are rules. But what's done is done. Come closer so I can see you. Do you have a name?

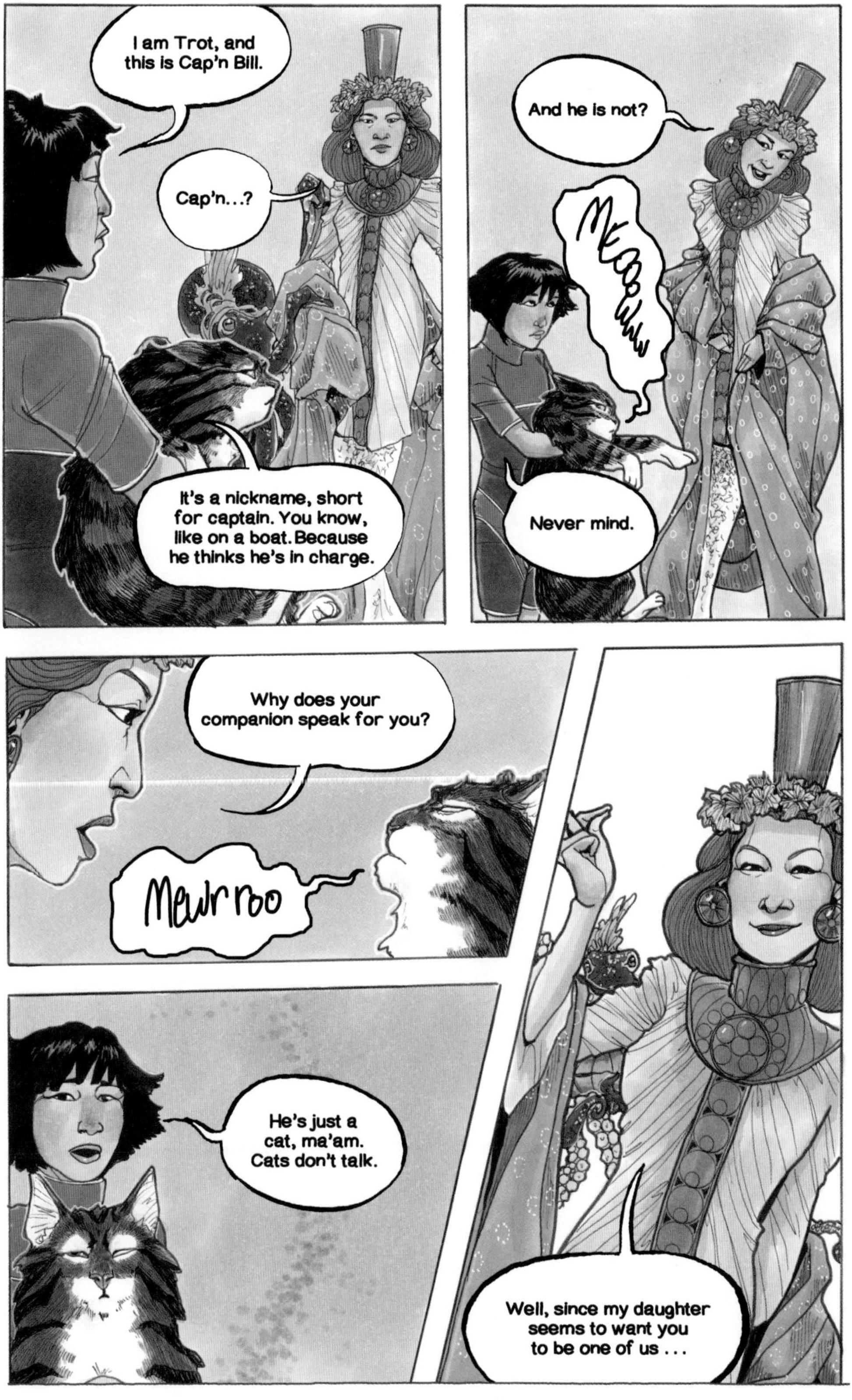
I am Trot, and this is Cap'n Bill.
Cap'n...?
It's a nickname, short for captain. You know, like on a boat. Because he thinks he's in charge.
And he is not?
Mrooowww
Never mind.
Why does your companion speak for you?
Mewrroo
He's just a cat, ma'am. Cats don't talk.
Well, since my daughter seems to want you to be one of us . . .

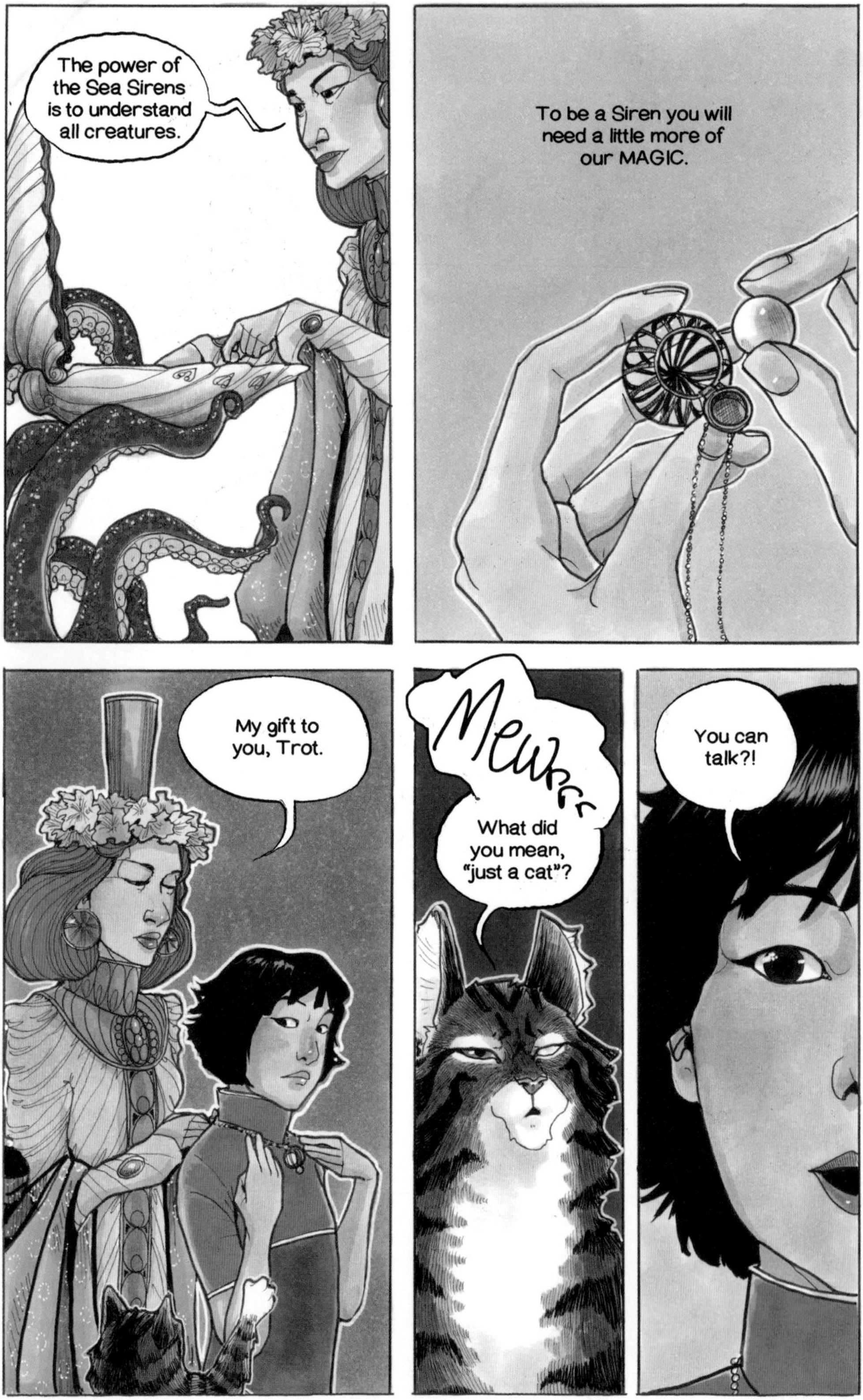
The power of the Sea Sirens is to understand all creatures.
To be a Siren you will need a little more of our MAGIC.
My gift to you, Trot.
Mewrrr
What did you mean, "just a cat"?
You can talk?!

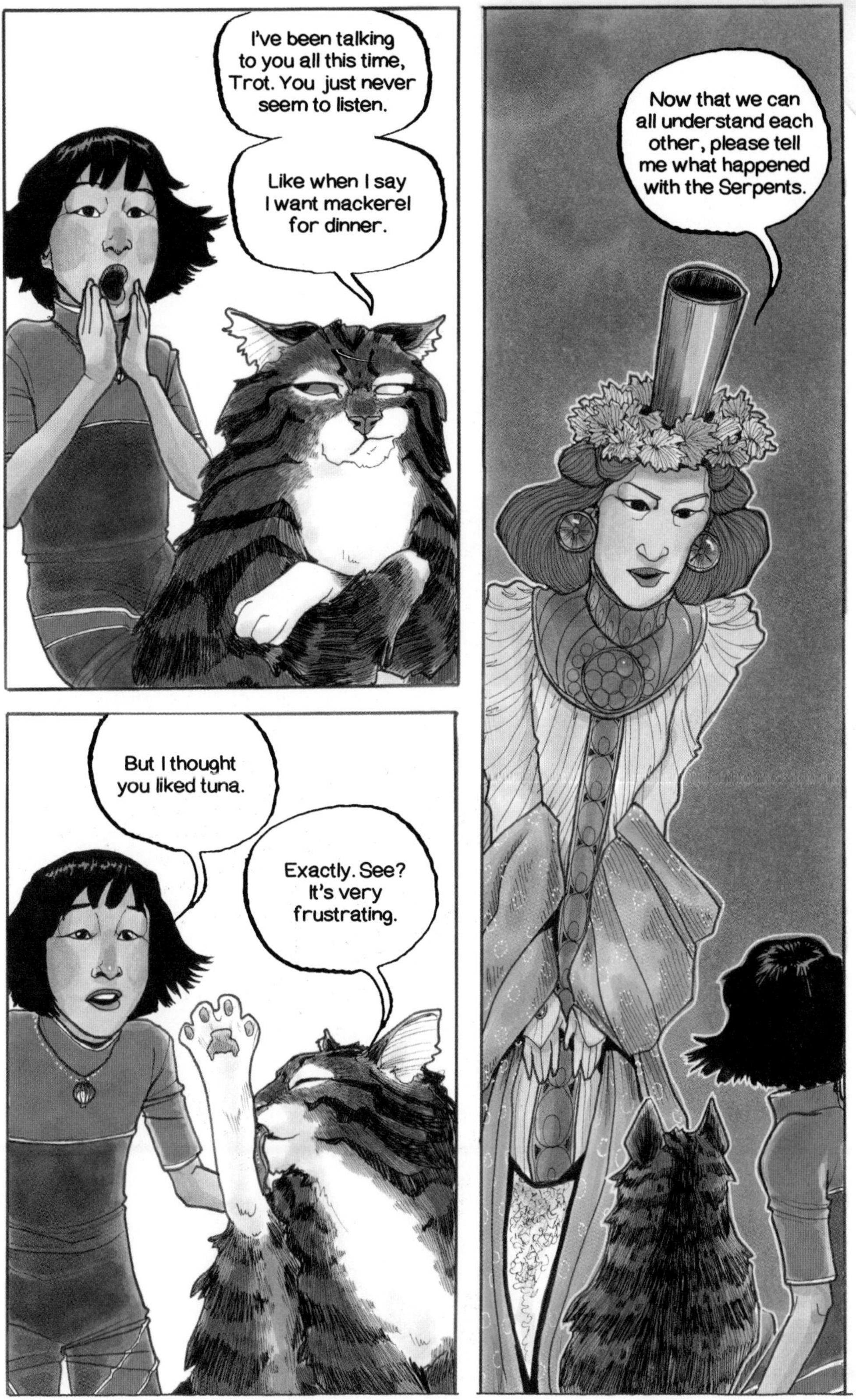
I've been talking to you all this time, Trot. You just never seem to listen.
Like when I say I want mackerel for dinner.
But I thought you liked tuna.
Exactly. See? It's very frustrating.
Now that we can all understand each other, please tell me what happened with the Serpents.

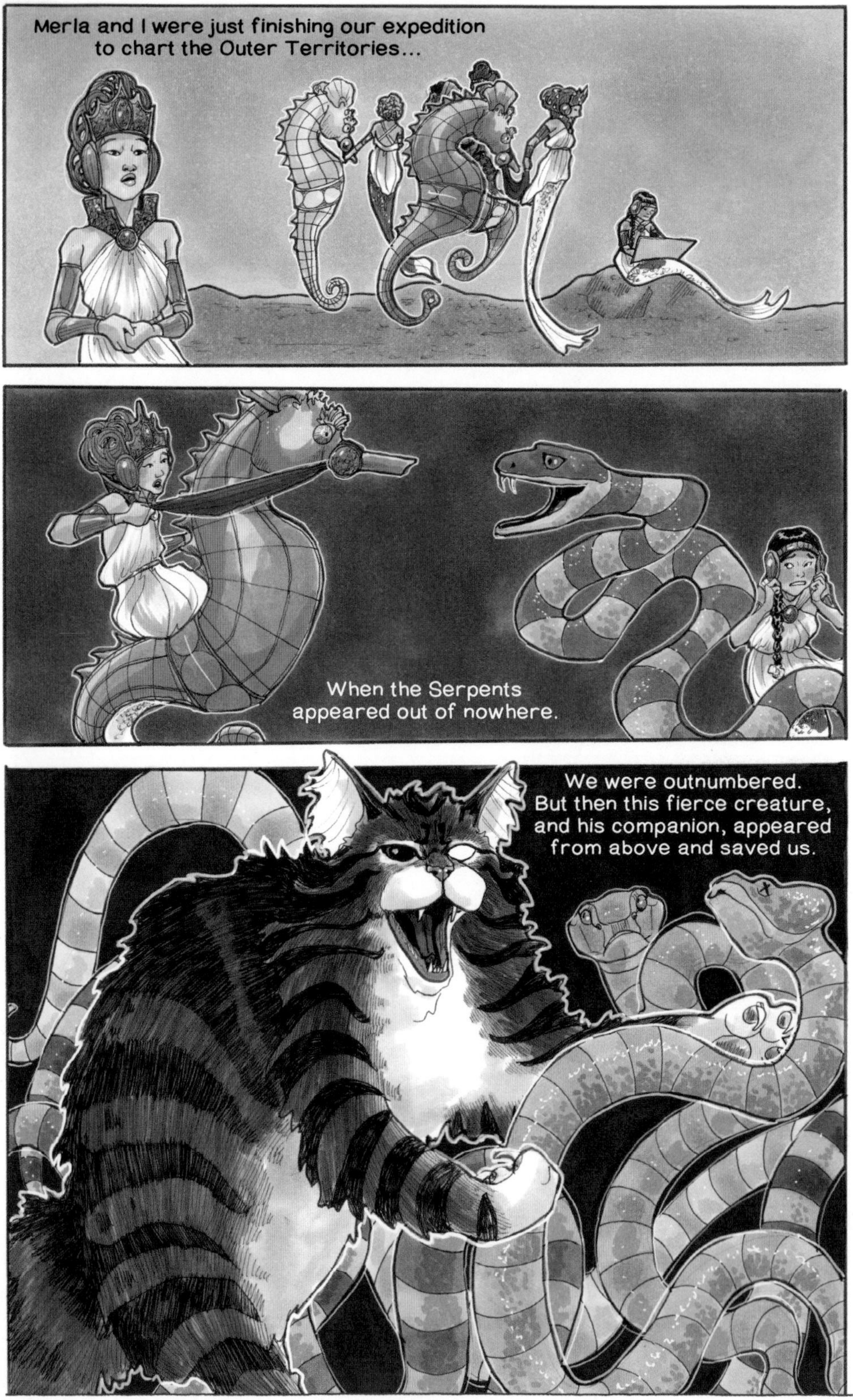
Merla and I were just finishing our expedition to chart the Outer Territories...
When the Serpents appeared out of nowhere.
We were outnumbered. But then this fierce creature, and his companion, appeared from above and saved us.

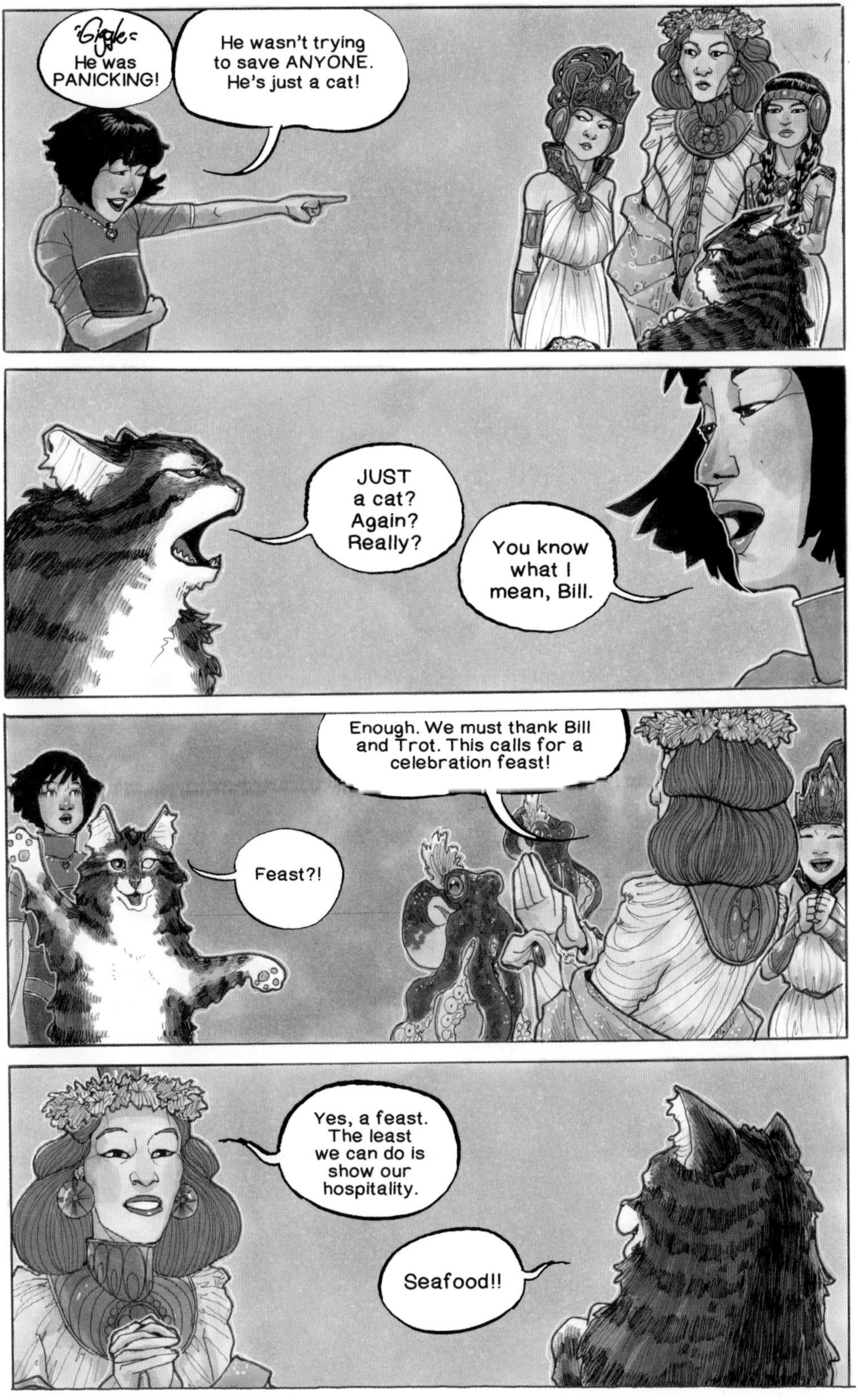
Giggle
He was PANICKING!
He wasn't trying to save ANYONE. He's just a cat!
JUST a cat? Again? Really?
You know what I mean, Bill.
Enough. We must thank Bill and Trot. This calls for a celebration feast!
Feast?!
Yes, a feast. The least we can do is show our hospitality.
Seafood!!

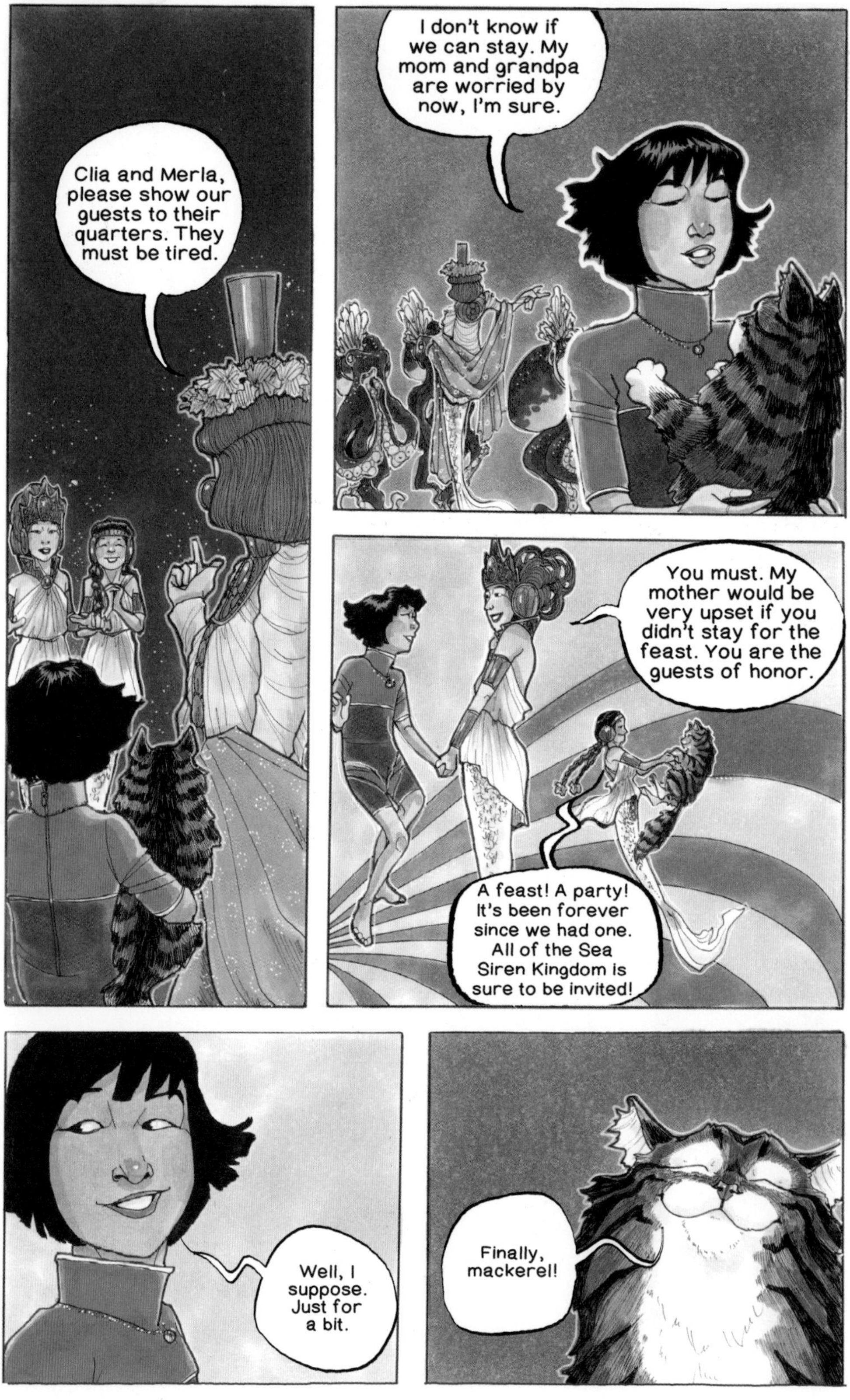
Clia and Merla, please show our guests to their quarters. They must be tired.
I don't know if we can stay. My mom and grandpa are worried by now, I'm sure.
You must. My mother would be very upset if you didn't stay for the feast. You are the guests of honor.
A feast! A party! It's been forever since we had one. All of the Sea Siren Kingdom is sure to be invited!
Well, I suppose. Just for a bit.
Finally, mackerel!

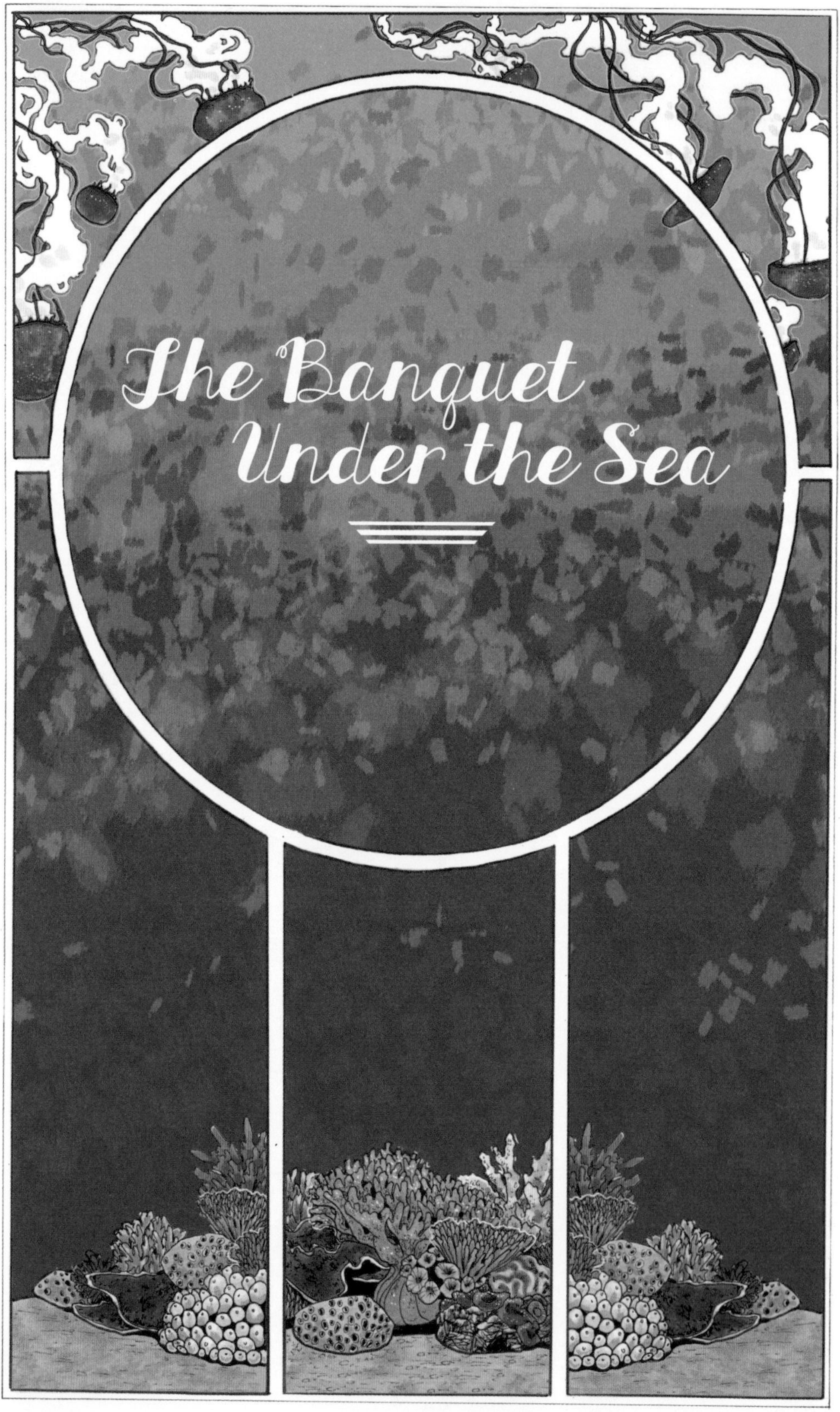
The Banquet
Under the Sea

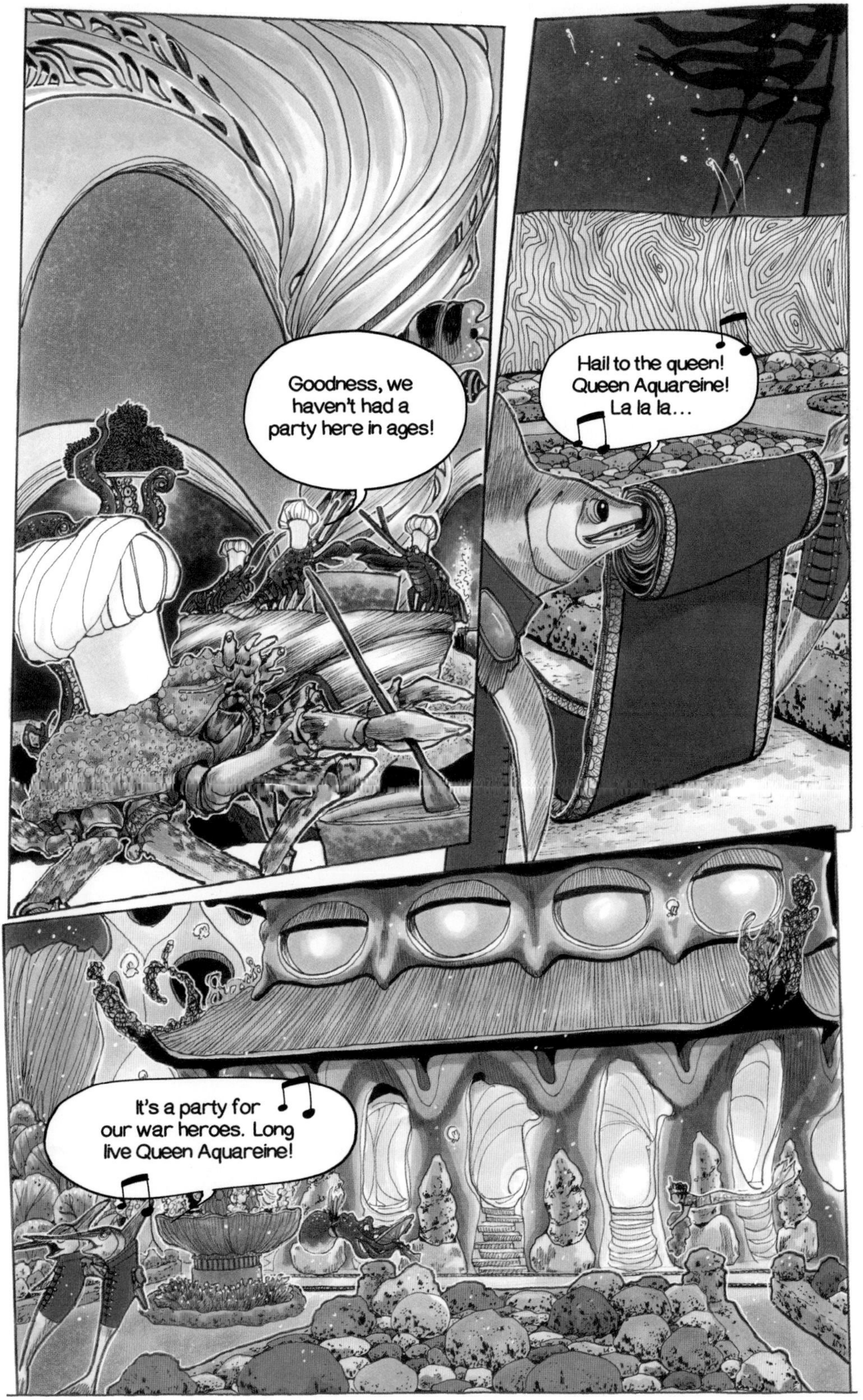
Goodness, we haven't had a party here in ages!
Hail to the queen! Queen Aquareine! La la la...
It's a party for our war heroes. Long live Queen Aquareine!

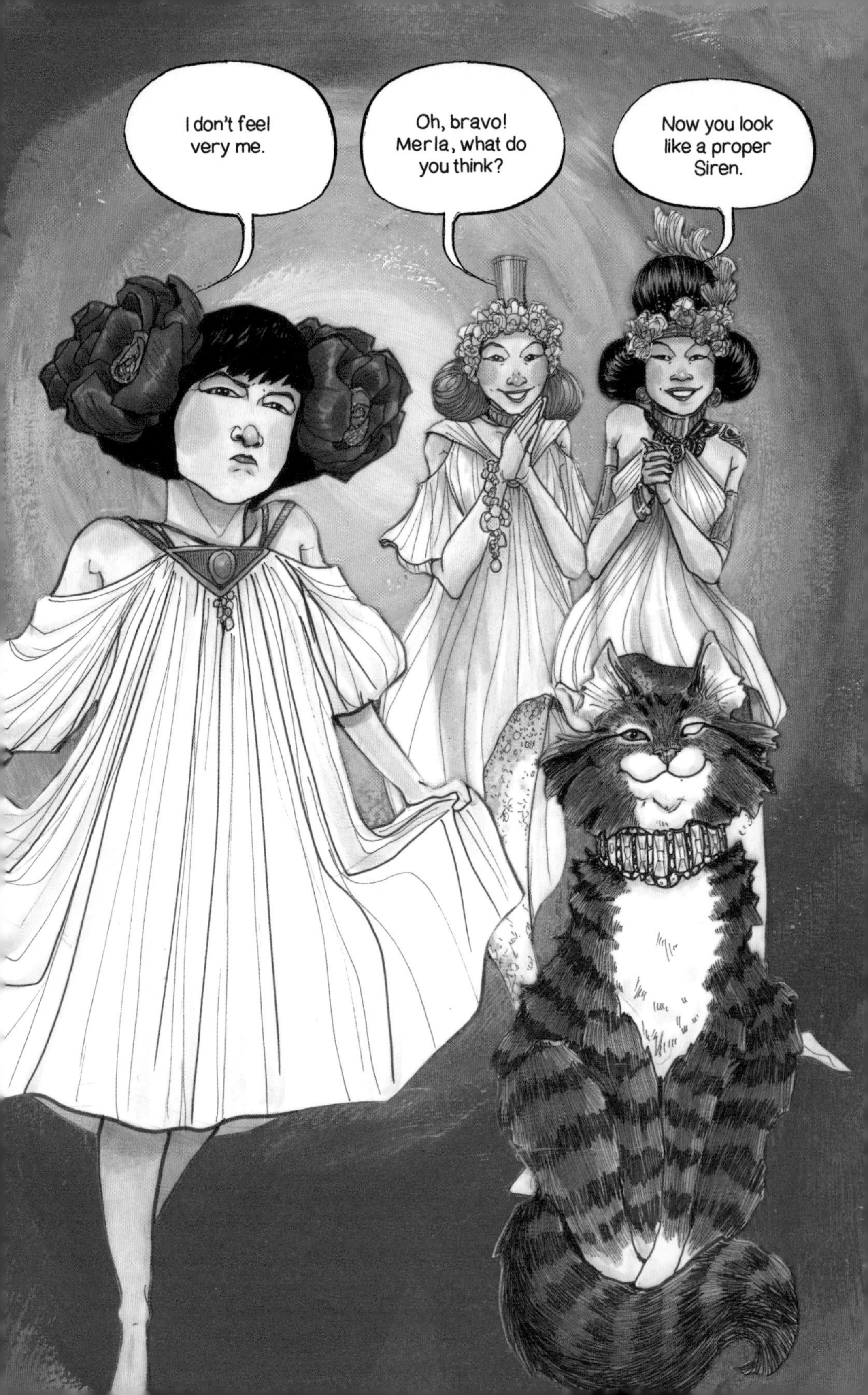
I don't feel very me.
Oh, bravo! Merla, what do you think?
Now you look like a proper Siren.

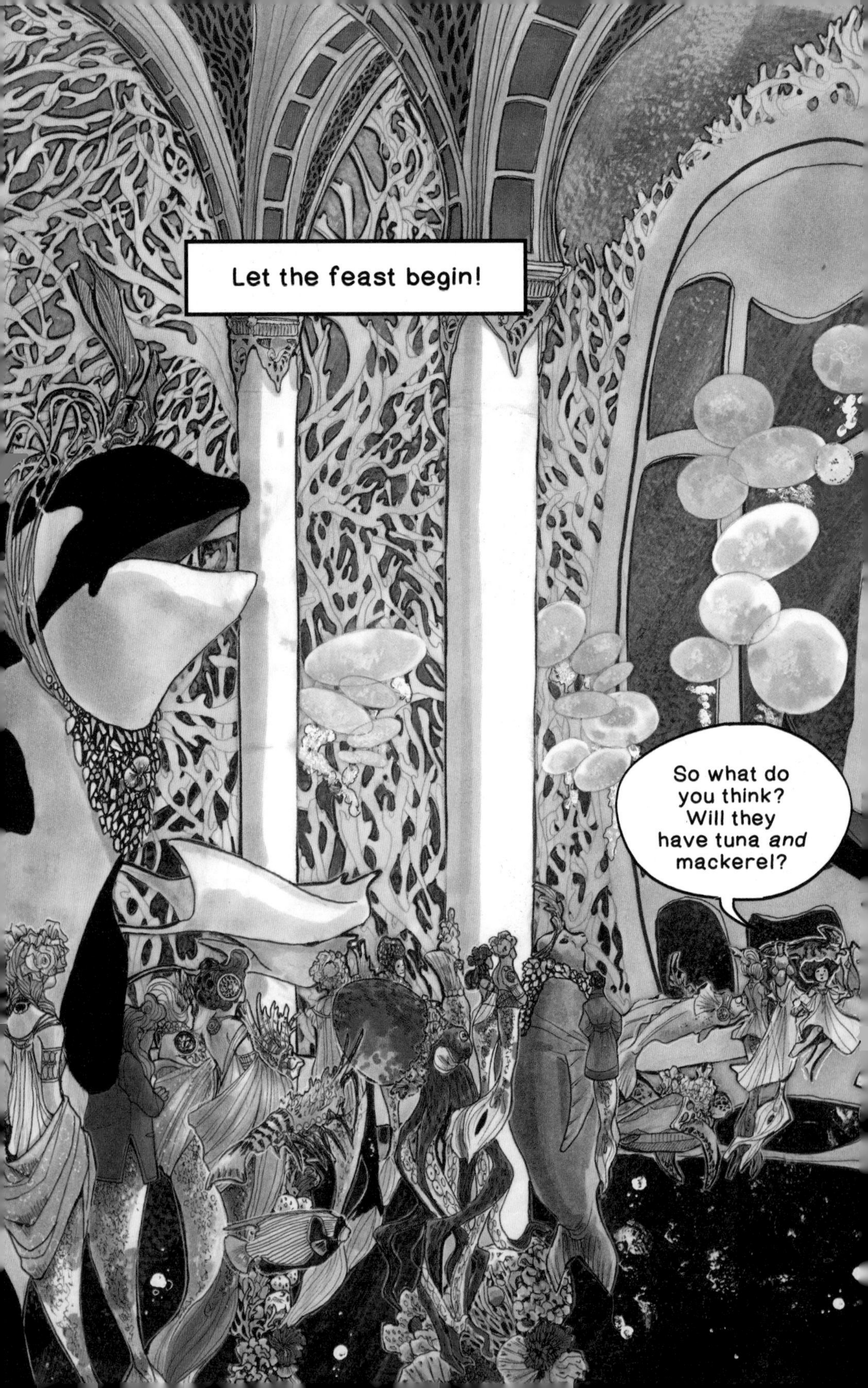
Let the feast begin!
So what do you think? Will they have tuna *and* mackerel?

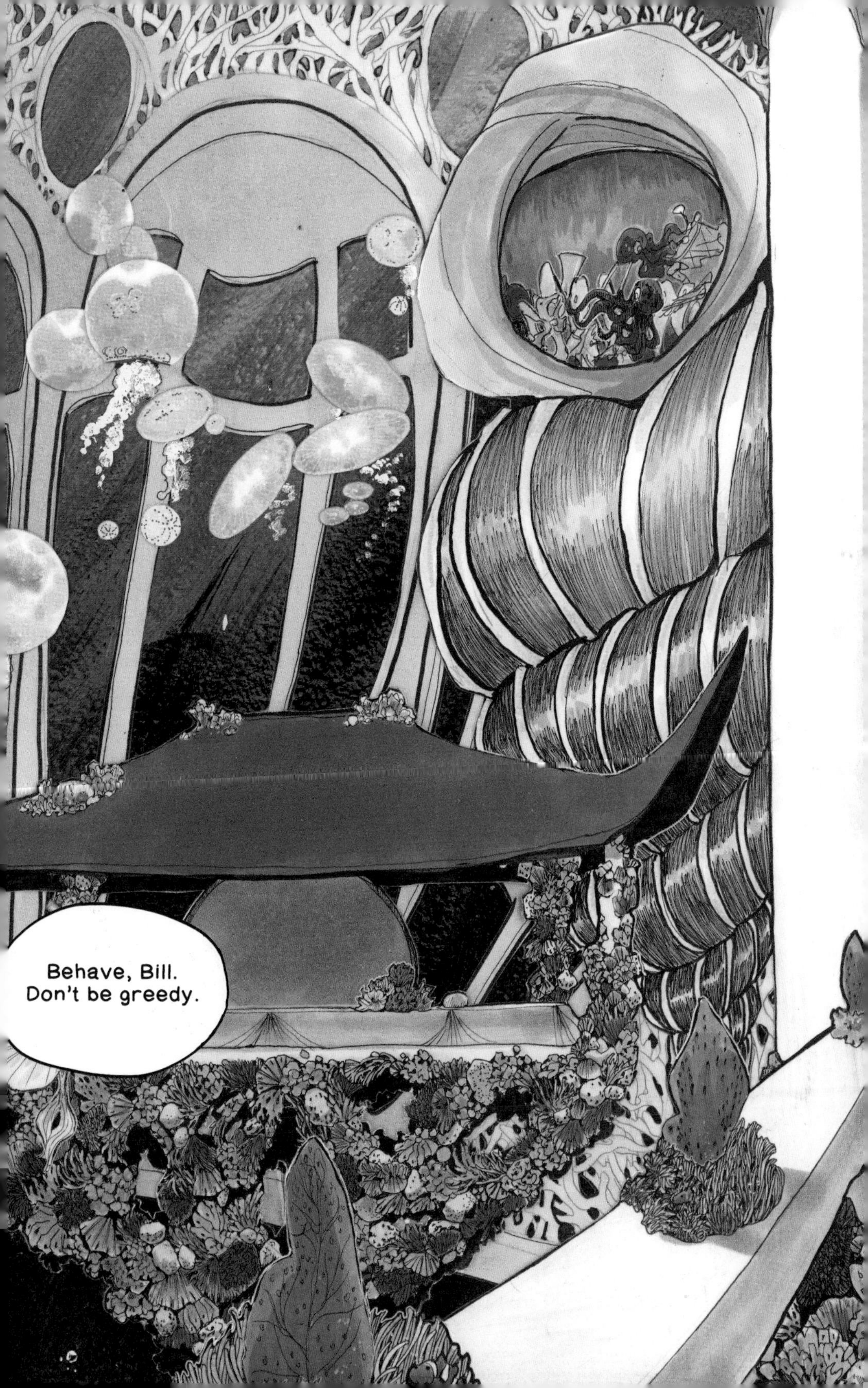
Behave, Bill. Don't be greedy.

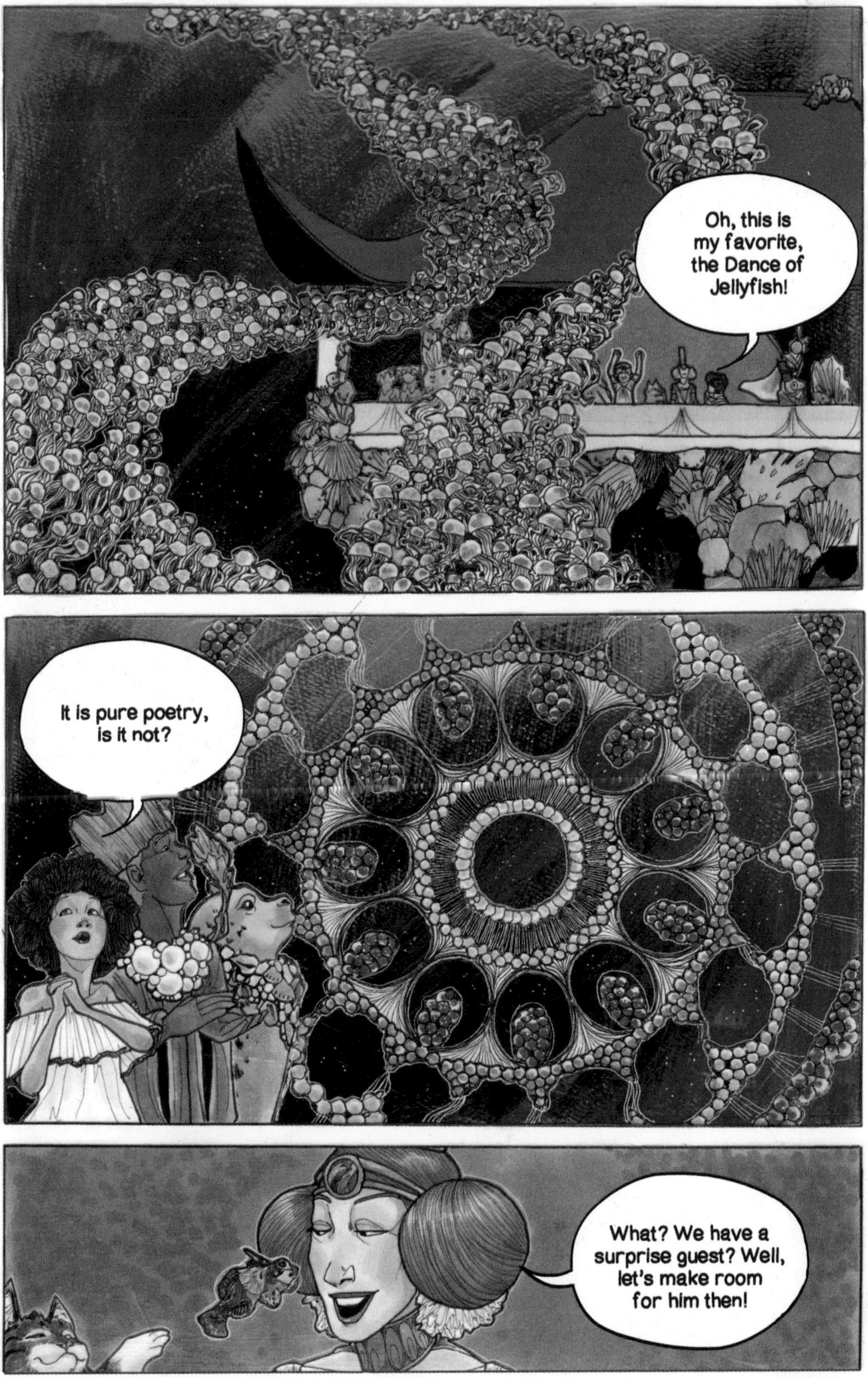
Oh, this is my favorite, the Dance of Jellyfish!
It is pure poetry, is it not?
What? We have a surprise guest? Well, let's make room for him then!

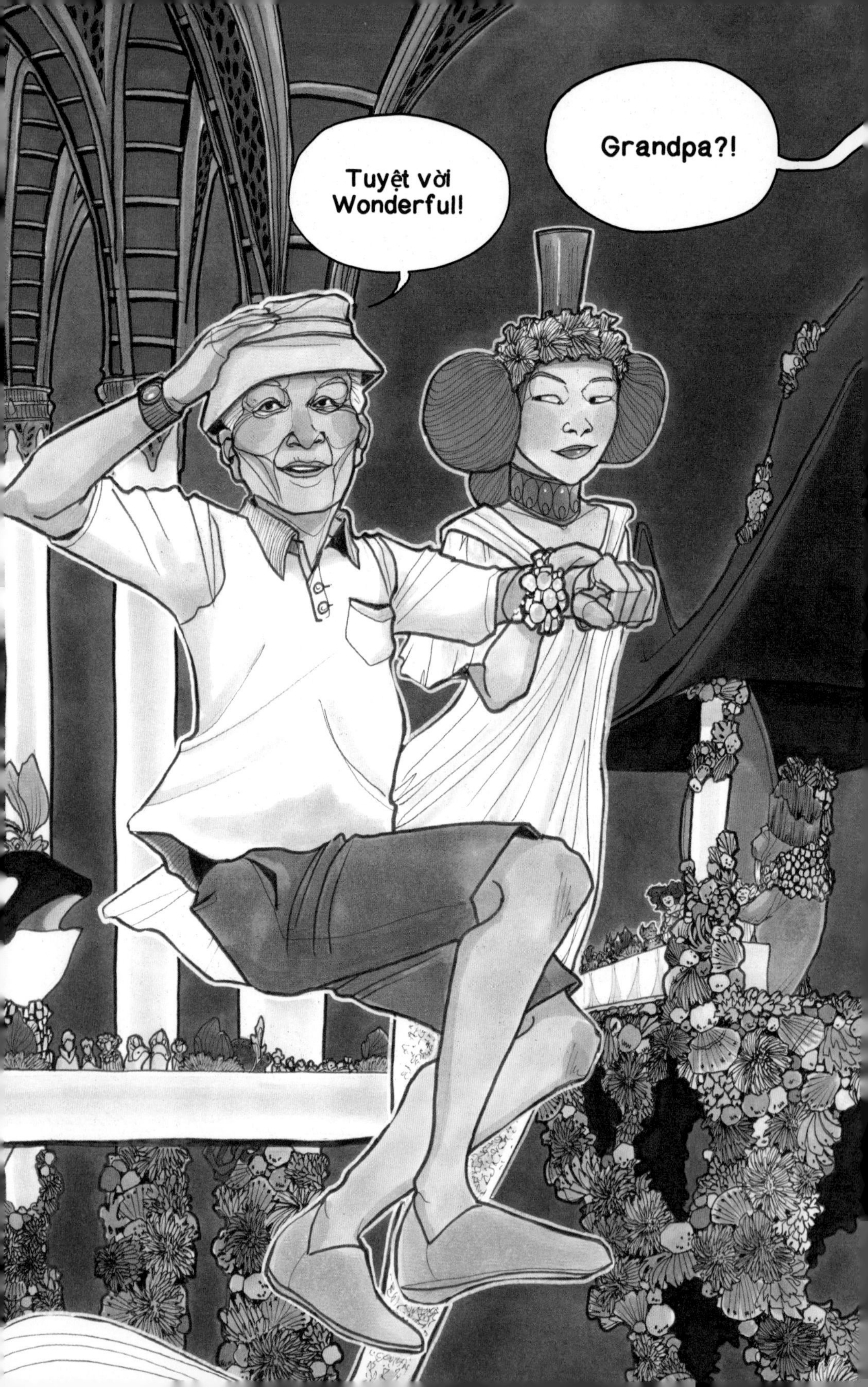
Tuyệt vời
Wonderful!
Grandpa?!

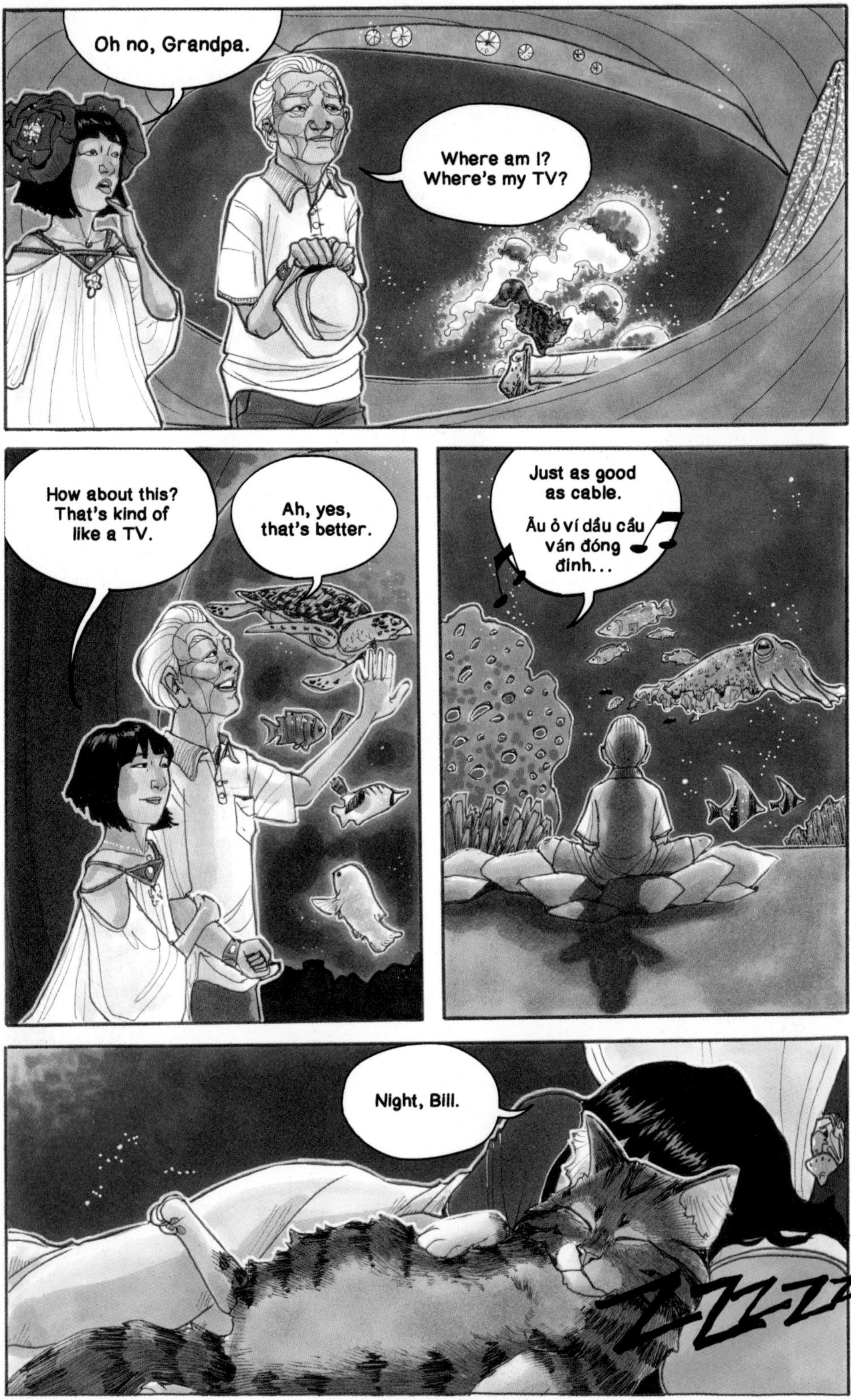

Oh no, Grandpa.
Where am I? Where's my TV?
How about this? That's kind of like a TV.
Ah, yes, that's better.
Just as good as cable.
Ầu ơ ví dầu cầu ván đóng đinh...
Night, Bill.
ZZZZZ

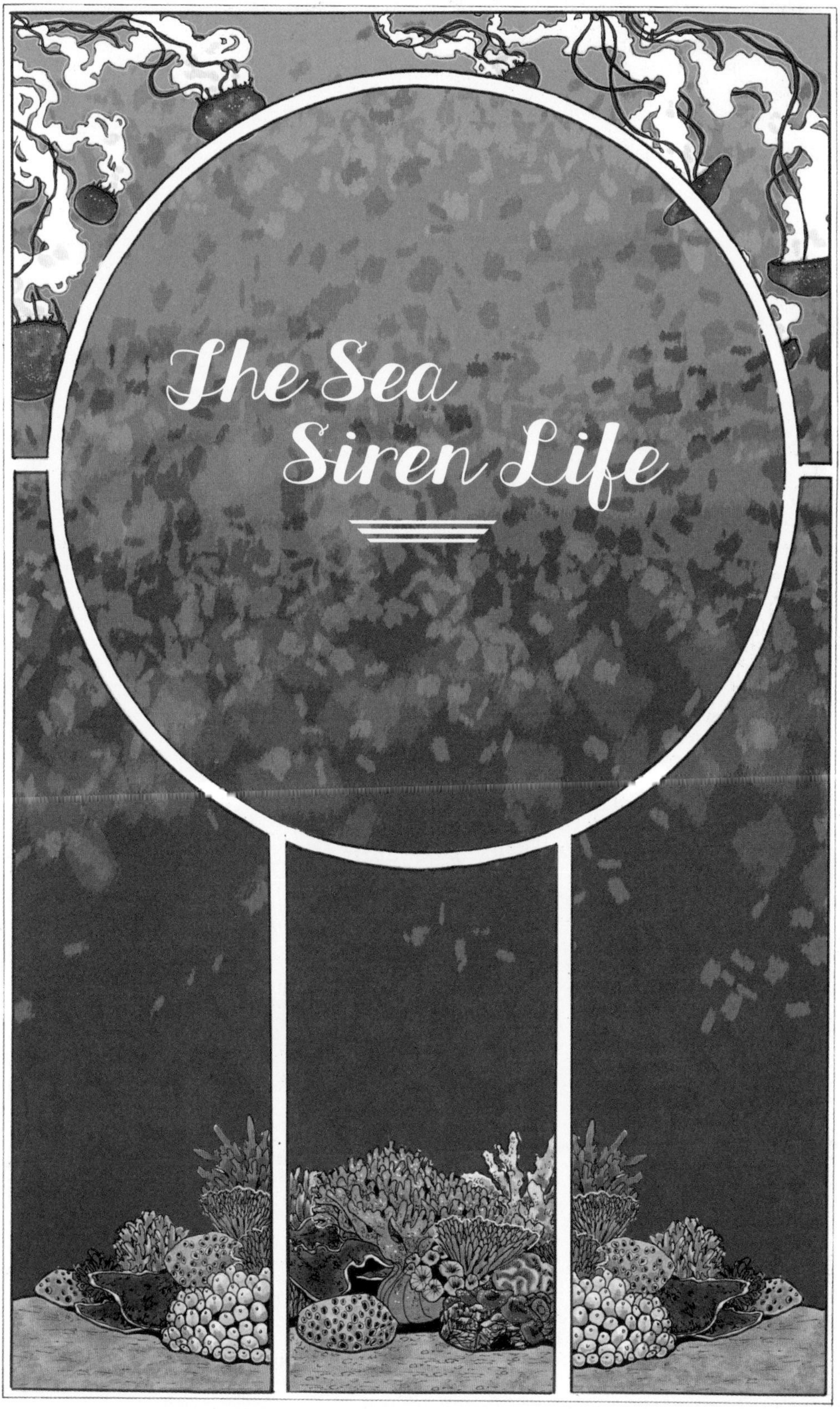
The Sea Siren Life

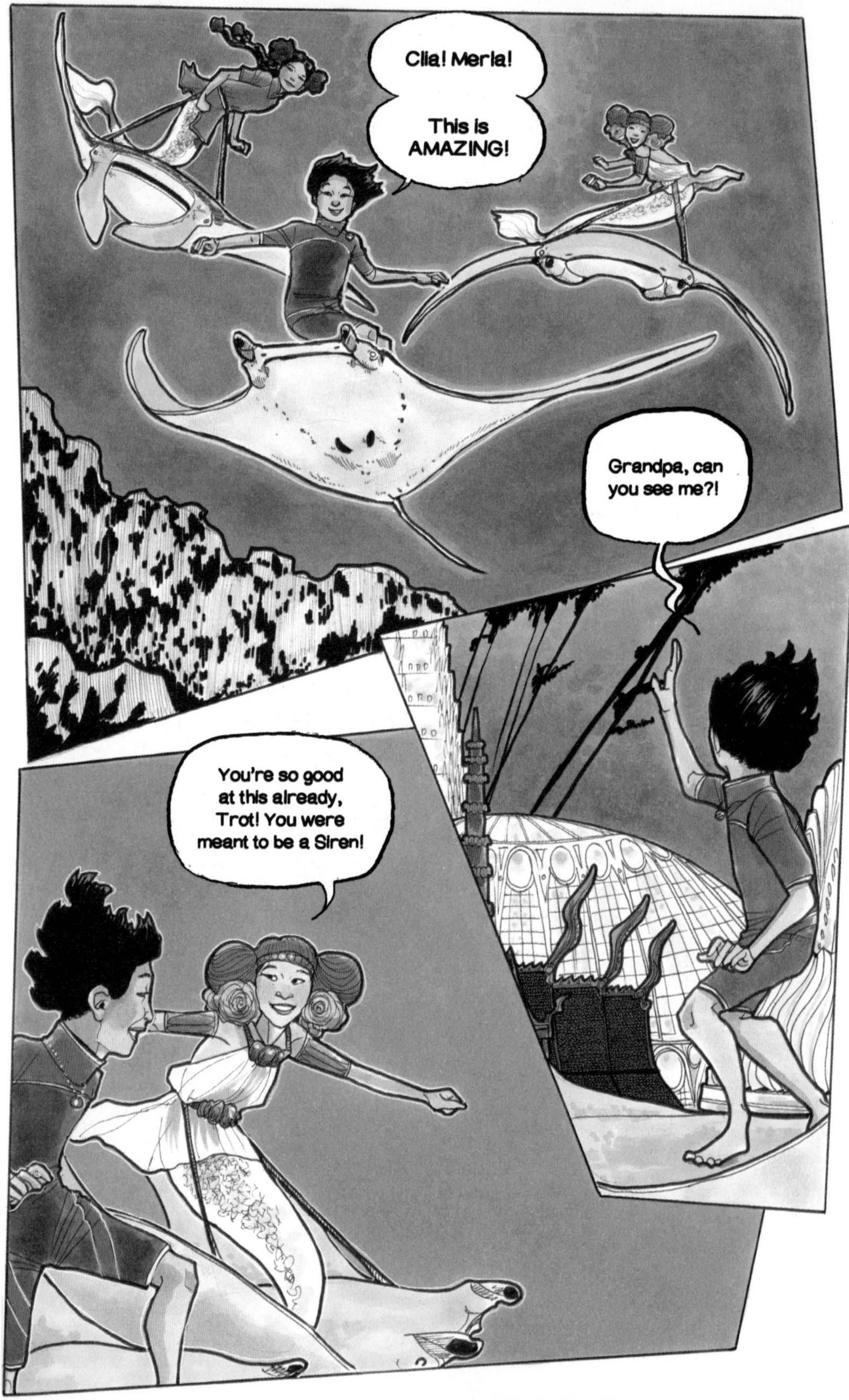
Clia! Merla!
This is AMAZING!
Grandpa, can you see me?!
You're so good at this already, Trot! You were meant to be a Siren!

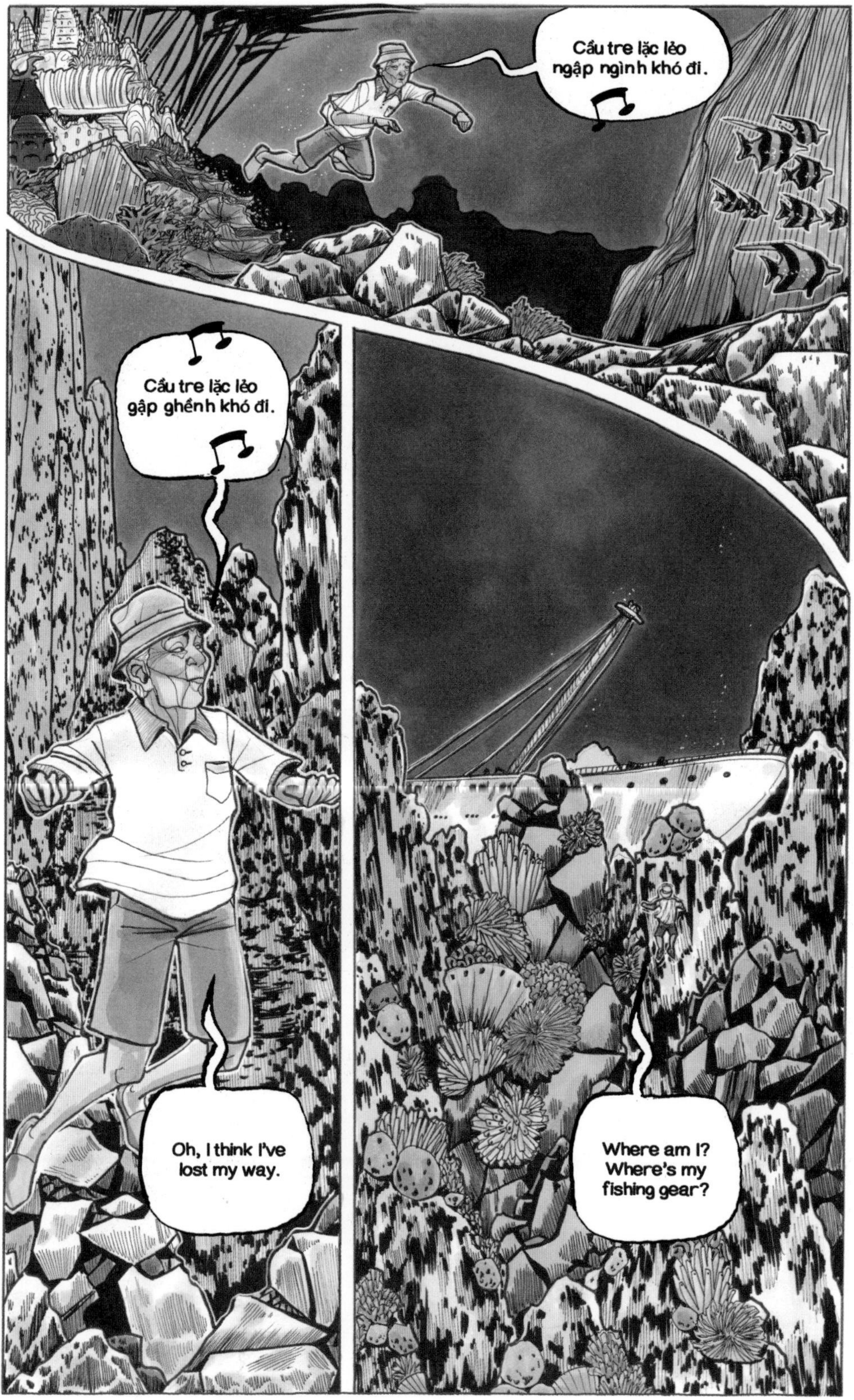
Cầu tre lặc lẻo ngập nginh khó đi.
Cầu tre lặc lẻo gập ghềnh khó đi.
Oh, I think I've lost my way.
Where am I? Where's my fishing gear?

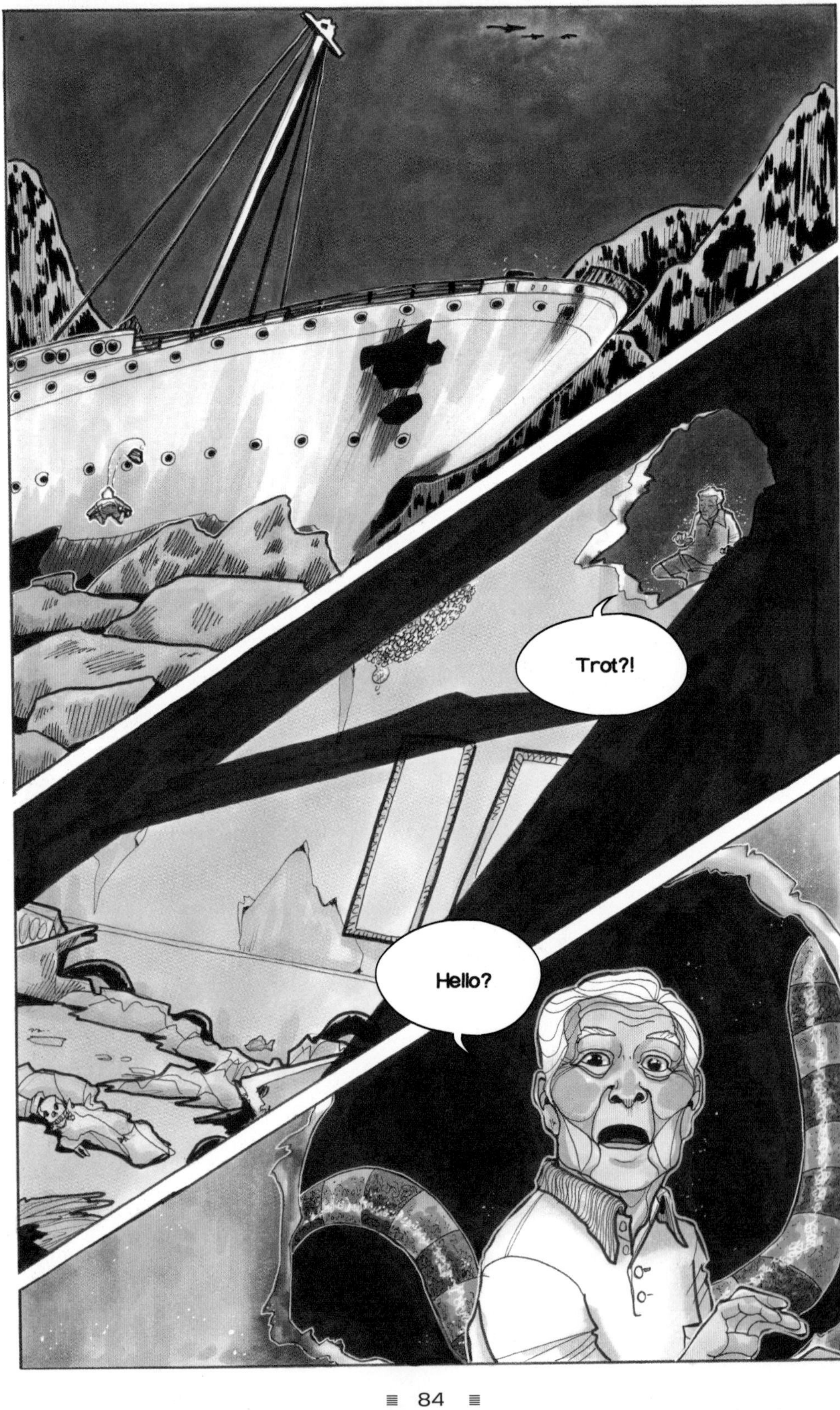
Trot?!
Hello?

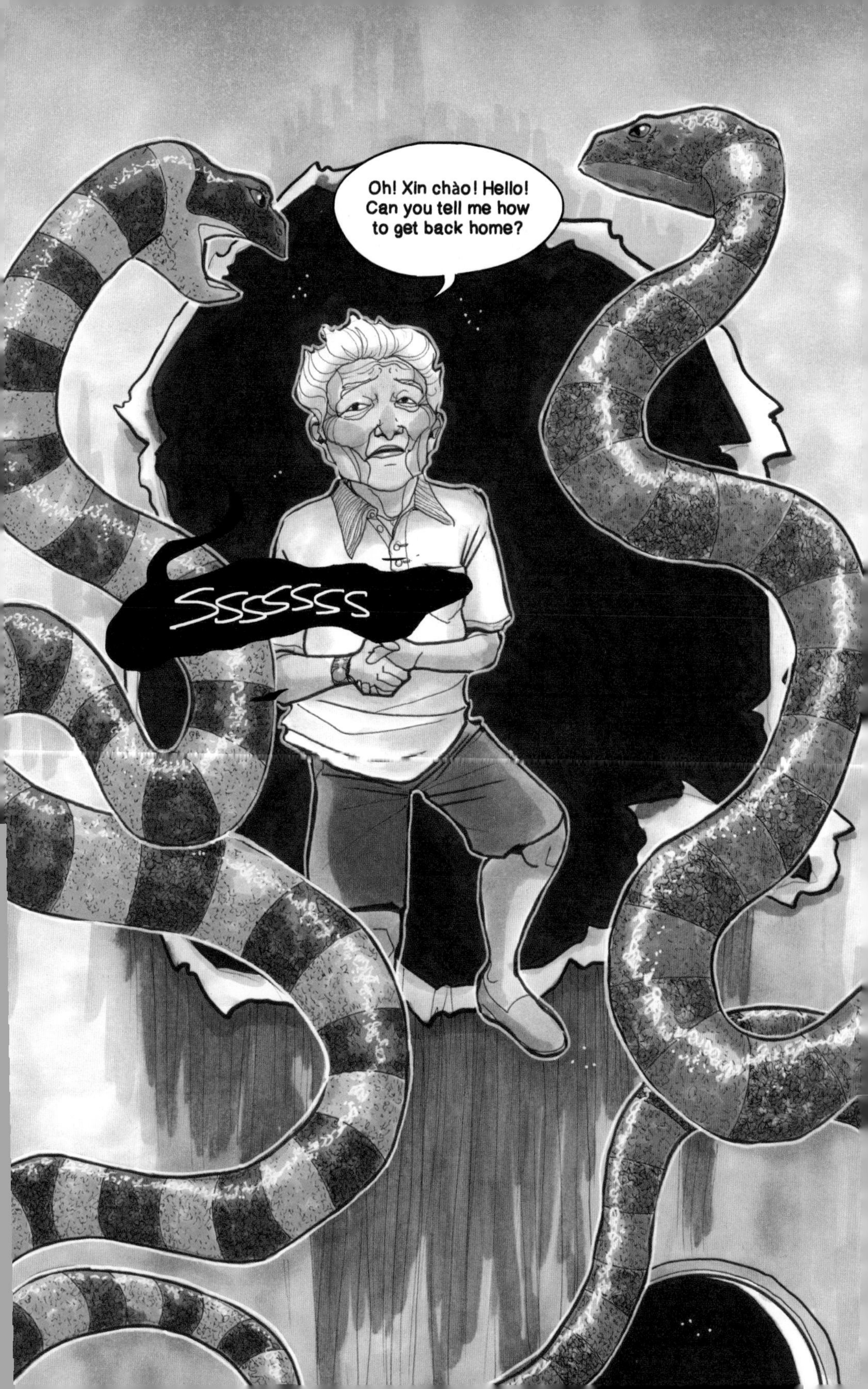
Oh! Xin chào! Hello! Can you tell me how to get back home?
SSSSSSS

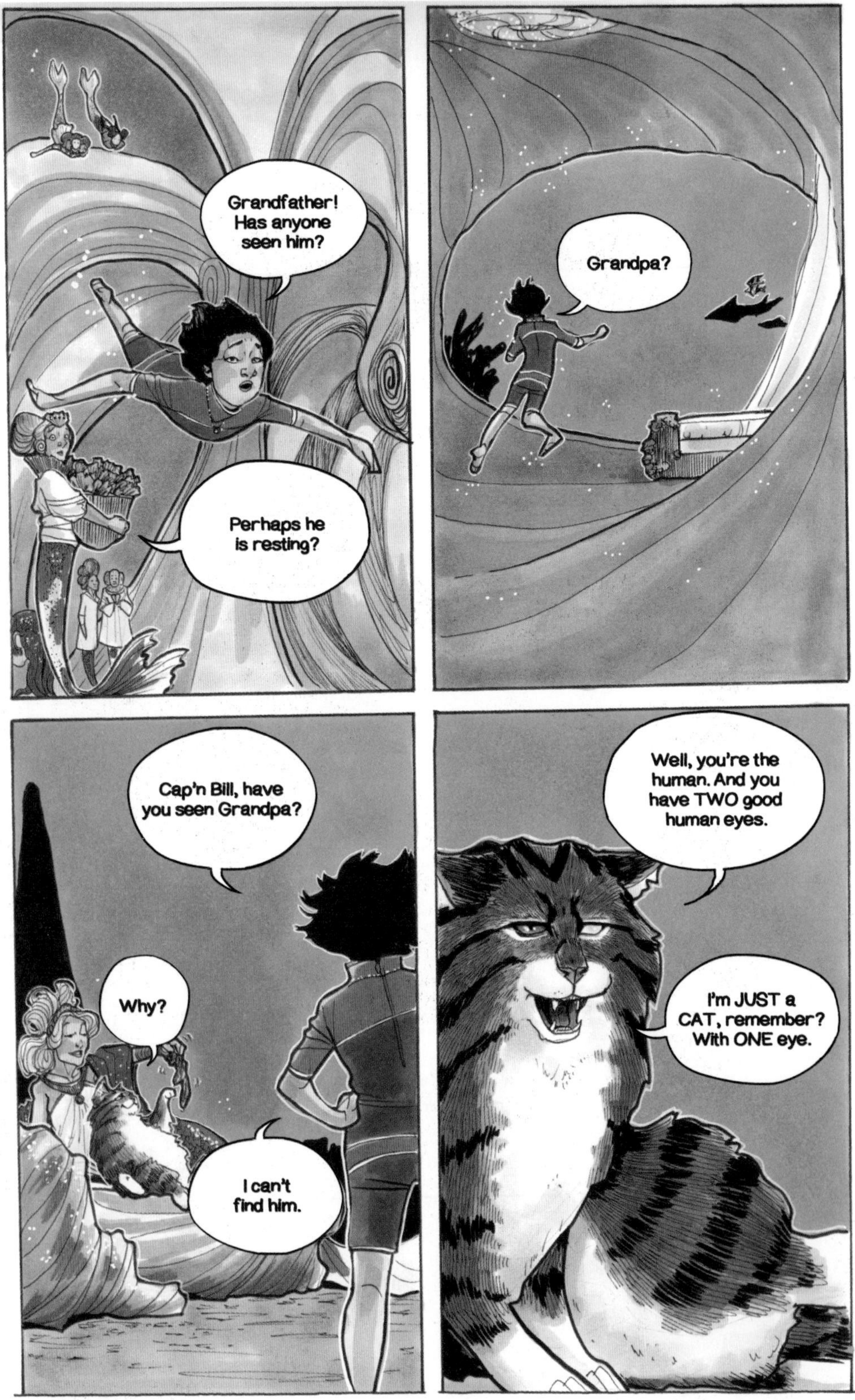
Grandfather! Has anyone seen him?
Perhaps he is resting?
Grandpa?
Cap'n Bill, have you seen Grandpa?
Why?
I can't find him.
Well, you're the human. And you have TWO good human eyes.
I'm JUST a CAT, remember? With ONE eye.

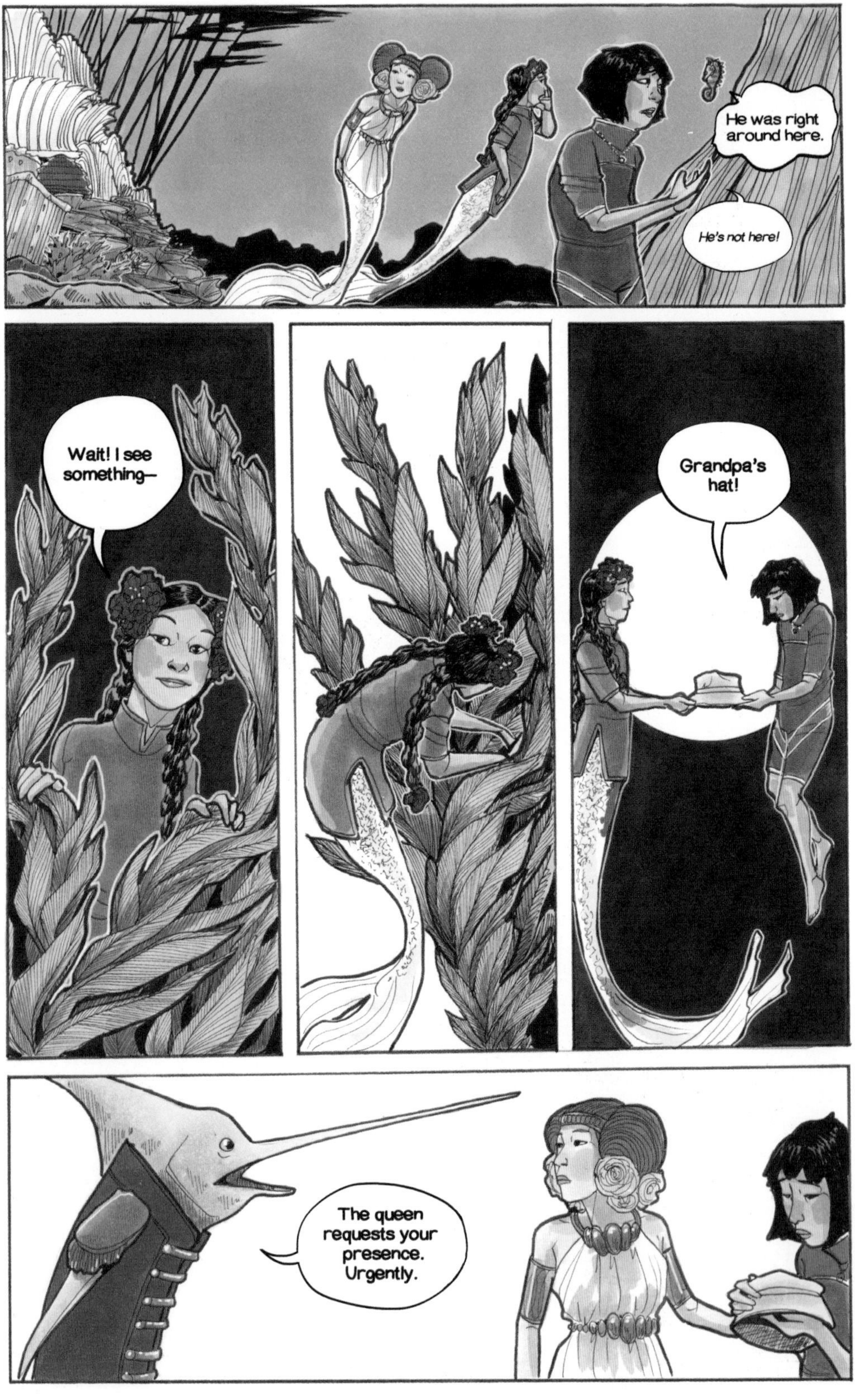
He was right around here.
He's not here!
Wait! I see something—
Grandpa's hat!
The queen requests your presence. Urgently.

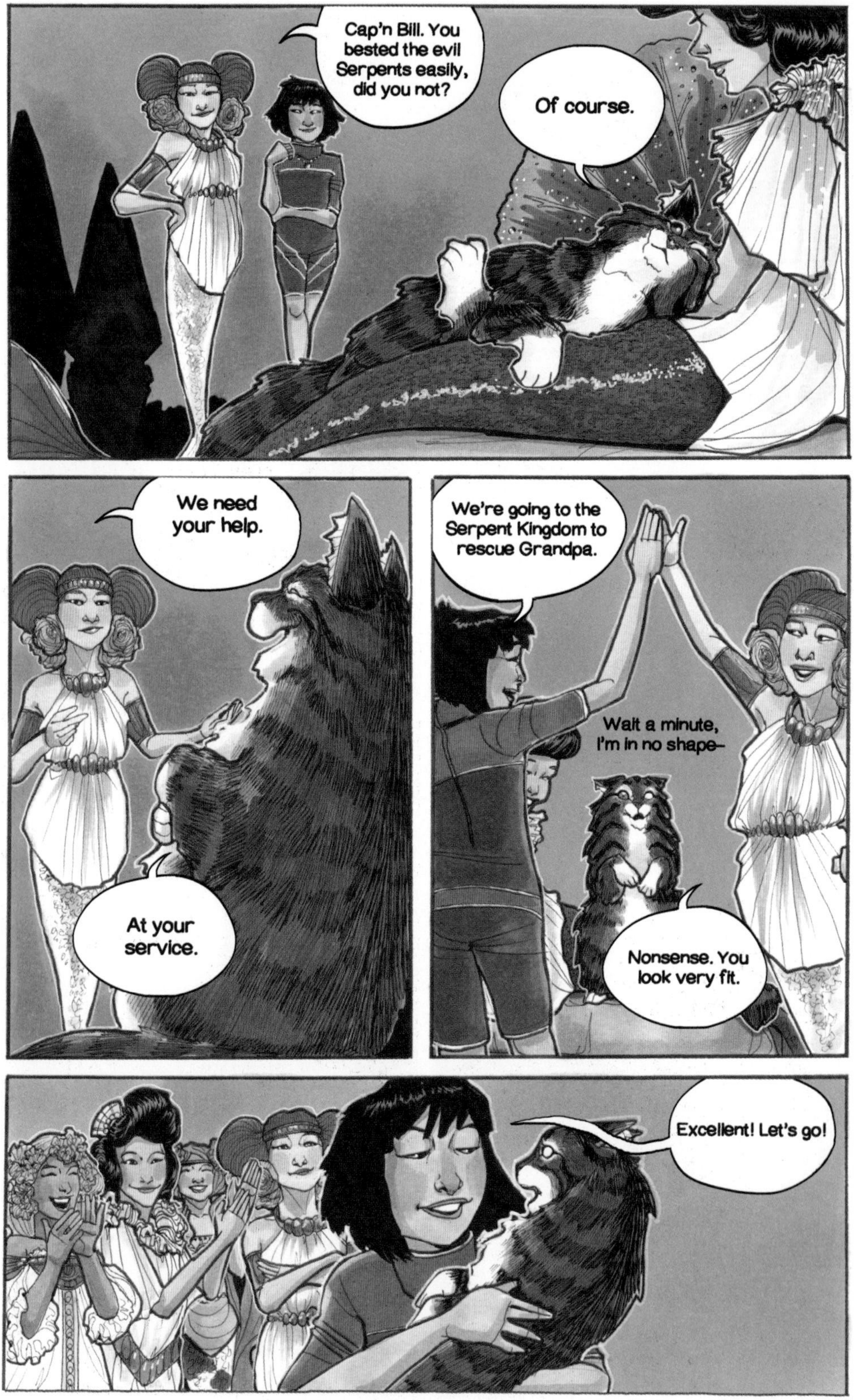
Cap'n Bill. You bested the evil Serpents easily, did you not?
Of course.
We need your help.
At your service.
We're going to the Serpent Kingdom to rescue Grandpa.
Wait a minute, I'm in no shape–
Nonsense. You look very fit.
Excellent! Let's go!

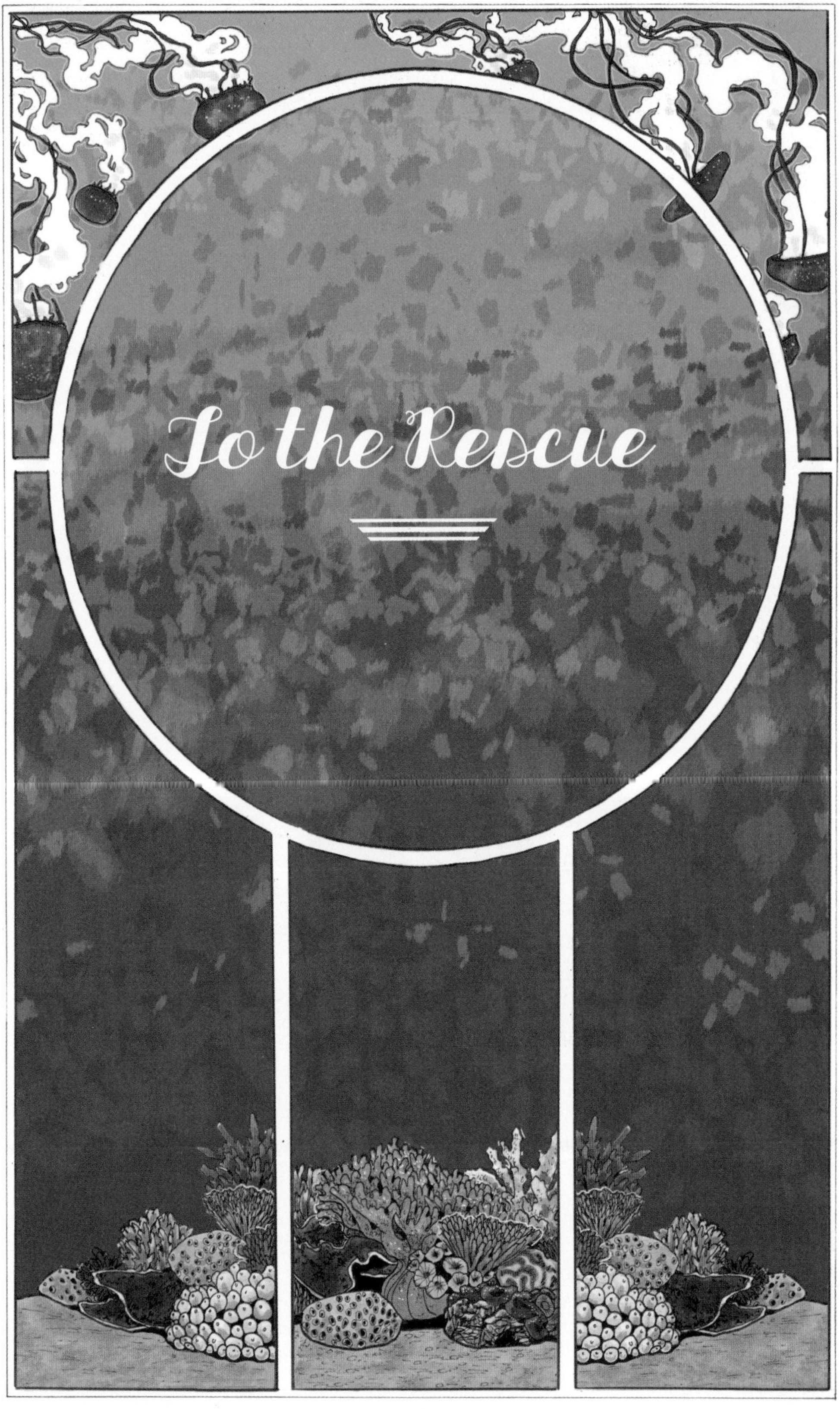
To the Rescue

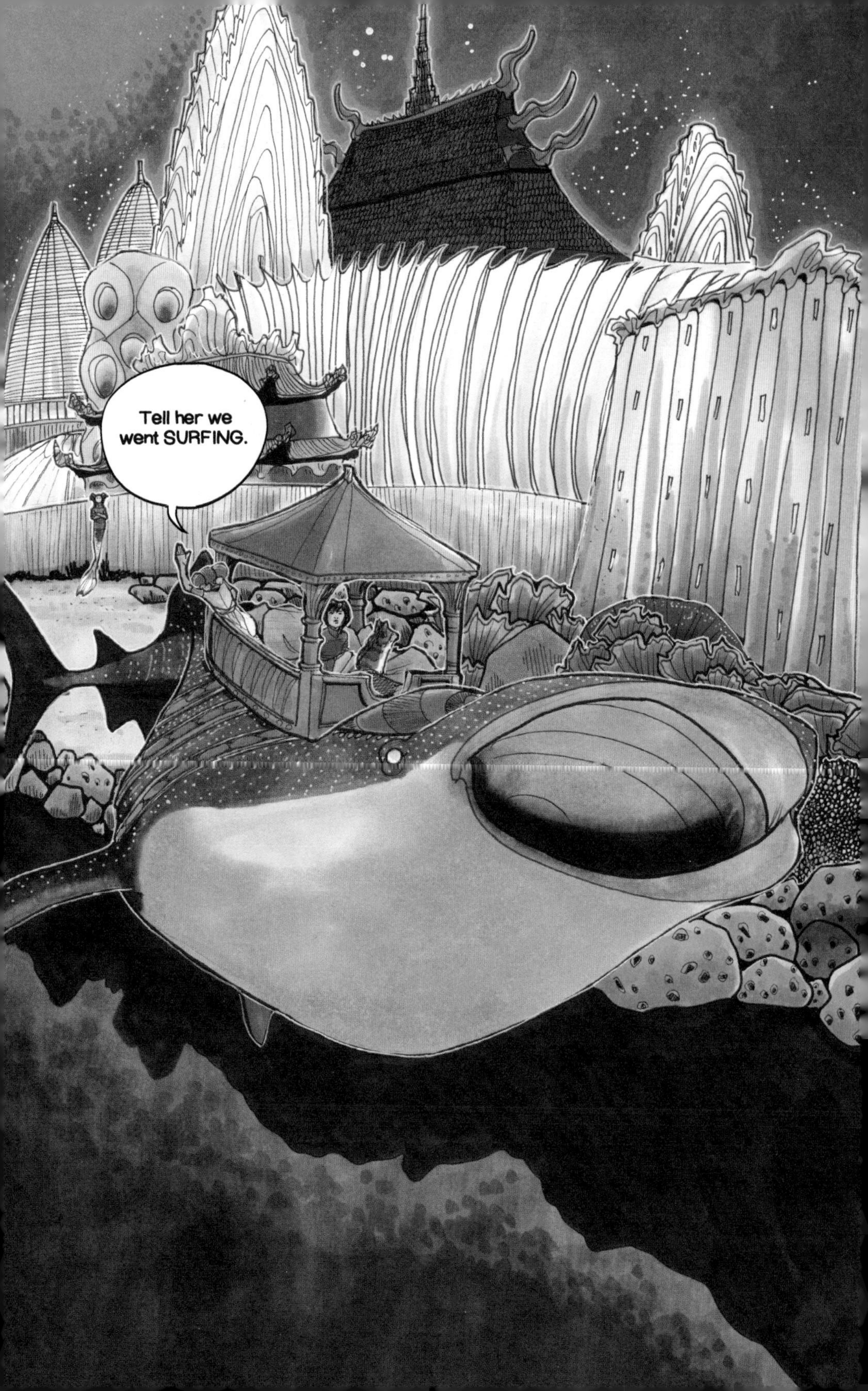
Tell her we went SURFING.

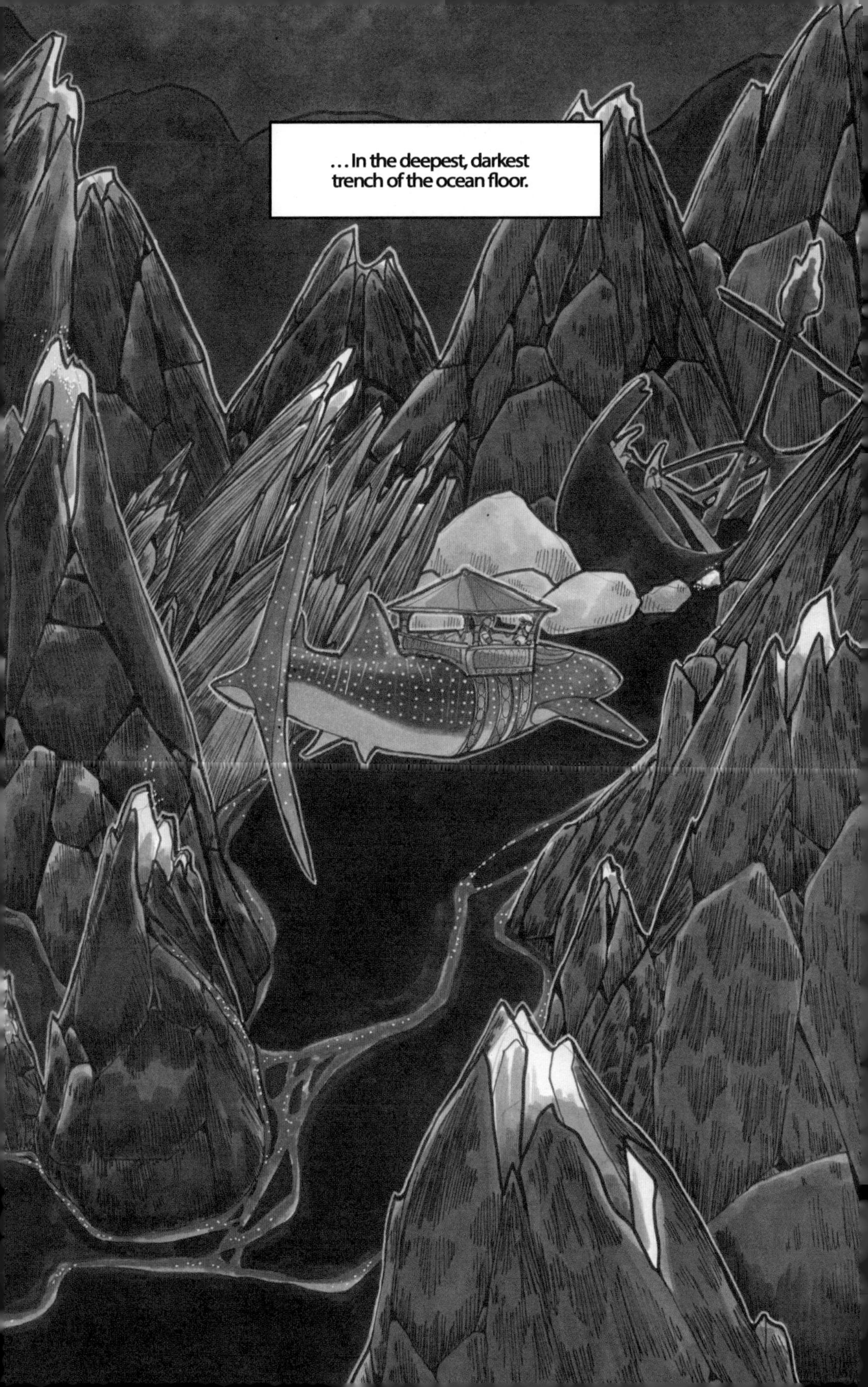
. . . In the deepest, darkest trench of the ocean floor.

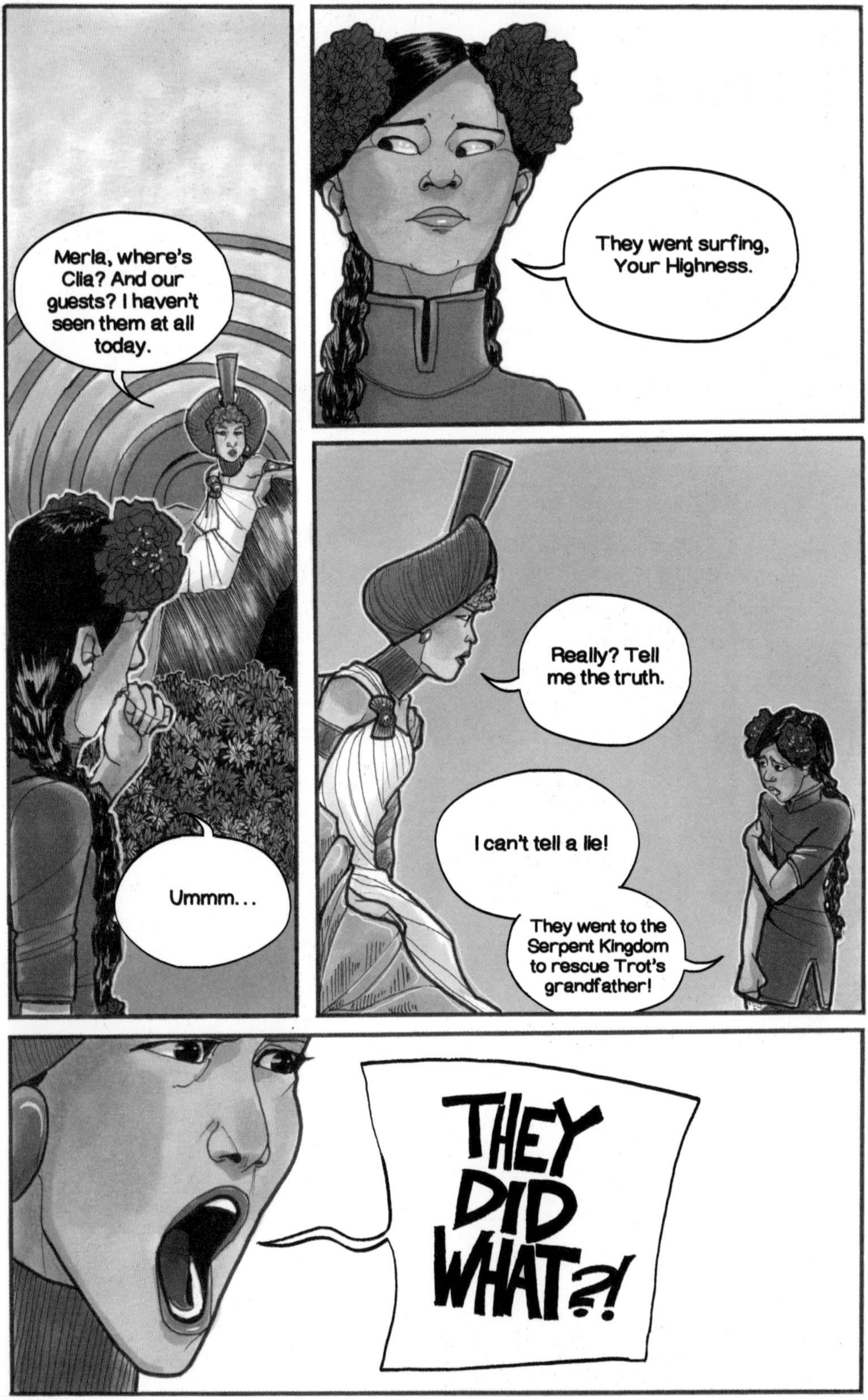
Merla, where's Clia? And our guests? I haven't seen them at all today.
Ummm...
They went surfing, Your Highness.
Really? Tell me the truth.
I can't tell a lie!
They went to the Serpent Kingdom to rescue Trot's grandfather!
THEY DID WHAT?!

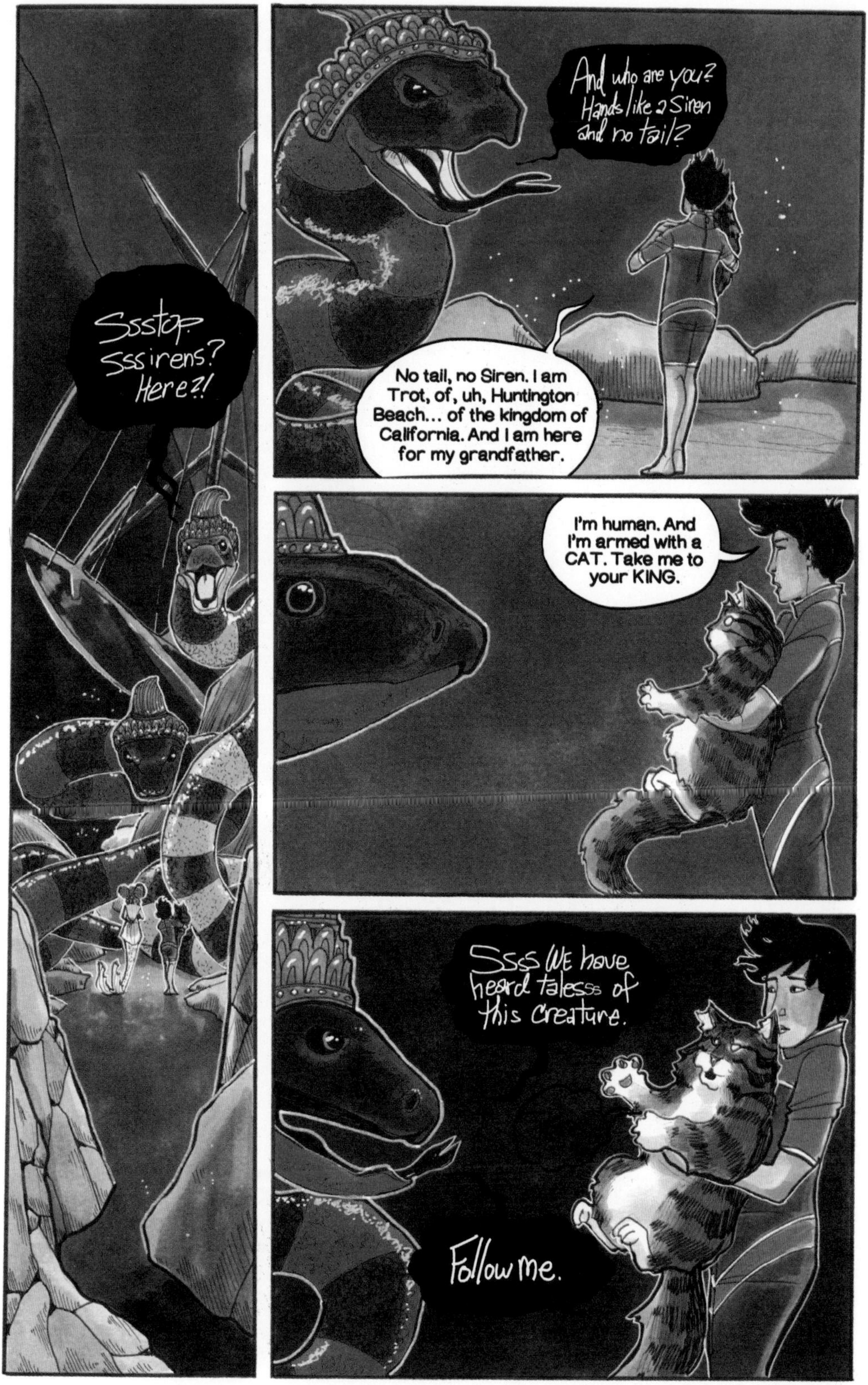
Ssstop. Sssirens? Here?!
And who are you? Hands like a Siren and no tail?
No tail, no Siren. I am Trot, of, uh, Huntington Beach... of the kingdom of California. And I am here for my grandfather.
I'm human. And I'm armed with a CAT. Take me to your KING.
Ssss We have heard talesss of this Creature.
Follow me.

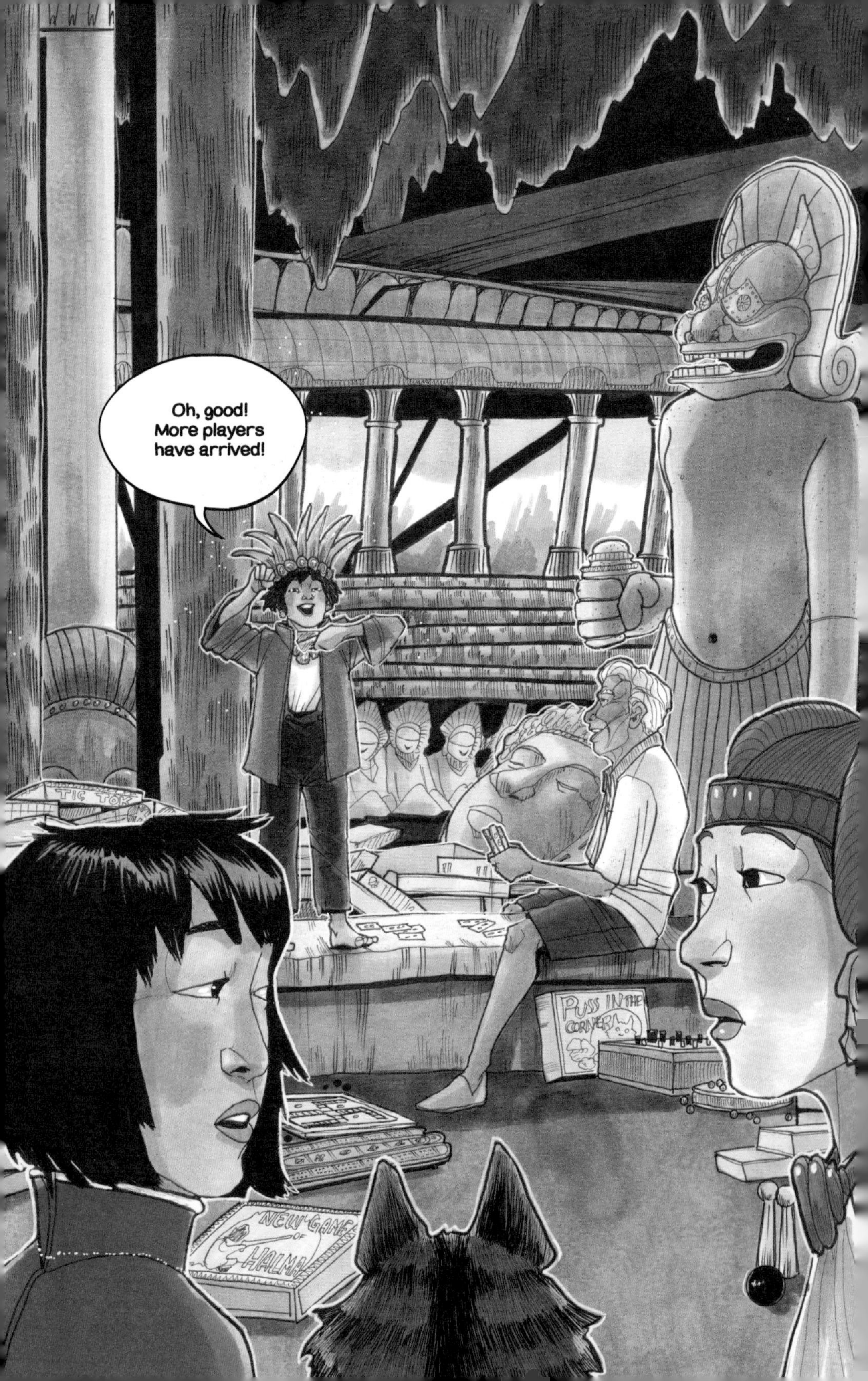
Oh, good! More players have arrived!
TIC TOK
PUSS IN THE CORNER
NEW GAME OF HALMA

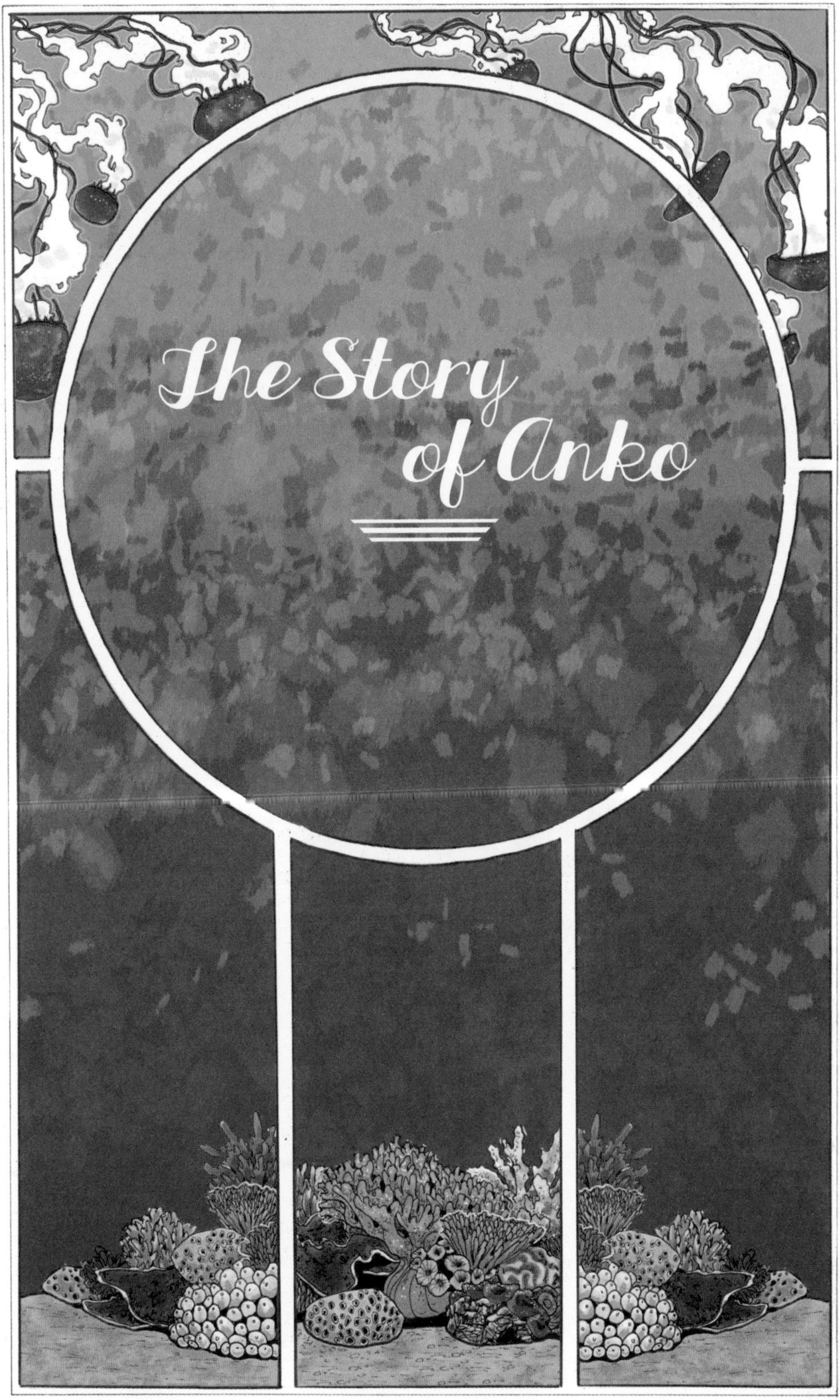
The Story
of Anko

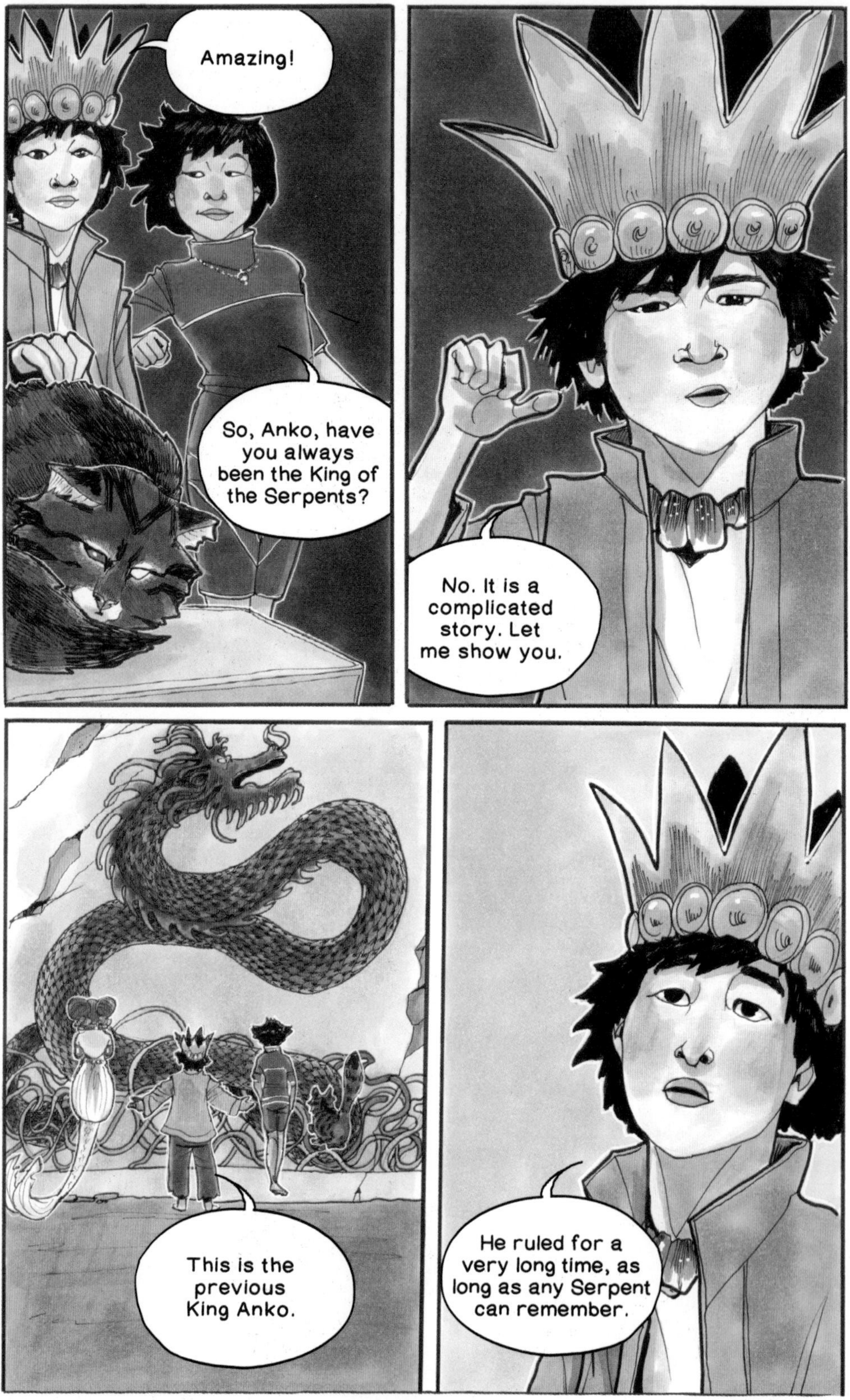
Amazing!
So, Anko, have you always been the King of the Serpents?
No. It is a complicated story. Let me show you.
This is the previous King Anko.
He ruled for a very long time, as long as any Serpent can remember.

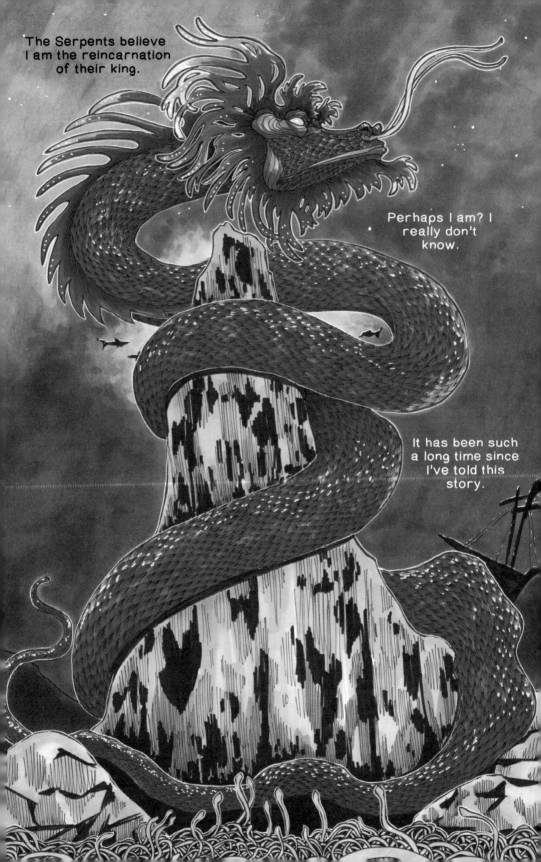

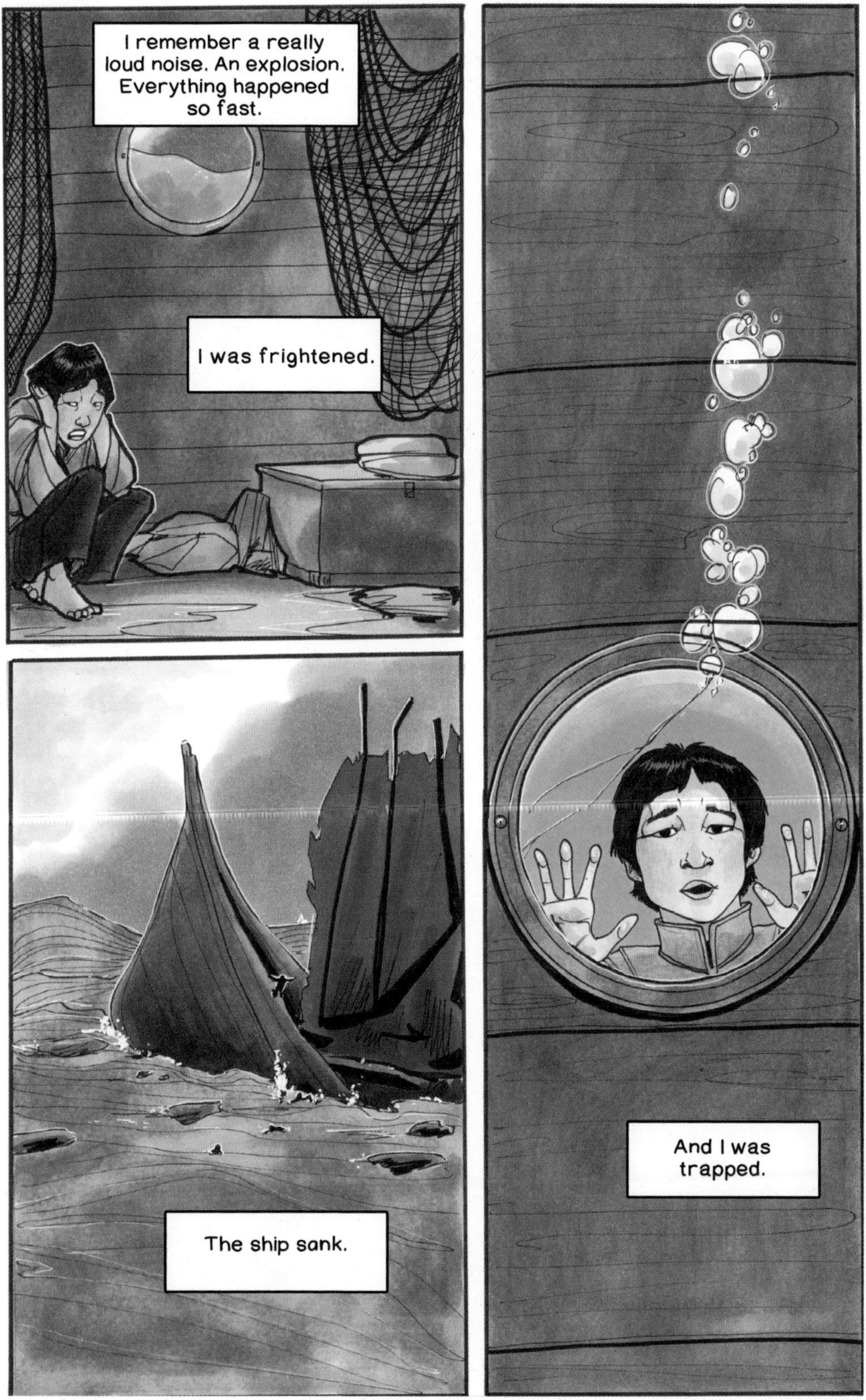
I remember a really loud noise. An explosion. Everything happened so fast.
I was frightened.
The ship sank.
And I was trapped.

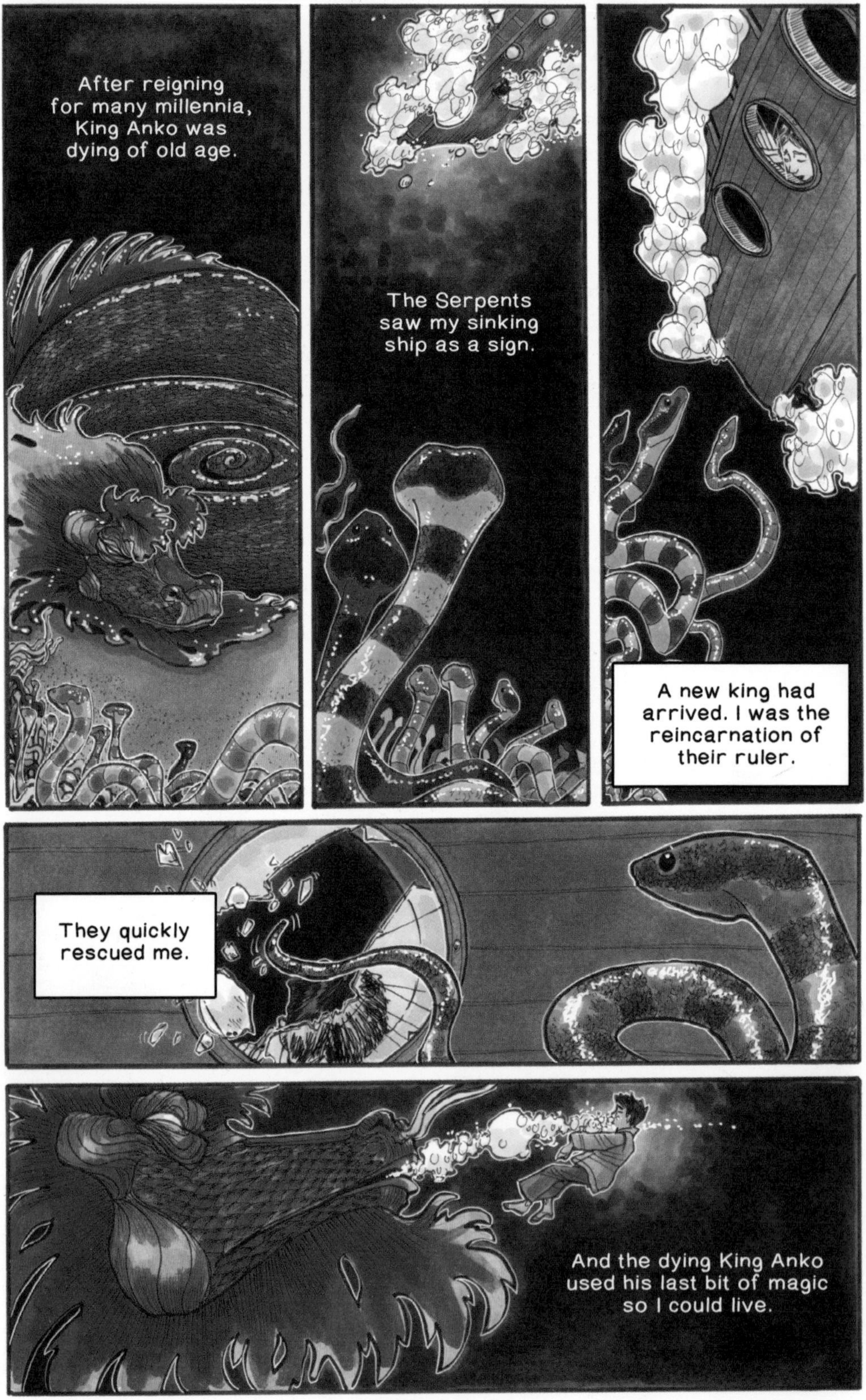
After reigning for many millennia, King Anko was dying of old age.
The Serpents saw my sinking ship as a sign.
A new king had arrived. I was the reincarnation of their ruler.
They quickly rescued me.
And the dying King Anko used his last bit of magic so I could live.

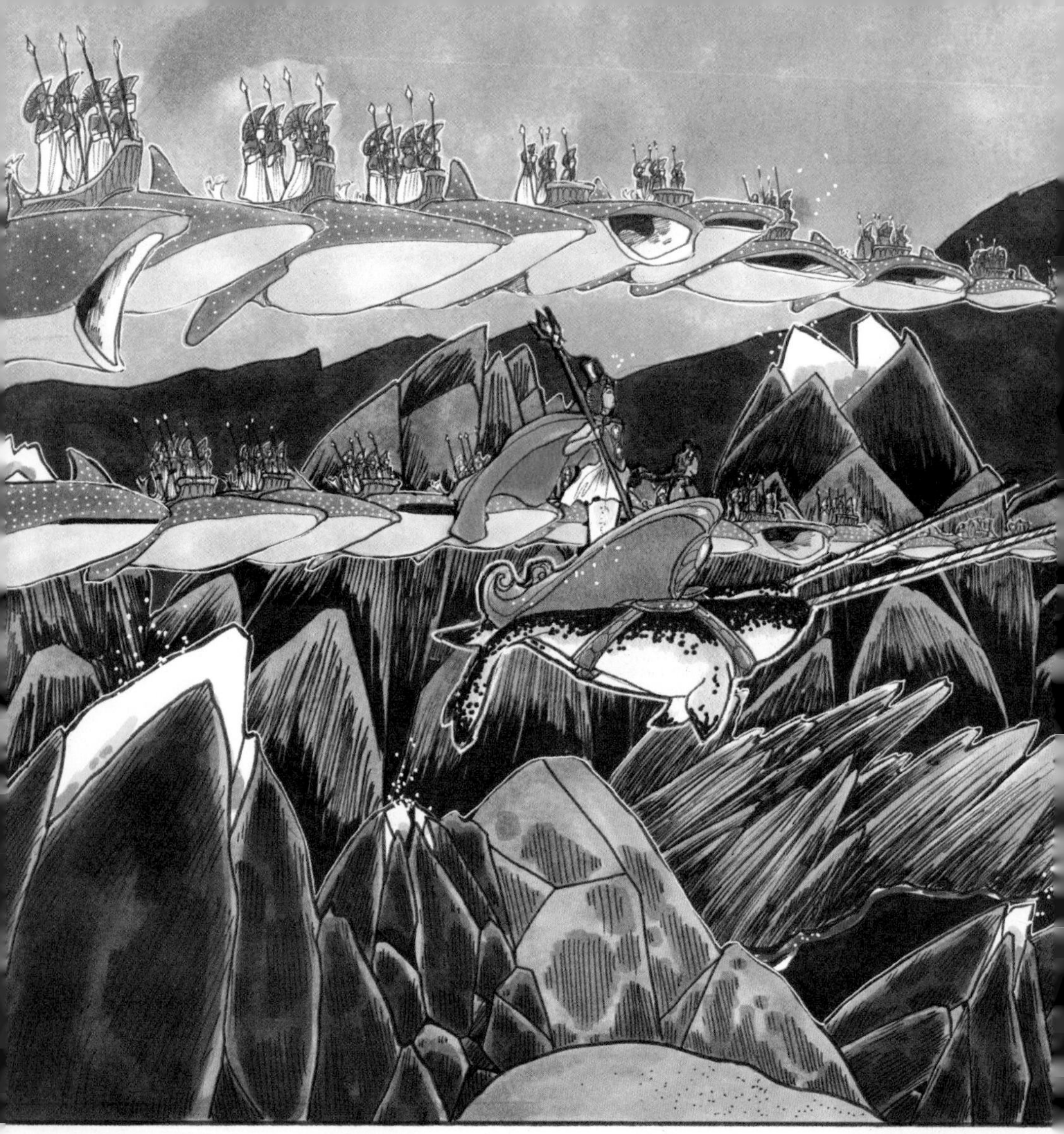

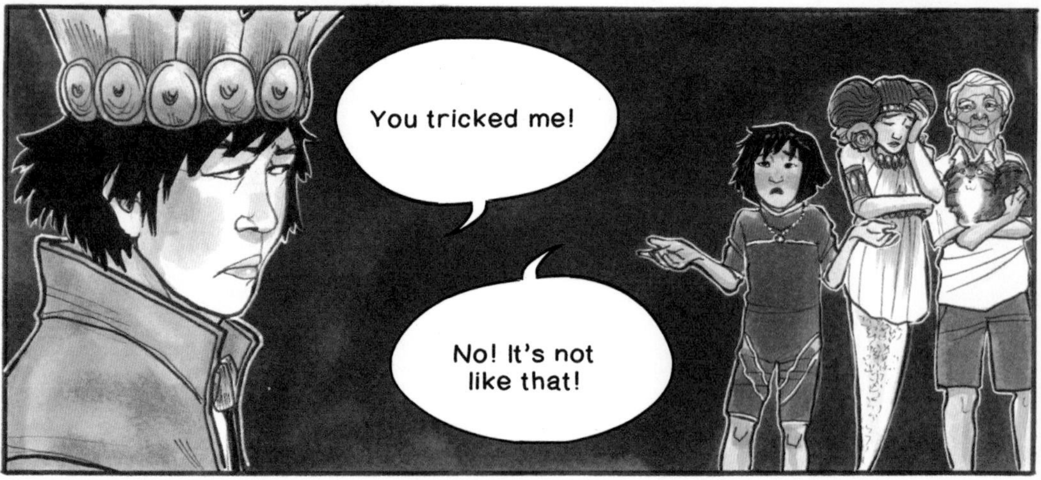
You tricked me!
No! It's not like that!

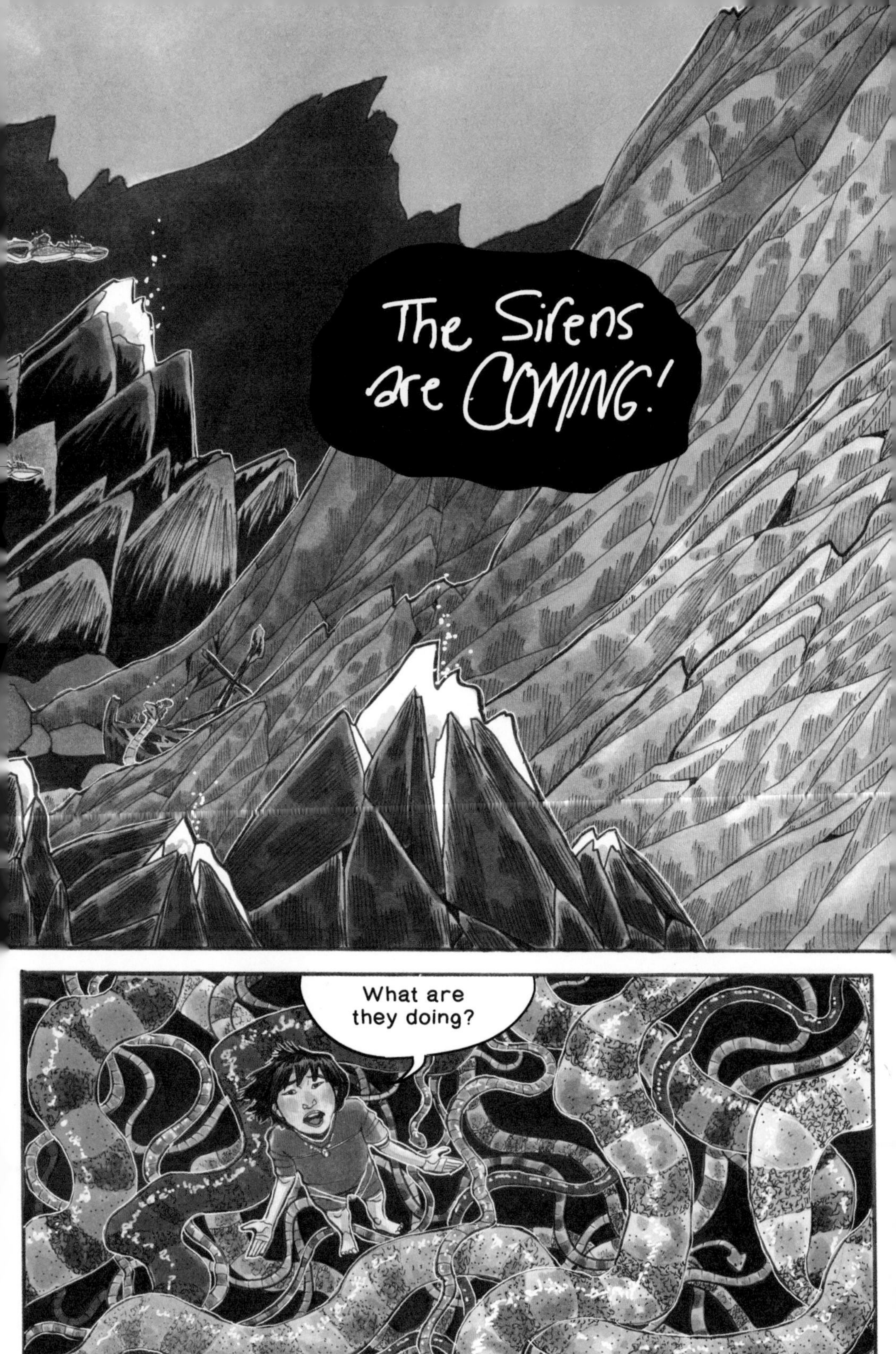
The Sirens are COMING!
What are they doing?

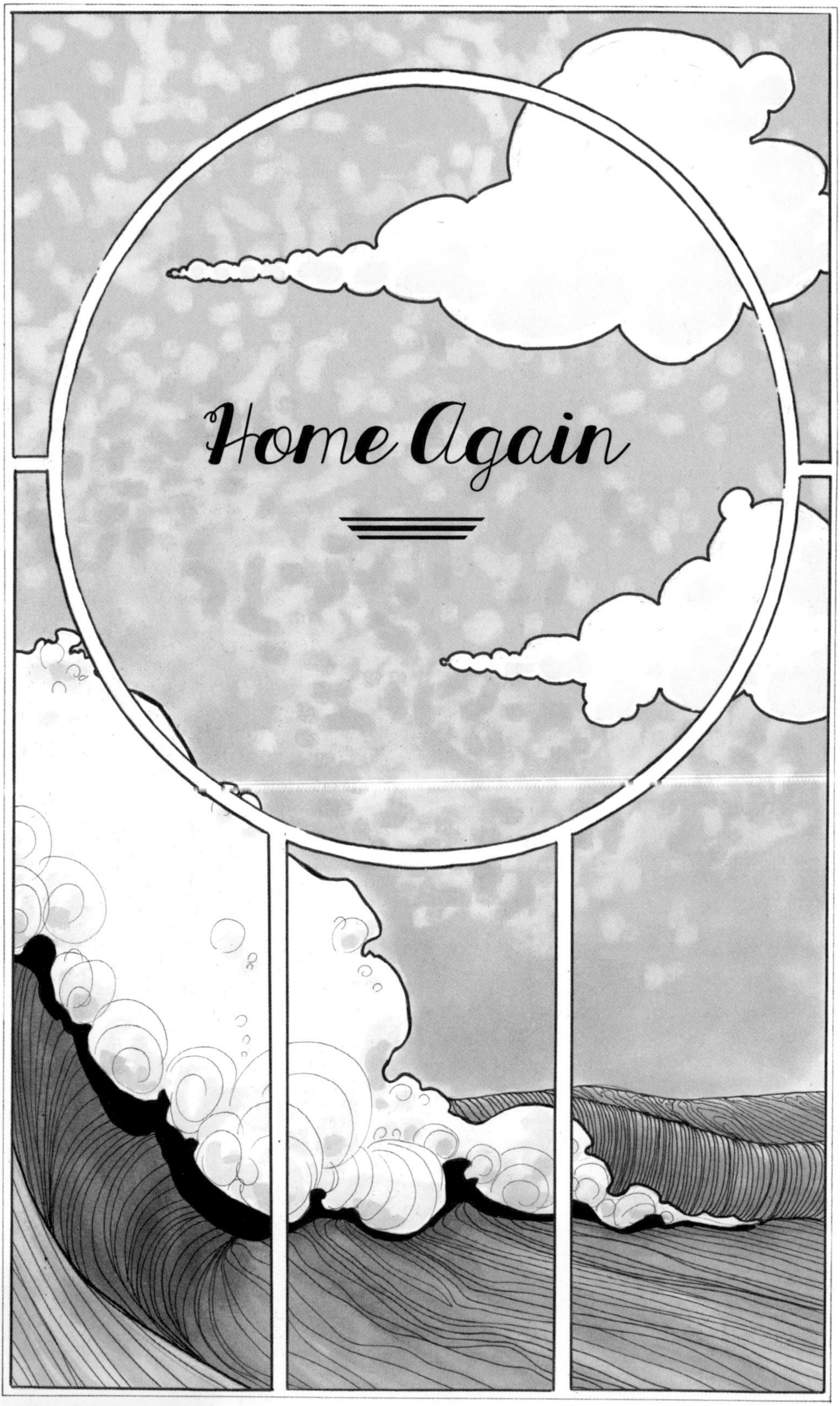
Home Again

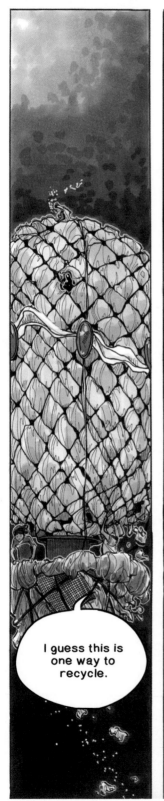

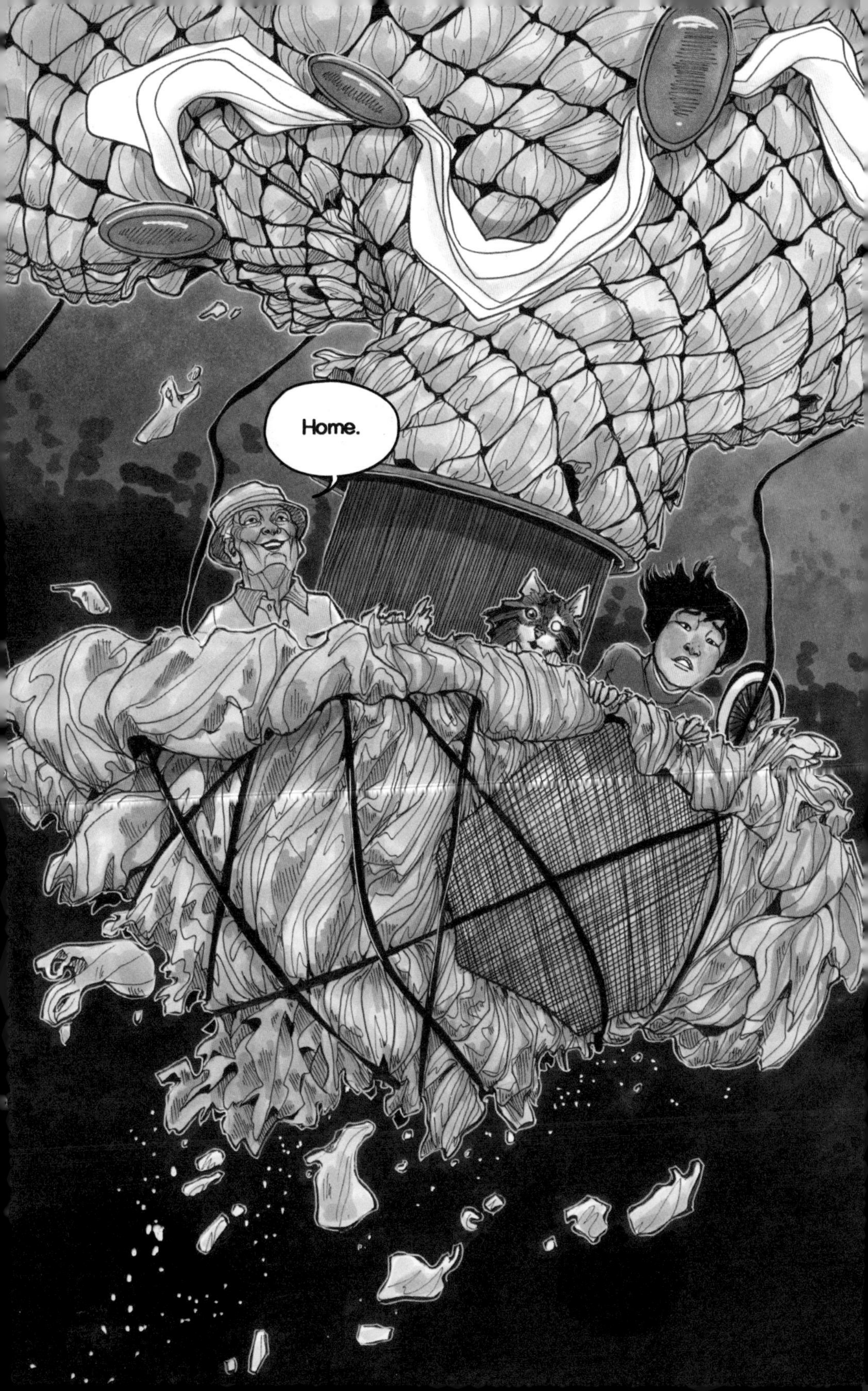
Home.

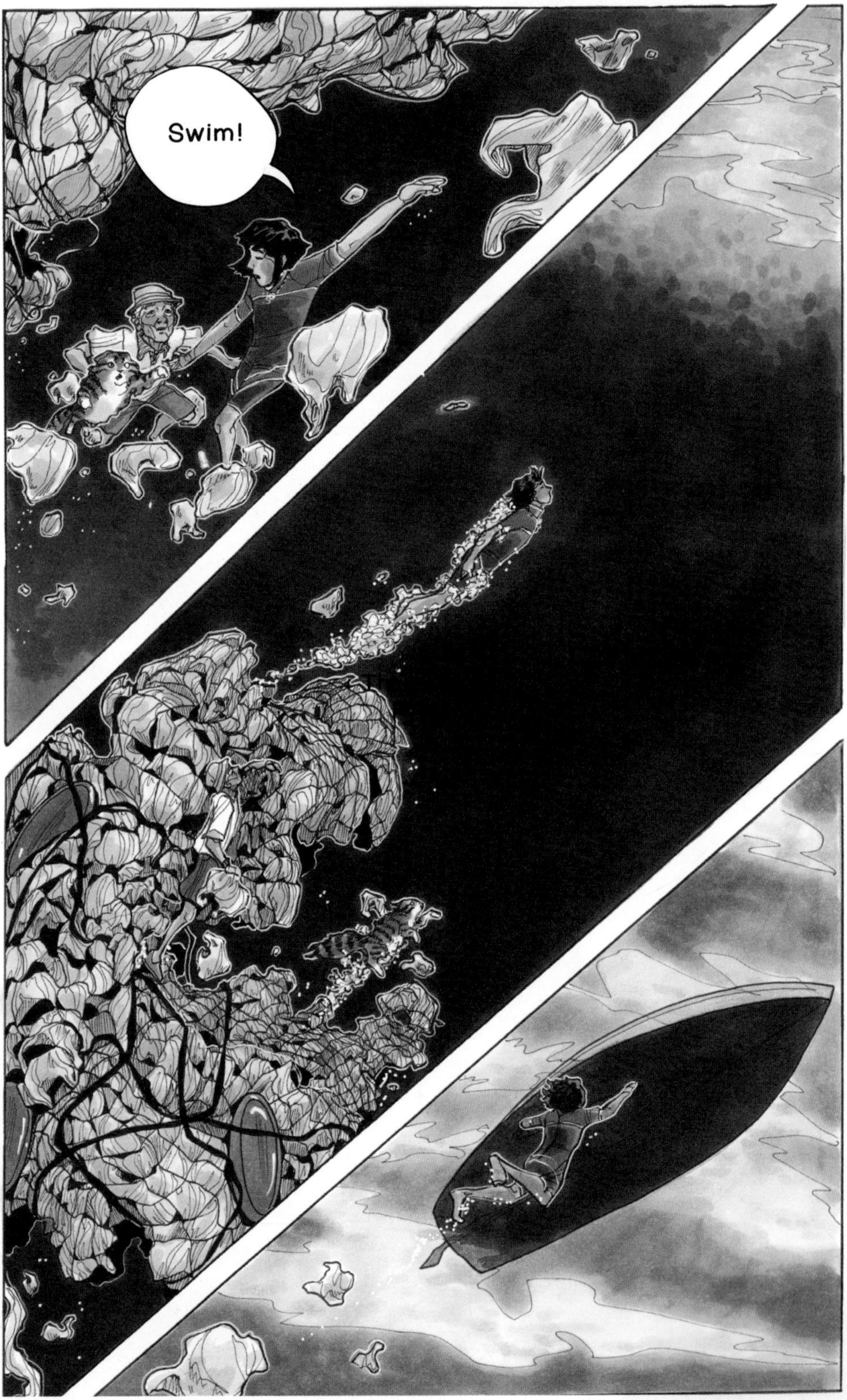
Swim!

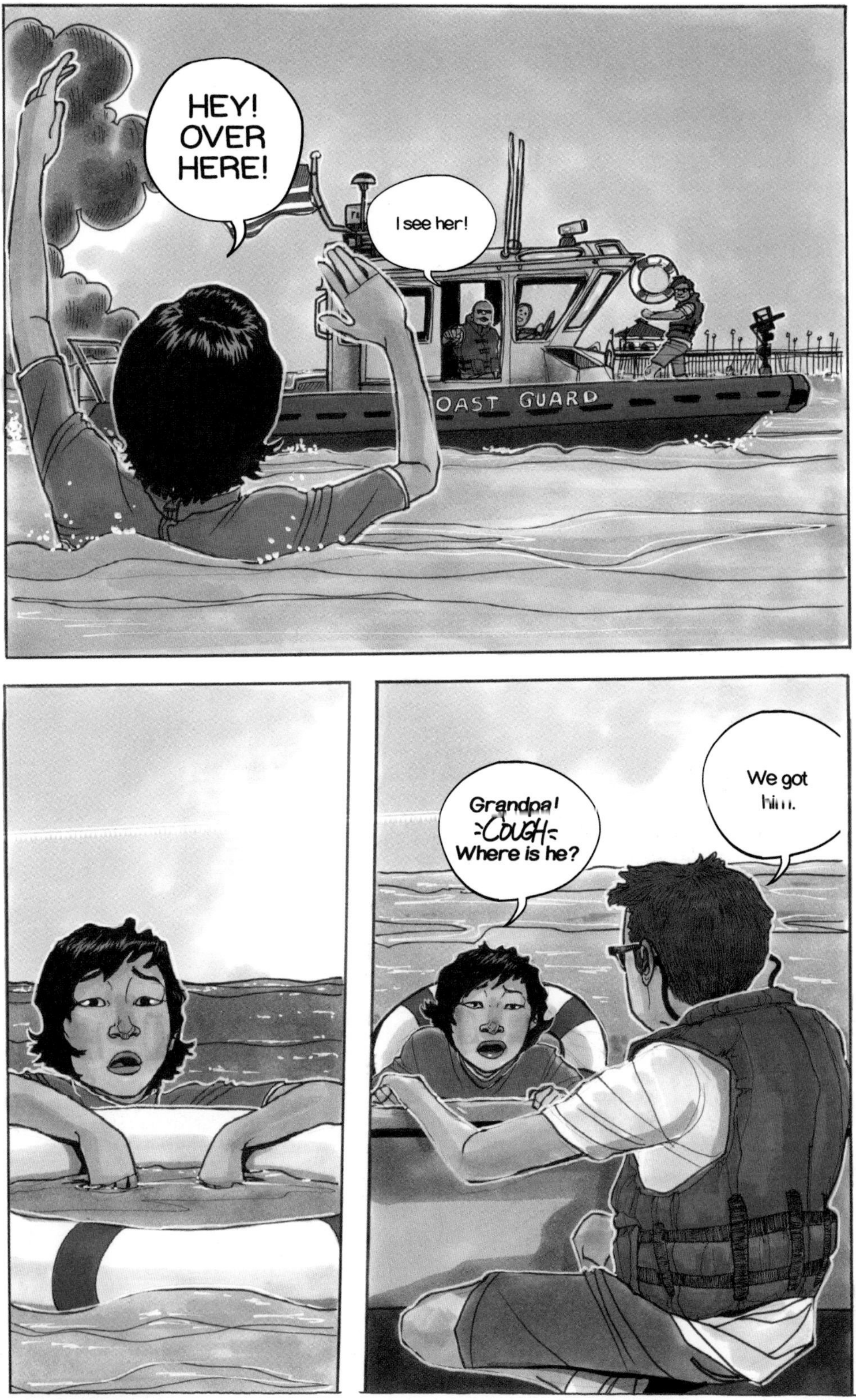
HEY! OVER HERE!
I see her!
OAST GUARD
Grandpa! =COUGH= Where is he?
We got him.

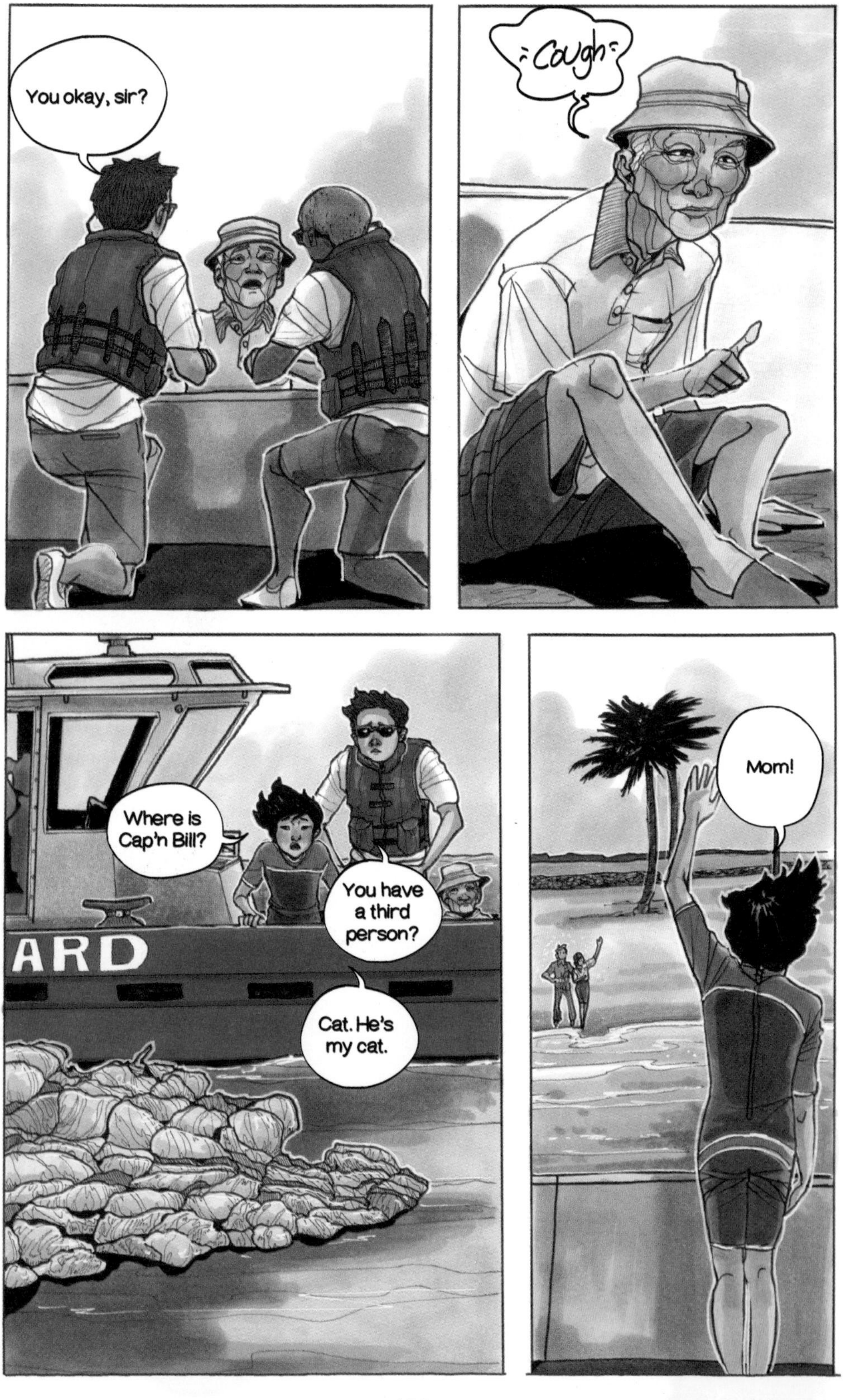
You okay, sir?
Cough
Where is Cap'n Bill?
You have a third person?
Cat. He's my cat.
ARD
Mom!

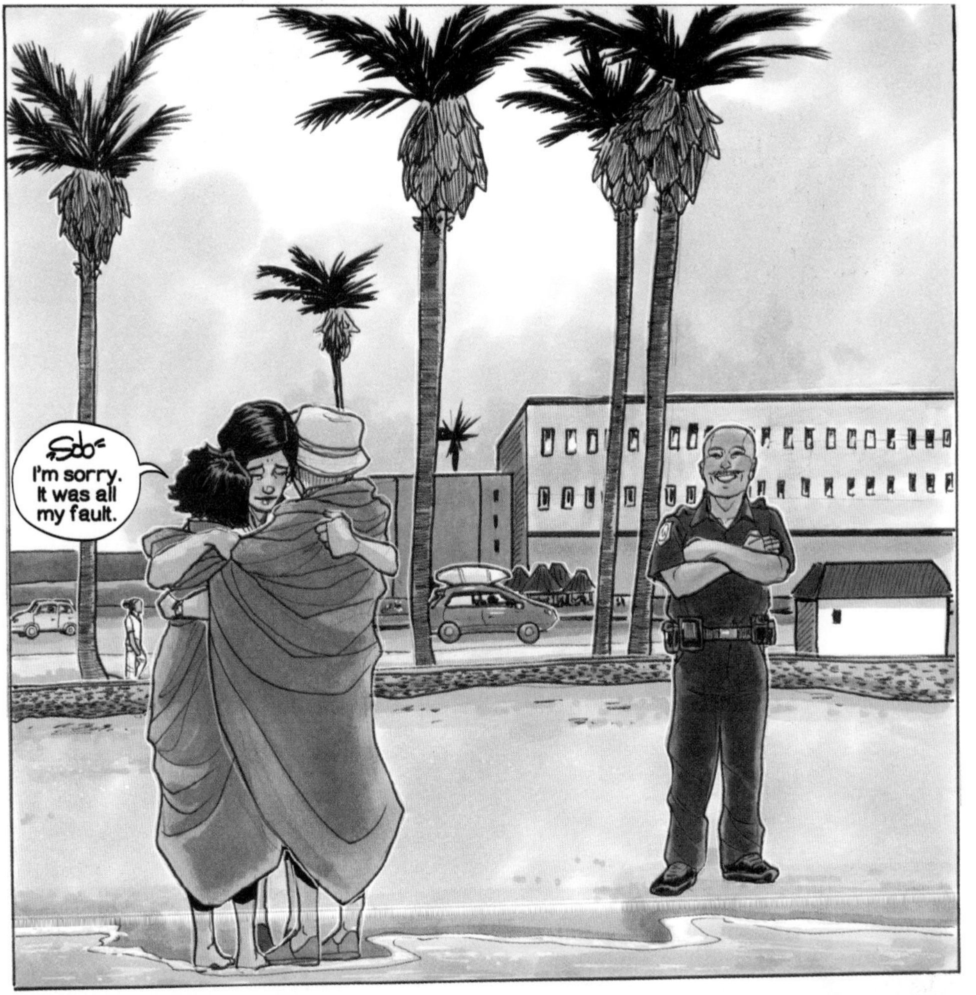
SOB
I'm sorry. It was all my fault.

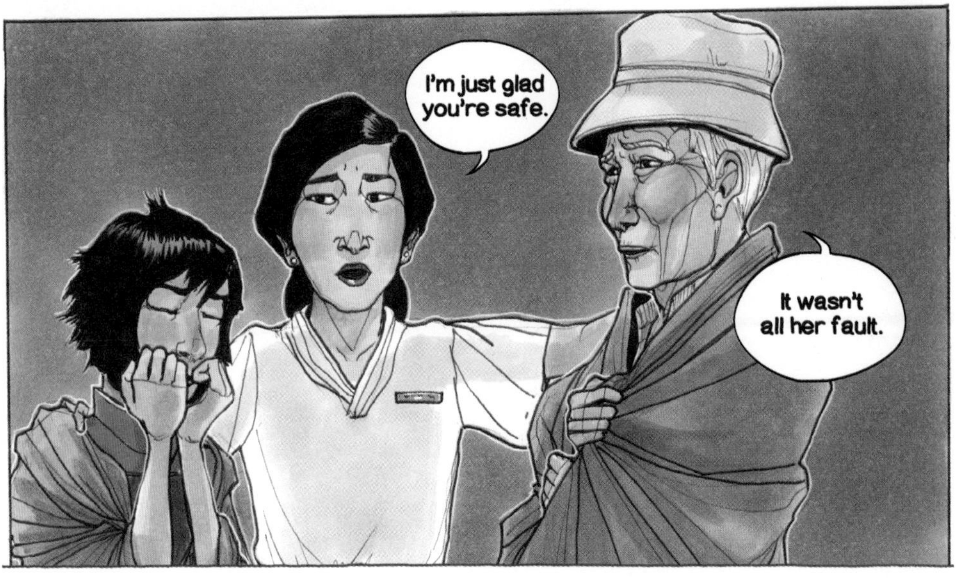
I'm just glad you're safe.
It wasn't all her fault.

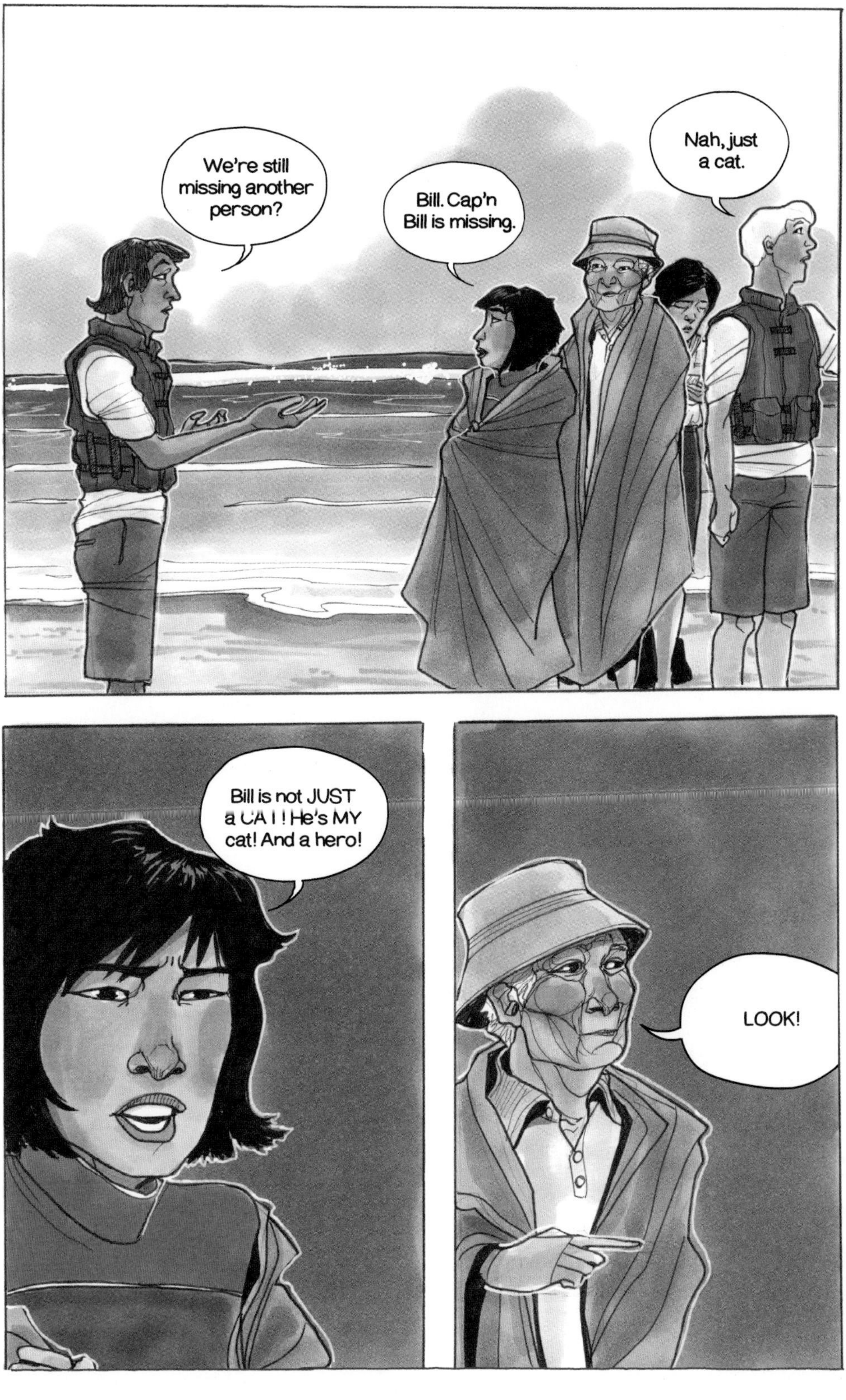
We're still missing another person?
Bill. Cap'n Bill is missing.
Nah, just a cat.
Bill is not JUST a CAT! He's MY cat! And a hero!
LOOK!

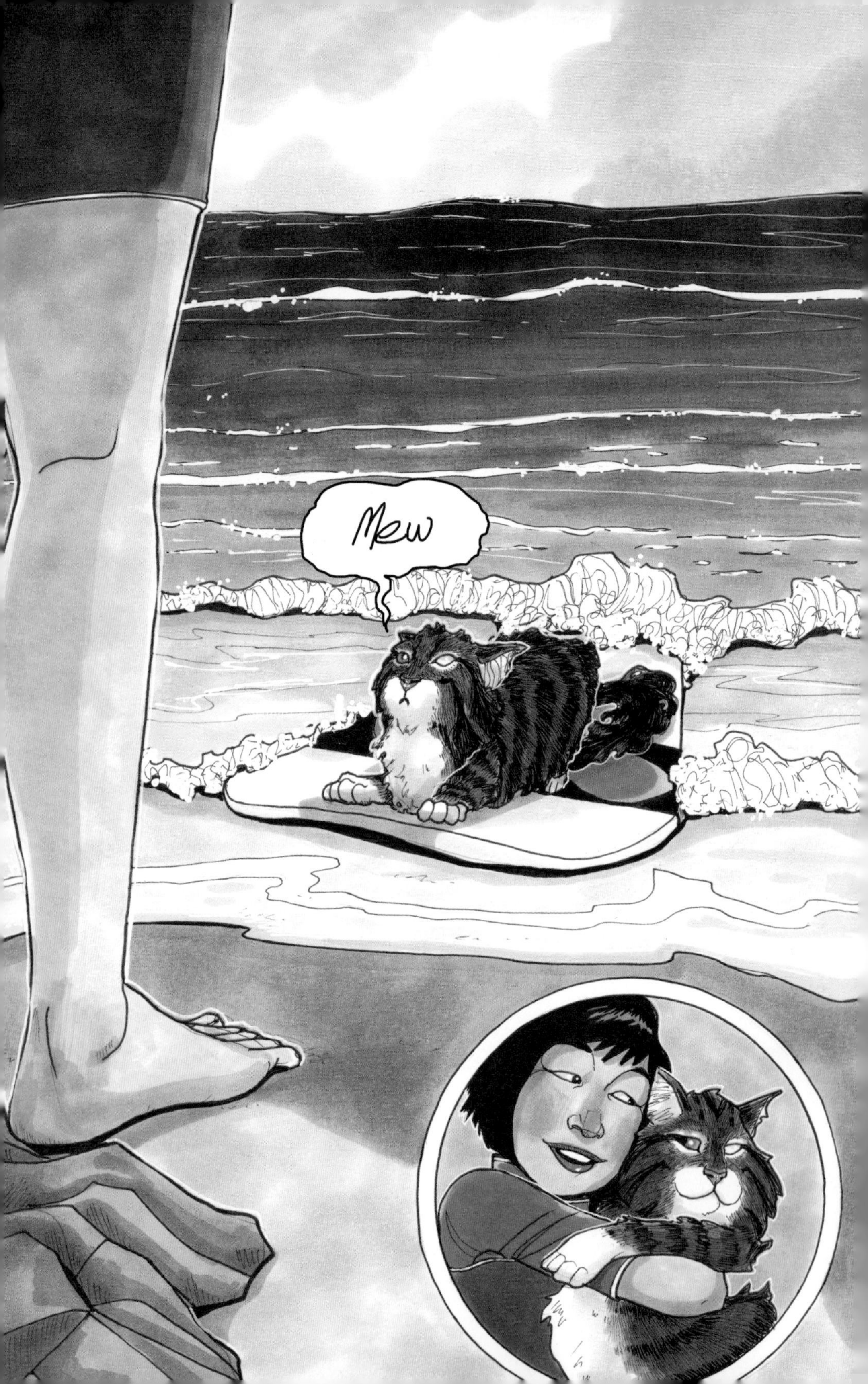
Mew

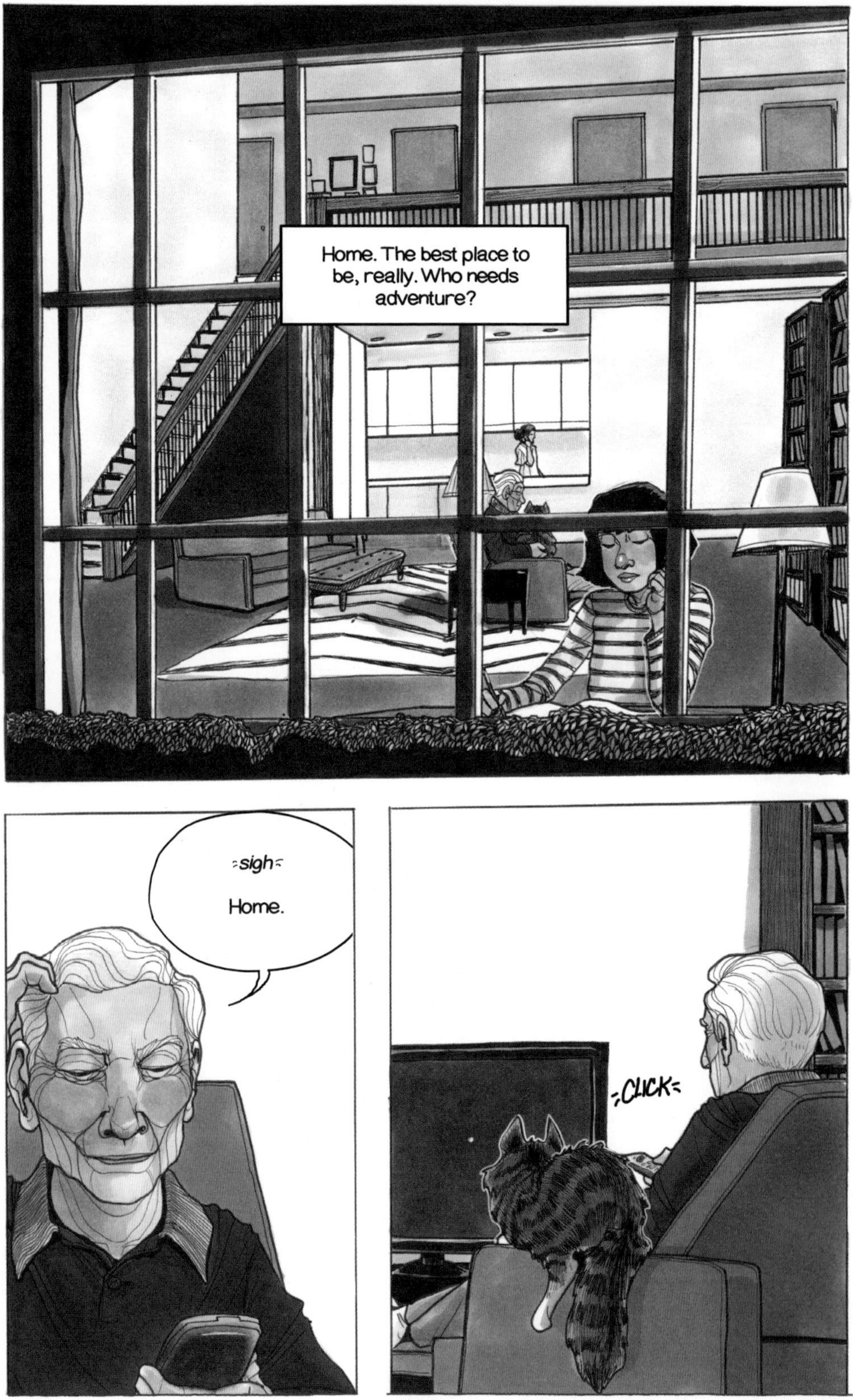
Home. The best place to be, really. Who needs adventure?
=sigh=
Home.
=CLICK=

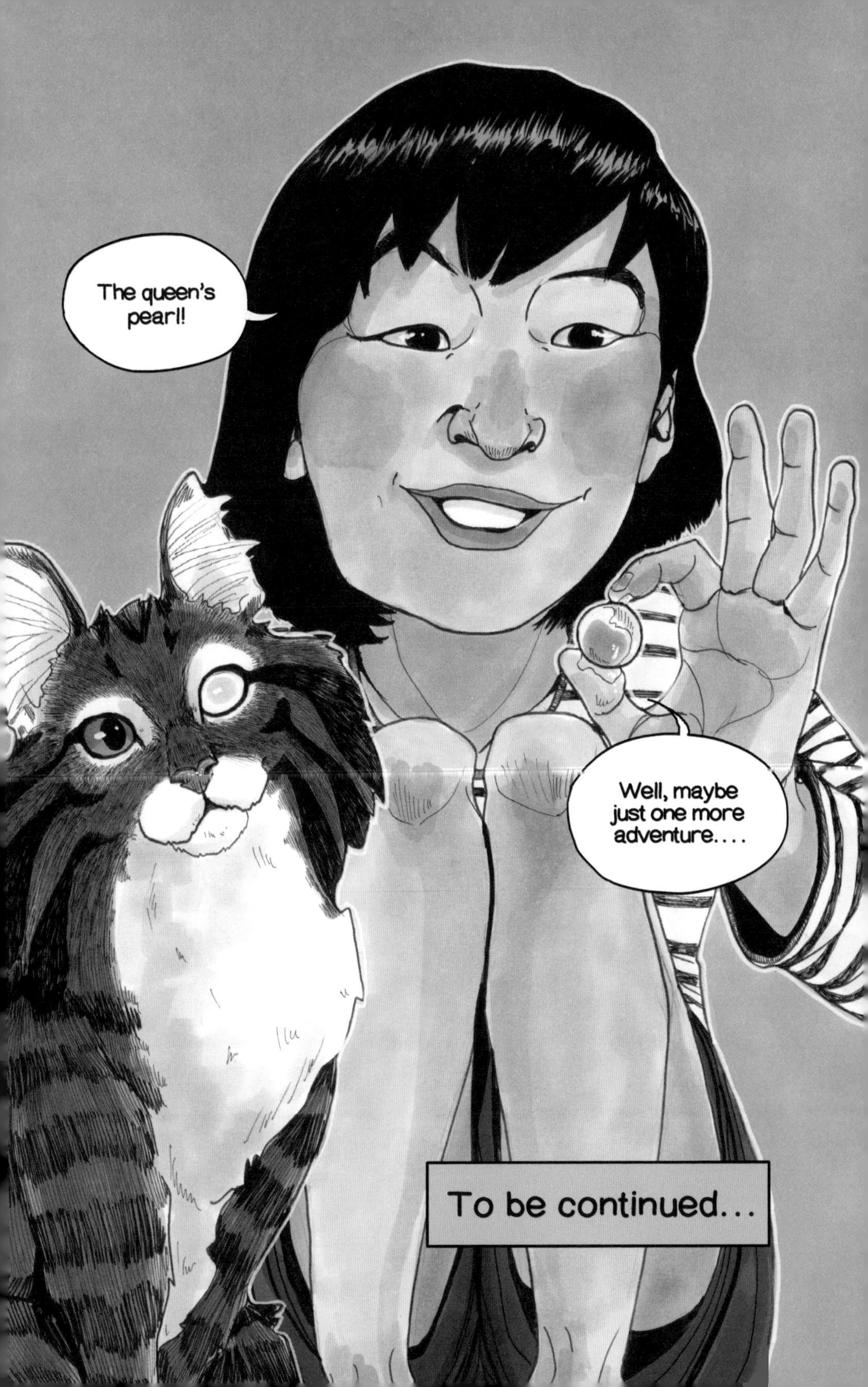
The queen's pearl!
Well, maybe just one more adventure. . . .
To be continued. . .

About the Artist

JANET K. LEE moved from Palo Alto, California, to Nashville, Tennessee, when she was eight years old and has been there ever since. Living so far away from an ocean, she never learned to surf like Trot, but she did have a kitten, Genie, as her first pet, rode a skateboard almost everywhere, and loved to draw. So she created her own newspaper, which featured her first comic strips, and passed that out to friends at school.

Fast forward to adulthood when Janet won an Eisner Award for her first graphic novel, *Return of the Dapper Men*. Now she illustrates comics full-time in a studio surrounded by four cats, one of which bears an uncanny resemblance to Cap'n Bill.

◣ About the Writer ◢

At age eleven, **AMY CHU** wrote her first book. It was about a princess and a magic poodle and went on to win the Best Book Prize in Mrs. Millard's sixth grade class.

Amy is now a professional comic book writer, creating stories for popular Marvel and DC characters such as Wonder Woman, Ant-Man, Deadpool, and Poison Ivy, as well as Green Hornet, Red Sonja, and The Princess of Mars.

Amy was born in Boston, Massachusetts, and has lived in New York, California, Iowa, Oklahoma, and Hong Kong. She now lives in Princeton, New Jersey, with her family and her extensive LEGO collection.

✒ About the Story ✒

SEA SIRENS was inspired by a few things new and old: fond childhood memories of being at the beach; real life stories of cats who like to surf; *The Dragon Prince* and *Why the Sea Is Full of Salt*, two collections of folktales and fairy tales from Vietnam; and a long-forgotten novel published in 1911.

That novel was *The Sea Fairies* by L. Frank Baum, the creator of the famous Wizard of Oz books. Baum wrote two underwater fantasy novels about a California girl nicknamed Trot and her adventures with mermaids and other creatures of the deep.

P.S. No serpents were harmed in the making of this book.

Acknowledgments

Shout out to Jimmy Gownley for his magical letters, Ngoc Cammuso for vetting the Vietnamese dialogue, Peter Nguyen and his family, Stephen Pruett, and all the women of the Comic Book Women support group. Last but not least, thanks to the wonderful team at Viking Children's Books. You guys really do make dreams come to life.